BOOKS BY JACK CAVANAUGH

An American Family Portrait series

The Puritans
The Colonists
The Patriots
The Adversaries
The Pioneers
The Allies
The Victors
The Peacemakers

African Covenant series

The Pride and The Passion
Quest for the Promised Land

Book of Books series

Glimpses of Truth
Beyond the Sacred Page

Songs in the Night series

While Mortals Sleep
His Watchful Eye
Above All Earthly Powers

The Great Awakenings series (with Bill Bright)

Proof

Postmarked Heaven
Death Watch (with Jerry Kuiper)
Dear Enemy

Dear
ENEMY

JACK CAVANAUGH

BETHANY HOUSE PUBLISHERS
Minneapolis, Minnesota

Published by Bethany House Publishers
11400 Hampshire Avenue South
Bloomington, Minnesota 55438

Bethany House Publishers is a division of
Baker Publishing Group, Grand Rapids, Michigan.

Printed in the United States of America

Library of Congress Cataloging-in-Publication Data

Cavanaugh, Jack.
 Dear enemy / by Jack Cavanaugh.
  p. cm.
  Summary: "American nurse Annie Rawlings finds herself behind enemy lines in
WWII, captured and alone with a wounded German soldier. Through shared danger,
faith, and a love of music, the two forge a bond that will be tested by prejudice and
the separation of time and continents"—Provided by publisher.
  ISBN 0-7642-2310-0 (pbk.)
  1. World War, 1939-1945—Fiction. 2. Enemies (Persons)—Fiction.
3. Prisoners of war—Fiction. 4. Soldiers—Fiction. 5. Nurses—Fiction. I. Title.

 PS3553.A965D427   2005
 813'.54—dc22   2005008958

In memory of my father

William J. Cavanaugh
1924–2005

A veteran of World War II
who found love upon returning home.
Buried at Ft. Rosecrans National Cemetery—
the setting for a scene in this story—
while this book was in production.

PROLOGUE

"Annie, everyone's staring at us!"

"They've never seen a bride in a cemetery before?"

Annie's gown rustled as she clambered out of the 1946 Chevrolet Suburban, which was polished to a sun-reflecting shine for the occasion. Hitching up her dress, she sailed down a grassy slope past row after row of tablet headstones, her red hair and white wedding gown flapping in the stiff onshore breeze.

Behind her, nineteen-year-old Celia Hanson set the parking brake, threw open the driver's side door, and, fighting the limitations of a bridesmaid's dress, hurried after her.

Celia was right. Everyone was staring at them. A gathering of grievers all dressed in black gawked from in front of the administration building. Without exception they wore black attire and scowls, interpreting Annie's bridal presence as disrespectful.

Three headstone rows away, standing over a World War I marker, two elderly women clutching flowers added their disapproval, tut-tutting loudly enough for Annie to hear.

And in a car that was meandering by, a family of faces pressed against the windows. The mother's jaw hung so low it was comical.

Annie didn't care. Since high school she'd discussed everything with Keith, and having second thoughts about getting married on one's wedding day ranked high on her list of important topics. She had to talk to him.

His headstone was of identical shape to all the others.

KEITH MITCHELL

5/15/1922–12/18/1944

LT US ARMY

"Well, Keith, what do you think? Am I crazy, or what?"

"If you ask me, I think you're crazy," Celia said, catching up to her. "But then, I hardly know you."

Annie couldn't help but grin. Celia sounded just like her older sister. In the short time they'd been together, Annie had also noted similarities in the sisters' mannerisms, and at just the right angle she could swear she was looking at Mouse.

"I mean, what's to think about?" Celia cried. "Stan's got the body of a Greek god, he's a blast to be with, and he's a surgeon! What's not to like?"

"He is all that, isn't he?" Annie agreed.

"And he loves you, right?"

"Without question."

"Well, there you go!"

But that was what was so puzzling. Give or take a few minor flaws—like his penchant for garlic and onions, and an overprotective nature that could at times be suffocating—Stan was perfect. Annie enjoyed being with him and could easily see herself growing old with him. And hadn't he waited for her when she told him she needed time to sort things out?

Annie let out a moan of indecision. She thought she had sorted things out. So why had she awakened on her wedding day feeling as though it was all a mistake?

"Wait," Celia said. "You love him, don't you? Tell me you love him."

"I love him."

"Then what's the problem?"

Annie sighed heavily. "There may be someone else."

"It's not because of . . ." Celia nodded toward the headstone. "Is it? Because if that's the case . . ."

Annie laughed. "No, Keith's place in my heart is secure. It's someone else."

"And you think you're in love with this other man?"

Annie's hands flopped at her sides. "No."

"No?"

"Well, maybe."

"Maybe?"

"That's just it! I don't know! I haven't known him long enough to know. But it's not fair to Stan for me to marry him as long as there's a doubt in my mind, is it?"

Annie plopped down onto the grass beside her husband's grave. Grass-stain warnings flashed in her mind. She didn't care. She'd worry about that later.

Celia carefully folded her own dress and sat down next to her.

From atop a ridge at Fort Rosecrans National Cemetery, the Pacific Ocean stretched before them all the way to the horizon.

"This other man. A former friend of Keith's?"

Annie grinned. "Actually, they were enemies."

Celia stared at her, stunned by a growing realization. "We're talking personal enemy, right? Like a rival?"

"Karl was my enemy, too."

Celia was nearly beside herself. "Wait. Don't tell me you're talking about an ENEMY enemy! I mean, during the war? Annie, tell me you're not saying you're in love with a Nazi!"

"I never said I was in love."

Celia cocked her head. Annie hadn't answered her question.

"And Karl was never a Nazi. He was pretty insistent about that."

Celia threw her head back. "Annie! Are you saying you may have feelings for a German enemy? A member of the Third Reich?"

"The war's over, Celia."

"It's not THAT over!"

From the tone in Celia's voice it was apparent that, like so many other people, she still harbored bitter feelings toward the Germans. Annie couldn't blame her. This was why Annie normally kept these feelings to herself.

They sat in silence for so long that Annie figured Celia didn't want to talk about it anymore.

"Did you meet him at the hospital?" Celia asked.

Annie smiled. Celia was just like her sister, always thinking of her friends.

"No. I met him in Belgium."

"During the war?"

"Yeah."

"How . . . when . . . I mean, wasn't it frowned upon to fraternize with the enemy?"

Annie laughed. "Very much so."

"Then, how did you meet him?"

"He shot Keith."

"Whoa! Annie!" Celia glanced at the headstone. "This is too much! You're telling me, this Karl, he's the one who—"

"Killed my husband."

For a moment, Celia was speechless. But only for a moment. "Did . . . did my sister know this Karl?"

Annie hesitated. Maybe now wasn't the best time to get into this.

"How much have your parents told you about Malmedy?" she asked.

"Not much. Whenever I ask, they tell me to wait until I'm older, or they change the subject, or they find something urgent to do like cleaning out the rain gutters."

"It's still hard for some people to talk about the war."

"They keep a picture of her on a table with a candle next to it like she was some kind of saint."

Annie smiled. "Saint Mouse. Marcy would have had fun with that."

"The two of you were close?"

"Closer than sisters. There's something about living with someone for years on death's doorstep that has a way of bringing people together."

Celia plucked a blade of grass and twirled it between her thumb and forefinger. "I still have a hard time believing my sister was over there. What was it like? Maybe if you talk about it . . ."

Annie bit her lower lip. Immediately, she regretted it. Now she'd not only have to check for grass stains, she'd have to fix her lipstick as well.

It was peaceful sitting here. Sunny, warm, with a blue vista stretching for as far as the eye could see. A fitting resting place for men whose last living memory was of frozen ground and mud and the mind-numbing thunder of mechanized conflict. The war seemed like a lifetime ago, a different world.

"Are you sure you want to hear this?" she said.

Celia settled in to listen.

Where to begin?

Annie took a deep breath. "Everyone told us it was the perfect time to get married," she said. "They were wrong. They didn't know that Hitler had plans that would ruin our honeymoon."

CHAPTER 1

On the first day of our honeymoon our leave was canceled. We were in Bastogne with plans to continue on to Paris. Oh, Celia, Bastogne is a gorgeous little medieval town. You really need to go there someday. There's this hotel on the Rue de Marche—the Hotel du Sud. It has a redbrick exterior with a quaint angled entryway on the corner. Inside, there's a twisting stairway, narrow halls, lace curtains, and there was the most exquisite handmade quilt on the bed.

We had just returned from a walking tour of the town. My feet felt like blocks of ice and I made a beeline for the bathtub, my second bath that day. It was a luxury we didn't get often, and I was going to soak for one long, decadent hour. You have to understand, we'd been sleeping in tents on cots or the ground for two years. Most of us couldn't remember the last time we'd taken a bath. If you were to ask me the week before the wedding what I was looking forward to most, being married to Keith Mitchell or soaking in a bathtub, truth be told, I would have had to flip a coin.

I was in the tub with bubbles up to my neck when the orders came down. We were to return to Malmedy immediately. Me, to the 67th Evac Hospital, and Keith to HQ. From what they told us, there were reports of isolated firefights in the Ardennes Forest. Canceling leaves was a precautionary measure, which only made interrupting our honeymoon that much worse. Had it been an emergency, we *would have understood. But nobody was taking the threat seriously. It was the Ardennes Forest, for crying out loud. This was the place where fresh recruits were sent to ease them into combat experience.*

Besides, this was a good six months after Normandy. By then our boys had broken the back of the German army. British General Montgomery had assured everyone that Hitler no longer had the resources to mount a major offensive. Monty was headed back to England for Christmas, and General Eisenhower was off somewhere playing golf.

But orders are orders. So we packed up. We weren't too happy about it, mind you. Little did we know that we were driving right into one of the biggest German offensives of the war.

———

From the passenger's side of the command car, Mrs. Annie Mitchell stared glumly through the streaks on the windshield. The only thing uglier than her mood was the weather. She could barely see the road for the snow and fog. Keith hadn't spoken since they left Bastogne.

"Think we'll make it to Paris for Christmas?" Annie asked.

Christmas was nine days away. If this recall really was a false alarm . . . well, she could hope.

Keith grunted. "Nothin' we can do about it. Orders are orders."

Annie slumped. It wasn't exactly the romantic response she'd hoped for. He could have said—

Honey, I've been dreaming of you and Paris for months. Somehow, we'll get there.

Or possibly—

Who needs Paris? We're married, that's all that matters to me, darling.

Instead, she got—

"Nothin' we can do about it."

Couldn't he be at least a little disappointed?

Annie sighed. She was just angry that their honeymoon had been interrupted. What did she expect from him really? She'd married Keith Mitchell, not Clark Gable, for crying out loud.

She got what she deserved. She'd gone compliment fishing and reeled in an old boot. It was just like her to do something like that. She always over-romanticized things. Take their first night together: For months she'd imagined it would be this wondrous joining, an almost spiritual merging of two souls. Reality was more like field maneuvers.

Face it, she told herself. *Keith is Buck Rogers fighting evil with his Thermic Radiation Projector and Disintegrator Gun, while you're Scarlett O'Hara during the siege of Atlanta with "Tara's Theme" swelling in the background. He's King of the Mountain, Capture the Flag, and Mumblety-peg; you're* Good Housekeeping *magazine, a jigsaw puzzle on a wobbly card table, and a Sunday afternoon drive.*

You're "Moonlight Serenade"; he's "In the Mood."

Annie blushed at the thought, then reminded herself it was no longer indecent to think such thoughts. She was a married woman now. Besides, it was true. Keith was always in the mood.

She glanced at her husband. Even beneath all the layers of winter clothing, he was trim and rugged. His gloved hands held the steering wheel with the grip of an athlete.

My husband, she mused. It was still difficult to think she and Keith were married.

There had been no shortage of contenders for Keith Mitchell over the years, girls who did their best to get their hooks into him. In the end, he chose her. She knew he would. She'd known since they were sixteen years old. The other girls may have been prettier, smarter, funnier, wealthier, but none of them knew Keith Mitchell like she knew Keith Mitchell.

So why now, after all this time, was she expecting him to be someone he wasn't? They'd exchanged marriage vows, not personalities.

Malmedy was still an hour away, and while the army may have cut short their honeymoon, that was no reason to toss aside their last hour together, was it?

Annie glanced down at her trousseau—a heavy jacket over a wool sweater, a wool olive drab shirt, a pair of men's fatigues, and

GI shoes that were two sizes too big. Beneath it all was long woolen underwear.

But romance was a state of the mind, wasn't it? Did it really matter what she was wearing, or how dreary and cold it was, or how inadequate the car heater? If two people were truly in love, wouldn't they find a way to turn such surroundings into a romantic rendezvous?

Annie slid seductively across the seat, linking her arm with his, laying her head against his shoulder. She hummed softly. "Moonlight Serenade." On the second verse, in a breathy voice, she sang:

"The stars are aglow and tonight how their light sets me dreaming.
My love, do you know that your eyes are like stars brightly beaming?
I bring you and sing you a Moonlight Serenade."

Keith looked down at her and smiled the smile of a newlywed husband.

"You know what I really miss?" he said.

"What, dear?" she said dreamily.

"Li'l Abner comic strips. Don't you? All the guys in the unit miss them, too." He let loose a loud guffaw. "Dogpatch. Daisy Mae and that skimpy little outfit she parades around in. Mammy Yokum." His face scrunched up to imitate Mammy. "Good is better than evil because it's nicer!" He laughed at his own rendition. "Remember that?"

By the way his comic review was spilling out, he'd obviously given this considerable thought.

"And Stupefyin' Jones! Remember her? She never said a word. All she had to do was stand there looking gorgeous and all the guys would freeze solid in their tracks, dumbfounded. Man, I miss reading that comic strip every Sunday afternoon! Best comic strip ever."

"Yeah, best ever," said Annie halfheartedly.

"You want to know what made me think of Li'l Abner?"

"What?"

"All this snow and fog. Reminded me of Lower Slobbovia. Remember Lower Slobbovia? The only place on earth worse off than

Dogpatch. Everything was always covered with snow and icicles. Look around! It's like we're in Lower Slobbovia right now, don't you think?"

"It certainly feels like it," Annie said.

"And then he spent the next twenty minutes telling me about a bazooka he and the guys named Joe Palooka," Annie lamented. "And how, for the new recruits, they printed the words 'Point this end at enemy' on the barrel."

Mouse grimaced in sympathy. "Oh, honey, once you and Keith get to Paris things will be different," she said. "He's just used to being around guys, that's all. There wasn't enough time for him to make the adjustment."

With Mouse and Nina sitting on the edge of a cot watching her, Annie unpacked her honeymoon trousseau from a standard army-issue duffle bag stamped with her maiden name: RAWLINGS. From the bag she pulled two new dresses, a nightie that had yet to be worn, an unopened bottle of perfume Keith had brought her from Bruges, and a bottle of champagne the nurses had given her for their first night in Paris.

Mouse reached over, took the top off the perfume bottle, and smelled it. "Whew! This stuff's honeymoon in a bottle! Forget Paris! Splash a little of this oo-la-la on, jump into Keith's foxhole, and let nature take its course!"

"Keith is at HQ," Annie said drolly, taking the bottle away from her.

"You're missing the point," Mouse said.

Marcy Hanson—Mouse—was a sprite of a woman with short curly hair and large brown eyes. To hear her tell it, when her little sister was two years old, the infant tried to say Marcy and it came out Mousey. The name caught on and was later shortened to Mouse. The daughter of a Methodist minister, raised in Owensboro, Kentucky, Mouse was a barefoot hillbilly and proud of it.

Nina Schaeffer, the third member of their trio, was everything

Mouse and Annie were not—tall, graceful, and gorgeous. With strik-
ing red hair, Nina could pass as a Hollywood starlet. The stunning
package contained an equally stunning intellect.

Nina was easily the most knowledgeable and experienced of the
nurses, having assisted her Chester, Maryland, physician-father since
the time she was eight years old. Nurse Schaeffer knew more medi-
cine than most of the doctors she assisted.

The three women had been together since Anzio, their first battlefield assignment. They'd stuck together through two years of
shelling, a shipwreck, mud, leaky tents, mind-numbing cold, pitch-
black nights cowering in shelters, and nightmarish amounts of blood
and death.

Short in stature, with hips too wide and a slight gap between her
two front teeth, Annie preferred to think of herself in intangibles.
She was the soul of the trio, the one who kept them going during
the seventy-two-hour marathon surgery shifts, the one who could
make intolerable working conditions tolerable, the one the nurses
came to when they were ready to slump to the ground, bury their
face in their hands, and wail. Annie had a way of picking a nurse up
from the ashes, dusting her off, and reminding her that the war
wasn't about her, that a nurse's job was to provide aid and comfort
to scared, lonely soldiers. Annie had that unique ability to be able
to reprimand and make a person feel good about herself all at the
same time.

She didn't know what she'd do if the army ever split her and
Mouse and Nina up. She never had sisters when she was growing
up. Now she had two. And the moment she'd returned from Bastogne, they were there for her.

"You want to hear my prediction?" Mouse said. "Give it two days.
Within two days all this nonsense about skirmishes in the Ardennes
will blow over, your leave will be reinstated, and you and Keith will
be in Paris for Christmas. Just wait, you'll see I'm right."

Annie offered a weak grin. She hadn't yet been able to shrug off
the disappointment.

"Thanks, Mouse, but we'll just have to—"

"Wait. I'm not done prognosticating," Mouse said.

"Prognosticating?" Nina cried. "Big word for such a little girl."

Mouse took exception to the comment. "Hey! We got big words in Kentucky, too! Maryland isn't the only state with big words, you know!"

Nina feigned surrender. "By all means, prognosticate away!"

"I predict," Mouse said with a flourish, "that you and Keith will make it to Paris . . ."

"All right," Annie conceded.

". . . and that within one year's time, the war will be over . . ."

"No objections here."

". . . and you and Keith will be settled in California in a little house overlooking the ocean . . ."

"A bit expensive for us, but okay, if someone will sell us a house overlooking the ocean, who am I to argue?"

". . . and you'll have a baby."

"Whoa!" Annie laughed. "A baby by the end of next year? That's a little fast, don't you think?"

"Not at all," Nina chimed in. "You're a patriotic person, aren't you? After the war the nation will need a new crop of Americans. You'll do it for your country."

"Government-issue children," Annie said. "Now, there's a thought. But let's just take one step at a time, shall we? Right now I'd settle for Paris, a little Glenn Miller music, 'Moonlight Serenade' on the Champs-Elysées . . ."

Mouse and Nina exchanged uneasy glances.

"What did I say?" Annie asked.

"Didn't you hear?" Nina said.

"Hear what?"

"Glenn Miller. His plane is missing. They think it went down in the Channel."

"No!" Annie cried.

"It took off yesterday from England. Nobody's heard from it since."

Annie collapsed onto the edge of her cot, surprised at how hard the news hit her. For months she'd been looking forward to Glenn Miller's Christmas concert. She wiped away a tear, embarrassed by the spillover of her emotions. She hadn't cried when her leave was canceled. Maybe it was all just catching up to her.

She reached into the duffle bag and pulled out two concert tickets and tossed them on the cot. "I guess some things just weren't meant to be," she said, her voice quivering.

"God willing, you still have Paris," Nina said softly.

Mouse cried, "Paris? What are you talking about? She still has a husband! There are some of us who would shave our heads and walk around bald for a year just to have a husband! And any time you want to toss yours away, you just let me know. I'll be the first in line to pluck him from the trash heap."

Captain Maude Elliott, the chief nurse, appeared in the doorway. "Rawlings!" she said.

"It's Mitchell now," Mouse corrected her.

Elliott paid no attention. "Skoglund's scrubbing for surgery," she said.

Nina stood. "Let me do it," she said. "Annie just got back. I'll assist Dr. Skoglund."

A wry grin formed on Elliott's face. "And we all know how that would go over." She walked away.

"I tried," Nina said apologetically to Annie.

"Thank you, but I'll be fine."

"We'll finish for you here," Nina said.

"Oh, and when you're done," Mouse said, "poke your head into the ward. We had two casualties this morning when the cathedral was hit."

"The cathedral was hit?"

"One of the soldiers is a New York Italian," Mouse said with a grin. "We all fell in love with him instantly. He has the voice of an angel."

"It's not his voice she's been drooling over," Nina said.

Annie found herself smiling again. It felt good.

"Oh, and Annie?"

"Yeah?"

"Be careful," Nina said, suddenly somber.

"Yeah. Be careful," Mouse echoed.

Annie's intuition prickled, not from what they said, but because of how they said it.

"What's going on?" she asked. "What aren't you telling me?"

"Just be careful, okay?" Nina said.

CHAPTER 2

*I*n a way, despite the disappointment, Annie was glad to be back at the hospital with Mouse and Nina. Was this normal—for a woman to feel uncomfortable on her honeymoon?

She didn't regret marrying Keith. It wasn't that. It was just . . . well, it was just strange . . . and, at times, embarrassing.

For instance, this morning, when she came out of the bathroom, there Keith was, sitting in a chair, wearing nothing but his shorts, cleaning between his toes with his socks. Then later, when she was soaking in the tub and Keith got the news that their leave had been canceled, he ambled in, sat on the commode real serious-like and gave her the news as though they were talking over a cup of tea at a café or something. And all the while Keith was talking, Annie was distracted by the realization of how totally naked she was beneath the bubbles.

All her life this kind of mingling of the sexes had been taboo, and now, all of a sudden it was supposed to feel natural and normal?

So, in a way, it was something of a relief to be back in the women's quarters at the 67th where it felt normal, if one could call a bunch of women living together in the middle of a war *normal*.

Rounding a corner, Annie nearly ran into a group of soldiers. There were five of them standing in the hallway. While it wasn't strange to run into loitering soldiers—there was always a group of them come to visit a wounded buddy—what was unusual about these soldiers was that they were armed. They held their weapons as though expecting to use them.

"Excuse me," Annie said, working her way past them.

They checked her out with grim expressions. That, too, was unusual. American nurses this close to the front lines were accustomed to being ogled. These men were on duty.

It made her wonder who was being prepped for surgery that would require this kind of security. A general, no doubt. If so, it made sense that Dr. Skoglund was performing the operation.

Lt. Colonel Eugene Skoglund was a talented surgeon. Their best. He was also kin to the devil. A man with a long face, hollow cheeks, horseshoe-bald head, wire-rimmed glasses, and incredibly nimble hands, Skoglund delighted in making nurses cry. It was a game with him.

During a surgical procedure, he'd ferret around with comments, questions, and criticisms—testing, probing, until he found a weakness. Then he'd attack. Mercilessly. Tears only egged him on. To Eugene Skoglund a surgery wasn't successful unless the procedure went well *and* he made at least one nurse cry. He'd rate his procedures accordingly. An unqualified success for him would be "a three-nurse session."

Every nurse at the 67th Evac had a Skoglund horror story that she used to scare new recruits. Annie must have heard a dozen Skoglund stories within days of her arrival. Given the chance of being overrun by Nazis or assisting Skoglund in surgery, the majority of the nurses at the 67th would take their chances with the Nazis.

Knowing that the OR rotation would inevitably put her and Skoglund at the same table, Annie did her best to prepare herself for it. She vowed that no matter what the man said or did, she would not let him get to her. She kept telling herself she was an army nurse, Skoglund a doctor; she would assist him in an efficient, professional, and, above all, dry-eyed manner. Anything he said to her not related to surgery was water off a duck's back. And if at any time he felt she was inadequate to the task, for the good of the patient, she would politely but firmly recommend he request another nurse.

The day of her first Skoglund-assist arrived. Annie was ready for him. She scrubbed methodically, professionally, and entered the OR confident that her hide was as thick as rhinoceros skin. Let him do his worst. Dr. Eugene Skoglund would not squeeze a single tear from her.

Within ten minutes of the initial incision Annie had to be relieved by another nurse and was running down the hallway in tears.

The man was a louse. He was a louse's louse.

Annie had never been so angry—at Skoglund for being a parasite masquerading as a man, but even more at herself for not being able to control her emotions and for having to be relieved from her duties. What upset her most was that she had failed her patient. The soldier on the table deserved better from her. Where would they be today if *he* had run from his post under heavy fire?

Doing an about-face, Annie marched back into the operating room and insisted on relieving the nurse who had relieved her.

This amused Skoglund. Apparently, he'd never had a nurse return to the scene of a mauling. He saw it as a fresh challenge. Could he make a nurse cry twice during the same operation? What a story it would make if he could force a nurse to be relieved twice from the same operation.

He gave it his best shot. He was cruel, crude, condescending, demanding, unreasonable, petty, and foulmouthed. He attacked her, her family, her lineage, her future children, her love life, her skills as a nurse, and all nurses in general. Annie took everything he dished out—though she was mightily tempted to stab him with his own scalpel when he made a filthy innuendo about Marcy.

For her part Annie was efficient, prompt, and polite. When the surgery was over, she looked Dr. Eugene Skoglund in the eye, apologized for being unprofessional earlier, and told him it would never happen again. She complimented his skills, saying that the sergeant on the table was lucky to have him as the surgeon of record. She then went straight to the chief nurse and requested that she be assigned to assist Dr. Skoglund with his next surgery.

The other nurses thought she was nuts, but they didn't try to talk her out of it. If she was assisting Skoglund, it meant they didn't have to.

For a month of surgeries, Annie's life was a whole new level in Dante's hell. Skoglund was merciless. Never before had anyone witnessed such creative cruelty.

Annie wished she could say she never let him get to her again, that he never made her cry again. But he did. Only she never gave him the satisfaction of seeing it. Through sheer willpower, Annie held back her tears until after surgery. She'd pay him a compliment, walk calmly to her bunk, then rip into her pillow until it was a soaked and battered bag of feathers. Then she'd go to the chief nurse and request Dr. Skoglund again.

After a month, either Skoglund exhausted his supply of cruelties, or he came to respect her. Annie didn't know which it was. All she knew was that he began acting civilly to her, at times even friendly.

Word got back to Annie that Skoglund had met with Chief Nurse Elliott and insisted Annie be assigned to him whenever he operated. At first, Captain Elliott resisted, saying she would never let a doctor dictate the nurses' schedule. Skoglund went on a rampage, making life miserable for everyone in the hospital until Chief Nurse Elliott conceded. Dr. Eugene Skoglund and nurse Annie Rawlings became an efficient team with the best save record in the battalion.

"What took you so long?" Skoglund barked as Annie entered the OR after scrubbing. "We're ready to begin."

She walked into a most curious scene. There were army soldiers everywhere. A team of them were lining the walls with mattresses.

With his hands raised to keep them from becoming contaminated, Skoglund was being fitted for a flak jacket by two soldiers. Two soldiers approached Annie with a similar jacket.

"Raise your arms," one of them said.

"What's going on?"

"Didn't Elliott brief you?" Skoglund asked.

"Captain Elliott told me to prep for surgery, nothing more."

Skoglund scowled. "One of ours," he said, nodding to a patient lying facedown on an operating table, "and one of theirs."

Annie moved in for a closer look. The two soldiers fitting her for the flak jacket complained, telling her to stand still.

The wounded American had metal fins four inches long protruding from his back. Metal and flesh was a common sight in a military OR, but not usually on so grand a scale, greatly escalating the grotesque factor.

"An unexploded bazooka shell," Skoglund said. "It's live."

Annie's stomach did a somersault.

That explained the mattresses and the jackets and all the grim expressions. The extra men in the operating room were members of a bomb squad.

"And him?" Annie asked of the German.

"Not life threatening."

"So why is he here?"

"That's the Kraut who fired the bazooka. I want him right next to me if this thing goes off."

From the look on the German's face, he understood his situation. Strapped to the gurney, with no protection other than a hospital sheet, he was scared and sweating profusely. His eyes were wide and darting after every sound. He blinked repeatedly from the sweat that kept getting in his eyes.

He stared up at Annie. If he was looking for pity, he'd come to the wrong nurse. His boyish face didn't fool her. The man was a trained killer. Put him back in the field and he'd kill again. Give him half a chance and he'd kill her and everyone in the OR without a second thought. That's the way German boys were trained from the time they were young.

The memory of a third-grade friend flashed in Annie's mind. Claudia, a pretty girl before a bullterrier tore into her. The dog had been trained to pit-fight in Tijuana by one of Annie's North Park neighbors. Claudia didn't have a chance. She was skipping rope in front of her house when the dog attacked. Had it not been for a neighbor knocking the dog senseless with a two-by-four, the pit bull would have killed her.

The German in the OR was no different from that dog. He was one of Hitler's whelps.

"Let's get to it," Skoglund said.

A square-jawed sergeant took a position on the opposite side of the operating table. There were no introductions.

"I'll cut here and here," Skoglund said, pointing with a gloved finger.

The sergeant bent down to get a closer look. He nodded. He was sweating.

Annie handed Skoglund a scalpel. She noticed her hand was shaking. Skoglund noticed it, too, but said nothing.

Steady as always, Skoglund made the first incision. Annie was amazed at his control. Nearly every day he held a patient's life in his hands. Today, not only the patient's life was in his hands, but everyone in the room.

So this was what Mouse and Nina weren't telling her earlier. They were under orders. Had to be, otherwise they would have said something. Captain Elliott probably didn't want word to slip out onto the wards and circulate among the patients. And Nina—bless her heart—Nina had offered to stand in for her.

The fact that she shouldn't even be here wasn't lost on Annie. She was supposed to be on her honeymoon, on her way to Paris. If something should happen to her . . .

She thought of Keith. Surely God wouldn't take his wife of one day from him. An image of Keith being given the news that his bride had been blown up during an operation flashed in her mind.

The first incision complete, Skoglund positioned himself to make the second incision.

An artillery round whistled overhead. Looking up, the sergeant cursed. The next instant the walls and floor shook from the explosion. Annie was thrown against Skoglund. His hand hit one of the protruding fins.

Time froze—that half moment between the instant a time bomb

ticks its last tick and the explosion. In that half moment no one breathed, no one moved, no heart beat, no pulse pulsed. Everyone in the room just stared at one another, afraid that the slightest movement would set time to ticking again and that moment would be their last.

Outside, a truck rumbled past the hospital.

The sergeant's eyes bulged in disbelief that they were still alive.

The German on the operating table began shouting. A corpsman gagged him.

"I'm sorry," Annie said.

Skoglund said nothing, which was very much out of character for him, meaning he was just as scared as the rest of them.

He steadied himself, then made the second incision.

Another shell screamed overhead. Another explosion. This one louder. Closer.

"I'm ready to extract," Skoglund said.

The sergeant stepped him through the procedure. How to touch the explosive. How to hand it off once it was out.

Another shell whistled and exploded just as Skoglund was reaching for the imbedded mortar, shaking the OR table.

Skoglund withdrew, set himself, then made another attempt, his long fingers handling the unexploded shell with a mother's touch, gently increasing the pressure, slowly tugging, backing the ordnance out, the edges of the incisions lifting up.

But the shell didn't come out.

The sergeant winced.

Skoglund tried again, tugging harder.

The sergeant's wince increased.

"It's snagged on something," Skoglund said. "I'm going to have to reach inside to free it."

The sergeant shook his head. "I don't know . . ."

"Should I pull harder?"

The sergeant scrunched his face with indecision.

"Well, I've got to do something!" Skoglund shouted.

"All right. Reach in there," the sergeant said reluctantly. "Just be careful."

"Be careful. That's your expert instruction?"

Skoglund took a deep breath. Slowly he slid a bloody finger down the side of the bomb into the patient's back.

He probed. He shook his head. "I can't get it. Rawlings, make the incision wider."

My name is Mitchell now, Annie thought. But she didn't say it. She'd just have to trust that the men carving her headstone would get it right.

"Doctor, I'm not trained . . ."

"I suppose you want to hold the bomb while I cut!" Skoglund snapped.

Annie exchanged glances with the sergeant. She reached for a scalpel. She'd never made a surgical incision before.

Skoglund raised his elbow so she could get to the patient. Annie ducked under his arm. Her face was inches from the bomb.

Trying not to look at it, she placed the scalpel at the end of the incision to widen it.

Overhead an artillery shell whistled.

The explosion shook the floor, the walls. Dust and debris fell from the ceiling.

The operating table rocked.

On reflex, Annie pulled back to keep flesh from jumping into blade. She bumped Skoglund's arm.

The sergeant ducked instinctively. The German flailed his head from side to side, his screams muffled. And Annie was certain her luck had run out.

The next thing she knew, Skoglund took a step back from the table. The mortar was in his hands. The bump had knocked it free.

A pair of bomb disposal technicians raced to Skoglund's side. They guided his hands as he placed the bomb inside a heavy container. Once it was in, they quickly carried it out of the OR.

For a moment, nobody moved. Nobody talked. Nobody

breathed. They just looked at one another, shocked that they were all still alive.

Another shell screamed overhead, as if to remind them that there were still plenty of opportunities for them to die in this war.

The soldiers began clearing out of the OR.

"What do you want me to do with him?" the sergeant asked of the German.

"Get him out of my operating room," Skoglund barked.

The prisoner, still gagged, was wheeled out the doors.

"Shall we finish?" Skoglund said to Annie.

He bent over the patient. Annie assisted him in cleaning and suturing the wound.

CHAPTER 3

The only sound in the scrub room was the splashing of water in the sink as Skoglund and Annie washed following the surgery. It was just the two of them.

Annie anticipated a lecture. There would be a dressing down. She deserved it. Bumping a surgeon's arm during a procedure, not once but twice, was inexcusable. She could have gotten them all killed. Artillery shells were no excuse. She'd assisted surgeons with explosions going off around them with a frequency that would rival a Fourth of July celebration, and never once had their line of incision been anything but perfectly straight.

Skoglund cleared his throat.

Here it comes, she thought.

But instead of attacking her, he attacked a fingernail, rinsed it, and went at it again.

Why didn't he just yell at her and get it over with?

Finished washing, Annie dried her hands. She tossed the towel into the bin. Still, Skoglund said nothing.

Should she stay? Maybe he was going to let her off the hook. That would be a first. She made a show of straightening the stack of towels, and when he still didn't say anything, she turned to leave.

"A word, nurse," Skoglund said.

So much for getting off the hook.

Skoglund dried his hands in a deliberate manner, just like he did everything else. Annie waited for him. He didn't look at her, just his hands.

After a couple of uneasy minutes, he tossed the towel into the bin.

"Miss Rawlings," he said.

"Mrs. Mitchell," she corrected him.

"Yes . . . well, that is your new name, is it?" he said. "May I call you Annie?"

"Um, yes, I suppose."

"Annie . . ." He stretched out his hands to her, palms up.

She looked at them, unsure what to do. She looked for a cut or abrasion, rash or redness. There was none. His fingers were slim and bony, but otherwise healthy. She was used to seeing the backs of them. They looked odd, ungloved and upturned.

He reached for her hands, cradling them in his. His hands were warm, large, and surprisingly soft. Standing opposite him like this made her feel extremely self-conscious.

"I have a confession to make," he said softly.

She looked up at him and his eyes attempted to hold her gaze, but Annie looked away. It was too much. They were too close. There was touching, and all Annie could think about was that Eugene Skoglund was holding her hands and that somehow she had to get them back.

"It was I who canceled your leave," he said.

That got her attention. It also stirred her anger. Everyone knew Skoglund was a prima donna who insisted on having things his way, yet this was going too far. So it wasn't rumors of skirmishes in the Ardennes Forest that had cut short her honeymoon.

"Did you hear what I said?" Skoglund asked her.

"Yes . . . yes, sir."

"I suppose you're angry with me."

Angry was an understatement. Her teeth were clenched so hard her jaw ached. But Skoglund was a superior officer to whom Captain

Elliott kowtowed daily. Whatever Annie thought or felt was irrelevant.

Somehow she managed to pry her jaw open long enough to say, "I'm sure you had your reasons, sir."

"Yes, yes I did. And that's what I want to talk to you about. I want to share my reasoning with you."

He wants to share his reasoning? Annie had to look at him to make sure this was the same Eugene Skoglund who was the temperamental surgeon at the 67th Evac.

He seemed to have trouble finding the words. In itself, this was odd. This was a man who was an expert at slicing and dicing people with his tongue.

"It's just that . . ." he stammered, "how do I say this? It's just that I simply couldn't fathom Christmas without you."

He gave her hands a squeeze.

Had his words been bolts of lightning, she couldn't have been more shocked. For a long moment, she just stood there, dazed, unable to comprehend what he'd said, unable to respond.

He looked down shyly, like a middle-aged schoolboy with a crush. He smiled a silly, slanted grin and said, "Since we've gotten to know each other . . ."

"Did you just squeeze my hands?" Annie said.

He looked at her, surprised.

"Did you?" she shouted, yanking her hands free. "Did you just squeeze my hands affectionately?"

Skoglund's hands hung between them, bewildered as to what to do with themselves. His long face grew even longer, with a sad, forlorn—Annie shuddered—lovesick expression.

"You do know why I was on leave, don't you?" Annie said.

"I realize I should have spoken to you sooner."

"Dr. Skoglund, I'm a married woman! You know I can't return your . . . your . . ." She found it impossible to complete the sentence.

Skoglund cleared his throat. His hands fell to his sides. He stepped back. This was obviously not the reaction he'd hoped for. But then, what was he expecting? Did he really think she'd fly into his arms and gush latent romantic feelings for him? What planet was he living on?

His demeanor changed. Suddenly he was Eugene Skoglund, M.D., again.

"Yes, well," he said flatly, "in war one never knows who's going to live from day to day, does one? Anyway, I thought it best to let you know how I feel. Good day, Annie."

Without looking at her, he strode out.

As the door closed behind him, Annie stood alone in the scrub room, dumbfounded. When her senses rallied, she shouted, "It's Mrs. Mitchell to you!"

———

That night Mouse couldn't stop giggling as they hung tinfoil angels and five-pointed stars on the Christmas tree in the ward.

"It's not funny," Annie said.

"On the contrary," Mouse replied. "I know funny, and Skoglund making a play for you in the scrub room is funny."

"He implied Keith could get killed! And the way he said it, it almost sounded like a wish!"

"All right, that part isn't funny."

"Did he get down on one knee?" Nina asked with a smirk. She placed a star on a high limb without having to stretch.

"No, he didn't get down on one knee. All he did was hold my hands and—"

"He held your hands?" Mouse cried.

"Oh, I'd pay money for a picture of that!" Nina laughed.

"You'd think he would have said something to you sooner," Mouse said.

"Not men like Skoglund," Nina said. "They don't want something until somebody else has it."

"What do you think he'll get you for Christmas?" Mouse said.

"Very funny. I'm glad my life is a source of amusement for the two of you," Annie said. "It was embarrassing. I mean, really! And sad, when you think about it. The man has no social skills. There's no other way to put it—as a human being, he's despicable. What makes him think any woman would want to have anything to do with him? The man . . ."

"Annie," Nina said.

". . . goes out of his way to make people hate him. And he's good at it! He doesn't have a friend in the world . . ."

"Annie."

". . . it's really pathetic when you think about it—that he'd moon over me all this time and not say anything until after I got married . . ."

"Annie! Hush!"

"I won't hush! It was disgusting! The flesh on my arms was literally crawling. It was as though bugs were—"

Nina punched her in the arm.

It was then Annie saw Dr. Eugene Skoglund standing in the doorway watching them.

Annie felt her face turn Christmas red.

"Dr. Skoglund! We were just . . . um, decorating the tree. Would you care to join us?"

Had the 67th Evac Hospital been holding auditions for a production of *A Christmas Carol*, Eugene Skoglund's expression would have easily nailed him the part of Ebenezer Scrooge.

He left without saying a word.

"Oh, good grief!" Annie cried. "Why didn't you stop me?"

"I tried!" Nina said.

"Well, you didn't try hard enough!" Annie's hands fell helplessly at her sides. "You could have stuffed one of these tinfoil angels in my mouth!"

She felt horrible. Worse still when she realized that now she was going to have to apologize to Skoglund.

CHAPTER 4

With Christmas only nine days away, and with the wards nearly empty, our thoughts turned to celebrating the season. The war was still on, Celia. It was never so peaceful that you could forget that. But with the exception of a few ill-timed enemy artillery rounds—which were more annoyance than threat—everything was quiet. We were completely unaware that Hitler had just launched three armies, thousands of pieces of artillery, and two dozen armored divisions at us.

The approaching invasion was a bold and desperate move that caught everyone by surprise. The Ardennes Forest was considered too dense for an offensive thrust of any significant size. Even two days into it, when initial reports began filtering in, our military leaders were so convinced it was impossible, they refused to believe it.

At the 67th Evac—completely oblivious that the Germans were headed our way—we were fighting a battle of a different sort. Sides were forming as to whether or not we should invite our German prisoner patient to the Christmas party. He was the fellow whose bazooka shell found its way into the back of one of our boys. What made the decision even more volatile was that following the surgery the American boy had gone into shock and died.

———

"He's the enemy!" Nina cried.

She shot a disapproving glare at Mouse, the kind mothers use when a child says something stupid.

"Can't you see that? He's not wanted here."

Mouse was unmoved. "This is Christmas and he's one of God's creatures!"

"He killed one of our boys and who knows how many others, and nearly blew the OR to bits!"

"He's a patient!"

"He's a Nazi!"

"It's Christmas! It's what Jesus would do!"

Nina turned to Annie. "She's hopeless! You reason with her."

Mouse grinned at what she perceived was a tactical blunder. "You'll get no help from Annie. She agrees with me. Don't you, Annie?"

Annie's two best friends looked to her to settle their argument, each expecting her to side with them.

Until now Annie had kept silent, and for good reason. She was of two minds. Her Christian upbringing sided with Mouse. Personally, having a German in the room would spoil the whole party.

"They don't celebrate Christmas anymore, do they?" she said. "I mean, didn't Christianity die out in Germany years ago?"

Disappointment registered on Mouse's face. Annie's heart sank.

"Ha!" Nina cried in triumph.

Mouse didn't hear it. She approached Annie. "That's not the point. It's not whether *they* act like Christians; it's whether *we* act like Christians."

Annie couldn't bear that she'd disappointed Mouse, but what was done, was done. "It's just that . . . I think it would be an insult to our own boys to include him."

All Christmas spirit had drained from Mouse's face. She turned and left the room.

Nina patted Annie on the arm as they watched their friend leave. "She'll get over it," Nina said. "You'll see. By tomorrow morning she'll be bouncing on her cot singing, 'Santa Claus Is Coming to Town.'"

The ward bustled with activity as the nurses arrived with goodies from their Christmas packages from home—cookies, cake, fudge, chocolate—though not the really good stuff. That was being saved for Christmas Day.

A parade of patients entered from other wards. Some walked in on their own; others were wheeled in, either in chairs or rolling beds. The first thing they saw when they came through the door was the Christmas tree in the corner, prompting grins and, for some, tears.

"That's all of them," a nurse said, pushing a wheelchair with a redheaded, freckle-faced soldier who grinned so hard it looked like he'd burst.

"Not all," Mouse said.

Coming in behind Nina, she wheeled the German patient into the room.

Festive sounds shut down abruptly as if someone had turned off a spigot.

Mouse pushed her patient through the silence.

"Get the Kraut outta here!" a soldier shouted.

"Come on, boys!" Mouse cried cheerily. "It's Christmas! Show a little Christmas spirit!"

A nurse distracted the vocal soldier with a piece of fudge. The other nurses who were scattered throughout the room took the cue and did the same. Annie asked the soldier closest to her to describe his typical Christmas back home. While he launched into an enthusiastic description suitable for a Norman Rockwell painting, Annie kept one eye on Mouse as she wheeled the German into a corner on the fringe of the festivities. Soon he was forgotten completely.

Nina introduced the entertainment for the night. Earlier that day a fawning band of nurses surrounded Private Antonio Scarpetti's bed, pleading and begging with him until he agreed to sing a couple of Christmas songs. He was the one Nina had mentioned earlier who had the voice of an angel and the body of Michelangelo's *David*.

As Scarpetti maneuvered on crutches toward the Christmas tree, Annie could see what all the fuss was about. Mouse's description of him was an understatement. A New York Italian, he was dark and swarthy with an infectious grin. And his voice! The best way Annie could think to describe it was that once Scarpetti started singing, no one paid any attention to how he looked.

He sang without accompaniment, which was just as well because a piano would only distract from the clear, vibrant tone of his baritone voice. With the first phrase of the first song, he took his audience captive.

> "O holy night, the stars are brightly shining,
> It is the night of our dear Savior's birth!
> Long lay the world in sin and error pining,
> Till He appeared and the soul felt its worth."

Annie closed her eyes. Despite their festive intentions, the mundane decorations took away from the beauty of sound and word as they blended into such soul-aching purity that Annie was transported to a different time and place where the stars shone innocently upon a much simpler landscape where the coming of the Christ child made a difference in the world, where peace was not just a word, but deeply felt by . . .

The song ended much too soon, and when Annie opened her eyes, she did so with a piercing disappointment that she was forced to return to a world with such bland colors and crude decorations that couldn't begin to disguise a world at war.

"Antonio! Sing 'White Christmas'!" a bouncy, bright-eyed nurse cried. She looked and acted as if she was the president of his fan club.

"Forgive me," Scarpetti said, touching a hand to his chest. "I do not wish to disappoint, but please, no. I have seen too many of my buddies lose feet and toes to frostbite. Let us leave it to our comrades in the Pacific to dream of a white Christmas, shall we? Do you have another request?"

He turned down the nurse's request with such charm that if she was disappointed, she didn't show it.

"How about 'Silent Night'?" she squealed.

"That, my sweet lady, I can do."

Adjusting his crutches, Scarpetti's eyes lifted heavenward as his voice took up the tale of Bethlehem with lyrical ease, and by the second verse Annie had once again escaped the bonds of the war with eyes closed.

"Darkness flies, all is light,
Shepherds hear the angels sing,
Alleluia! hail the King!
Christ the Savior is . . ."

A nudge in the ribs brought her rudely back to the hospital ward. With a frown she opened her eyes and saw Nina.

"In the doorway," Nina whispered. "Someone wants to talk to you."

Annie moaned. The only hospital personnel not at the party were some of the doctors, Skoglund being one of them. Annie's shoulders slumped. Why now? Why must the man insist on ruining her Christmas?

With the greatest reluctance, Annie swiveled out of her chair and started toward the door.

"Keith!"

There in the doorway, leaning against the doorjamb with a goofy grin on his face, was her husband. His appearance took her so by surprise that Annie's heart skipped a beat. She ran to him, not caring that the entire ward was watching her, and she didn't stop until their faces were intimately close.

"What are you doing here?" she whispered excitedly, pressing against him. He tried to answer, but his words made no sense. Her nose and cheek and lips kept getting in their way with nuzzles and kisses.

"Come in! Join the party!" several nurses shouted.

Keith whispered to Annie, "I only have thirty minutes."

She took him by the hand and, ignoring the disappointed cries behind them, led Keith down the hallway into a deserted ward. The lights were off. She didn't turn them on. She closed the door and was roughly snatched up in a ferocious embrace. For a good five minutes neither of them spoke. They communicated in other ways.

Coming up for air, Annie said, "What a perfect Christmas present!" Her arms were around his neck, her forehead against his forehead.

"Officially, I'm not here," Keith said. "I'm picking up the CO's jeep from the motor pool."

Annie grinned. "I'll take you any way I can get you, officially or unofficially."

"Are you still up to a Paris Christmas?" he said.

Annie's heart leaped. "Really?"

"Mad Max—he's my new CO; actually, it's General Maxwell Conrad—anyway, he says there's no way the Germans are coming through the Ardennes. He says the reports we've been getting are nothing but a bunch of green recruits with the jitters."

"He's reinstating your leave?"

Keith nodded with a smile. "He's real antsy to get a command in the First Army. Says that's where the breakthrough into Berlin is going to happen and that the war's gonna be over in a few weeks and the last thing he wants is to be sittin' around here on his keester when it happens."

He interrupted himself to kiss her.

"Anyway, he's goin' into the forest tomorrow to see for himself—"

Keith looked around to make sure nobody was in the room.

"No one's supposed to know that," he whispered. "When he gets back, he's gonna brief Ike personally. He says you and me, we can be on our way to Paris in two days tops, but then he wants me back and ready for action."

Annie raised her eyebrows. "Sounds like your general and I both want the same thing—we both want you back and ready for action."

Her comment started another round of smooching.

"You'd like Mad Max," Keith said.

"I already do. He wants us in Paris."

"Remember Coach Sweeney?"

"Bear crawls and wind sprints."

Keith laughed. "Yeah, that's the one. Well, General Maxwell reminds me of the coach. You know, a real gung-ho kinda guy."

"Are we really going to get to Paris?" Annie squealed.

"First, you need to get your leave reinstated."

The bottom dropped out of Annie's good time. Skoglund. If she was going to get her leave reinstated, she'd have to make up with Skoglund.

Keith read her face. "Is that a problem? 'Cause if it is, Mad Max says just have your captain call him and he'll fix everything. He says he'll give your captain his personal pledge that we're going to have a quiet Christmas."

"I'll get my leave reinstated," Annie said optimistically.

"Great! I don't know if I'll be able to get a command car again, though," Keith said. "We may have to take a general transport to Paris."

As the thought of being in Paris sank in, Annie began to cry. She couldn't help it. It was really going to happen! She threw her arms around her husband.

"I'd walk to Paris just to be with you," she said.

With her clinging to his neck, he looked at his watch. "I've gotta go," he said.

She kissed him again and backed away, reluctantly. He pulled her close for more.

"Now I've really got to go!" he said.

It was all she could do to let him go.

"Oh, wait! I nearly forgot!" He fumbled in his pocket and pulled out a small box. He opened it in front of her.

"Keith! It's lovely!"

A necklace with two hearts entwined, nestled against a midnight blue field of velvet. In each of the hearts was a small stone.

"Our birthstones," he said.

He put the necklace on her, fastening the clasp with difficulty.

"It's my promise to you that we're going to honeymoon in Paris," he said.

"It's perfect!" Annie cried, fingering the hearts.

More kisses and then, just like that, Keith was gone.

Annie floated back to the Christmas party. Everyone sat in groups, talking, laughing, eating Christmas goodies—all except the German, who sat off in a corner by himself.

The moment Annie stepped into the room, the nurses converged on her, telling her how gorgeous her husband looked and how lucky she was to have a man who was so romantic. Annie showed them the necklace and told them that the Paris honeymoon was back on.

She didn't mention that Skoglund could nix her leave. If she mentioned it, it might come true.

For the remainder of the evening, Annie happily sang Christmas carols, rolled her eyes over Nina's hand-rolled chocolate truffles, and laughed at every joke and story. It was her way of weaving a happy Christmas that would culminate in Paris lights and an intimate rendezvous with her husband. If she believed it hard enough, even the evil power of an ogre like Eugene Skoglund couldn't break the spell and it would come true.

However, in the back of her mind, she knew that sometimes evil is stronger than dreams. So, in the morning, she would go on the offensive. She would apologize to Skoglund. It was a necessary first step. Captain Maude Elliott was of the old school of nurses who believed that doctors were gods and that a nurse's job was to appease the gods.

Once that was done, and with General Maxwell's personal assurance that the war was taking Christmas off, how could she possibly refuse Annie's request to reinstate her honeymoon leave?

With a plan of action settled in her mind, Annie turned her full attention to the party.

CHAPTER 5

*S*unday began with a boom.

Annie's cot shuddered. She bolted up into a sitting position.

Another boom.

All the nurses were up now, in a similar state of confusion—half asleep, half awake. Some grabbed bathrobes, others just their steel helmets, and ran into the hallways in their pajamas.

"German railroad guns, 170-millimeter," Mouse said. "One of the patients told me. Same kind that leveled the church."

For twenty minutes they stood in the hallway listening to screaming shells and explosions, wondering if they'd get any casualties.

It was 0530.

The shelling stopped. They stood around for a few minutes. All was quiet. There were no sounds of approaching ambulances outside. Everything settled down back to normal inside. Most of the nurses straggled back to bed.

At 0800 they were in the hallway again. Another round of shells. Closer this time. The brick walls shook. Dust fell from the ceiling. Everyone got dressed. Casualties began arriving shortly afterward.

Captain Elliott directed the litter bearers.

"Take this one," she said to Annie. "And prep for surgery."

Annie examined the man on the cot. Correct that—the *boy* on the cot. From the looks of him, a month ago he was playing baseball in the park with his high school buddies. He had an ugly abdominal wound. Annie led the litter bearers to the operating room.

On the way they passed the Christmas tree. Last night it was so pretty and festive. The music magical. Now, surrounded by moaning, bleeding men, the tree had lost all of its enchantment.

Annie scrubbed for surgery and then waited for the rest of the surgical team to arrive. She stood over the wounded man. He was barely conscious.

"Where's home?" Annie asked brightly.

"Omaha, Nebraska." The boy's voice sounded dry and raspy.

"What's your name?"

"Philip. Philip Jamieson."

"I'm Annie. We're going to take good care of you."

"Am I gonna die?"

Annie placed a gloved hand on his hand. She wished she could touch him flesh to flesh; the plastic glove had such a clinical feel to it.

"We don't let soldiers die this close to Christmas," she said.

Philip grinned. "Lucky I got wounded close to Christmas." A worried look crossed his face. "It's bad out there. The Krauts broke through our lines. Caught us by surprise. They rolled past us like we weren't even there."

"Where?"

"In the forest. Tanks. Artillery. Heavy equipment. Infantry." Tears filled his eyes. "There were so many of them! We dropped our weapons and ran."

"The Ardennes. Are you sure?"

The boy was meandering along the edge of consciousness, stepping on one side, then the other. He didn't answer her.

Annie didn't take his assessment of the situation in the Ardennes seriously. What Keith had said last night was true. A lot of the soldiers along the forest perimeter were young boys like this one seeing their first combat. They were sent here from basic training. If the Germans had indeed broken through the lines, they would have heard. The hospital would be issued orders to evacuate.

The OR doors swung open. Skoglund and the rest of the surgical team strode in. This was the first time she'd seen him since insulting him last night. It was the moment she'd been dreading.

"Dr. Skoglund," she greeted him.

He didn't acknowledge her. Taking his place at the table, he said, "Let's save this boy."

Annie prepared herself for the worst, expecting Skoglund to resume hostilities, to revert back to the way they were before he started liking her—the belittling, complaining, attacking, snarling, all of it.

It was worse than she'd anticipated. He gave her silence. Irritating, nerve-grating, cold, excruciating silence. He acted as though she weren't even there, as though the instruments appeared magically in his hand.

The clatter of metal tools dropped onto metal trays never sounded so loud. During the entire procedure not a single human sound was made. No one dared to speak a word. Time was in stasis. It was the longest, most agonizing surgery in Annie's life, and this from a woman who had endured stretches of seventy-two hours in battlefield conditions.

Forget Paris, Annie told herself. Skoglund would never agree to it, no matter how much she groveled.

But she had to try, didn't she?

"Dr. Skoglund!"

Annie ran to catch up with him, taking two strides to his one. There had been too many ears nearby while they were scrubbing out, and when Annie turned to get a towel, Skoglund had left.

"Doctor . . ."

He heard her. He kept walking down the hall, refusing to acknowledge her. Was she going to have to tackle him to get him to stop?

"Dr. Skoglund . . ."

She caught up with him. He pretended she wasn't there.

"Doctor, please . . ."

Grim-faced, his eyes fixed steadily on some faraway horizon as he kept walking.

"Doc . . . Eugene . . ."

She broke through. He blinked.

"I want to apologize for last night. We were . . . I mean, it was . . ."

He pulled up abruptly.

"Is there something I can do for you, nurse?" he said.

It was the old Skoglund speaking, the one who took pleasure in belittling nurses. Gone was any cordiality he'd shown her.

"Please accept my—"

"I don't have time for this," he said, starting off again.

She did her best to keep up with him. If he wouldn't listen to her apology, she couldn't force him. Still, she had to ask him about her leave. Paris depended on it.

"Hospital business, then," she said. "A scheduling matter."

"I'm listening."

She'd gotten this far. Now what? She'd been so concerned about approaching him, she hadn't thought about what she'd say.

"Um . . . my leave. I'd like it reinstated."

He stopped again. This time he turned to face her. A good foot taller, he towered over her.

"A request?" He smirked as he said it. "You're asking me for a favor?"

Annie pressed on. "I'm putting in for my leave to be reinstated," she said, "and I know Captain Elliott will consult you, and I was thinking—"

"You were thinking I could return the kindness you showed me last night?"

"About that," Annie said, "I feel really—"

"Denied."

With that, he was gone. Annie knew better than to chase after him. There was no reasoning with the man when he was in a mood. Her heart sank. She knew Captain Elliott would never let her go if Skoglund didn't approve it. Yet it was her only hope.

"The worst she can say is no," Annie muttered.

She proceeded to Captain Elliott's office, formulating an argument as she walked.

Just then a ruckus of engines and shouts erupted from the street. Men screamed for help. Annie ran outside.

Two jeeps and a truck crowded the entrance to the hospital. One of the jeeps had come up two steps and stopped just shy of the front doors. The soldier in the passenger seat clutched at a leg wound, moaning with pain. The driver held his hand against a gaping head wound. He kept blinking, his head tilting repeatedly to one side. If it hadn't been for the steps, the jeep surely would have crashed through the hospital doors.

Annie ran to assist the man with the leg wound who was screaming now.

The driver was delirious. "We had our hands up," he said to no one. "We had our hands up. Why did they shoot us? We had our hands up!"

Mouse appeared at Annie's side.

"Help me get this one on a litter," Annie said of the soldier with the leg wound. "We're going to get you inside," she said to him.

He nodded. His eyes rolled up into the back of his head.

"He's going into shock," Annie said.

They flanked him, ducking under his arms.

"On three. One . . . two . . ."

"Buckle my shoe," Mouse said as she lifted.

It was her trademark. She said it every time they lifted on the count of three.

They got the leg wound onto a litter. Two orderlies came for him. "You stay with him," Annie said to Mouse, "and I'll get the head wound."

She ran to the driver's side.

"They just opened up on us. Why? We had our hands raised.

They're not supposed to shoot if we have our hands raised. It's not right."

"Come with me," Annie said, helping him out of the jeep.

He obeyed blindly, as if hypnotized.

"We had our hands raised. We were surrendering."

The horn of a jeep blared.

Annie looked up just in time to see two army jeeps skirt around the vehicles in front of the hospital and race by. A flag with a single yellow star flapped wildly on the first jeep. Although Annie had never seen him, she recognized General "Mad Max" Maxwell from his picture in the *Stars and Stripes*. He sat forward in the front seat, his chin jutting forward with determination, looking like a charging cavalryman riding a boxy green steed.

The second clue that this was indeed Maxwell was sitting in the driver's seat.

"Keith!"

What was he doing? He'd told her that Maxwell was going into the Ardennes Forest to assess the situation. He hadn't said he was driving the general.

Keith didn't see her. His attention was occupied with a slow horse-driven cart that was blocking the road. The horn blared again as the jeep dodged around the cart toward the forest.

CHAPTER 6

ater that afternoon Annie sat between two beds in the ward. The hectic pace of admitting patients, getting them cleaned up and bandaged, starting IVs, dispensing medications, and delivering meals had slowed. Next came the paper work. There was always paper work to do. The army kept detailed records of everything.

Twenty-one patients had been admitted. The story they were telling cast a pall over the ward.

"We were moving south on N–23," Alex Black said.

Black was a private from Champagne, Illinois. A piece of shrapnel had severed an artery in his leg. His buddy in the next bed, Dick Hollander, had saved his life by shutting off the flow of blood by making a tourniquet, using a dead soldier's shirt and the stick shift that had been blown free from their jeep.

"At the Baugnez crossroads," Dick added.

"I'm familiar with the place," Annie said. "There's a café there."

"Yeah. Café Bodarwe, on the southwest corner," Dick said.

Hollander was from Great Neck, New York. He had a concussion and belly wound. Even though he was still woozy from surgery, he propped himself up on one arm to add to the story. It was a compulsion with them.

Annie's attention bounced back and forth between the two men as they spoke over each other.

"We had about thirty jeeps in the convoy," Alex said.

"And a couple of weapons carriers and a two-and-a-half-ton truck. Battery B," Dick said.

"Anyway, we'd just passed through Five Points . . ."

"Baugnez crossroads. We call it Five Points because it's the intersection of five roads."

". . . traveling south, when all of a sudden we came under fire!"

"A couple of German tanks spotted us."

"We were sitting ducks!"

"The next thing I know, the jeep lifts up beneath me and I'm flying through the air."

"We landed in the ditch."

"More German tanks appeared. An entire column."

"Our convoy was wiped out."

"We counted eleven dead," Dick said.

Alex blinked. From the look in his eyes, he was back in the ditch, reliving the moment. "Then the Jerries started rounding us up. We played dead, Dick and me. There was enough of my blood around, I guess, to make it look convincing."

"We waited for them to move on."

"That's when Dick put the tourniquet on me. He used Harold's shirt . . ."

"Harold was our driver. He was dead."

". . . and the stick shift from one of the jeeps."

"It was just lying there on the ground."

"Then he helped me out of the ditch and we made for the forest. We took cover there."

"That's when we saw what happened," Dick said.

"Yeah," Alex added somberly.

Neither of them spoke for a while.

"There was about a hundred of them, wouldn't you say?" Alex asked.

"A hundred easy," Dick replied.

"The Jerries assembled them in a field next to the café."

"They had their hands up in the air."

"That's when . . ." Alex choked back his emotion. "That's when they opened fire on them."

"Machine guns. Rifles."

"The tank column passed by them during the massacre. The Krauts watched from the tanks like it was something they seen every day."

"They still had their hands up," Dick said again.

"The Jerries started walking among them, kicking, prodding." Tears filled his eyes. "Paul . . ."

Dick winced. He explained, "Paul and Alex were close. He saw Paul go down."

"They shot him in the back of the head."

"They shot anyone who showed signs of life."

The two men fell silent.

Annie had listened to enough stories from patients over the years to know there was a time to say something and a time to be quiet. She allowed them their silence while inside she raged.

From what she'd already heard from other patients, these two men were not exaggerating. What happened at the Baugnez cross-roads was unthinkable. Barbaric. A gross violation of the rules of war. And typically, German. Twenty-one Americans survived the slaughter. Over a hundred didn't. They lay dead on the frozen ground, victims of an atrocity.

Just when she thought she'd grown accustomed to the horrors of war, something like this happened. The Germans made it even more inhuman, more barbaric. Just wait for the spring offensive, she thought, when the Allies resume their march toward Berlin, mowing down any German forces that stand in their way, like a scythe through wheat. Then, finally, justice will be done.

Something touched her shoulder. She jumped.

Annie turned. A disheveled Mouse stood behind her, her eyes red, her cheeks wet.

"Oh, honey!" Annie was out of her seat instantly. She led Mouse to the far side of the room. "What's wrong, dear?"

She suspected she knew. Since the jeeps arrived with the casualties, all anyone heard about were stories of friends watching friends get massacred. Mouse was such a sensitive soul. It was too much for her.

"Antonio . . ." Mouse muttered.

"Antonio? Scarpetti? The singer?"

Mouse nodded, overcome by tears. She barely managed to say, "He didn't make it."

"Oh, honey, I'm so sorry! What happened?"

She cradled Mouse against her chest. Mouse's voice was muffled as she said, "Blood clot. Broke free from his leg. Lodged in his lung."

Annie wept with her friend.

In the corner of the ward stood the Christmas tree with its tinfoil stars and angels. Less than twenty-four hours ago the young New York Italian had stood in front of it singing Christmas carols, helping everyone to forget the war for a moment. Now his voice was forever silenced.

"Why do we insist on killing everything that's good in this world?" Mouse cried.

———

As the day progressed, American jeeps and trucks rumbled through the streets of Malmedy with increasing frequency. A steady stream roared past the 67th Evac. Away from the Ardennes Forest. They were retreating.

With every passing vehicle, Annie thought of Keith. The last time she'd seen him, he was heading the opposite direction, heading into whatever it was they were fleeing from.

Late that afternoon Captain Maude Elliott called an emergency meeting.

"We just received orders. We're evacuating. Take only what you can carry. You have fifteen minutes."

Stunned, the nurses exchanged glances. This was supposed to be a safe area. They'd been making Christmas plans.

"Before you go," Captain Elliott said, "I've been ordered to select three of you to stay behind to work in the OR and care for the nontransportable patients." She looked down. "I can't bring myself to do that, so I'm asking for volunteers."

That was when Annie knew it was worse than they were letting on. Captain Elliott made life-and-death decisions every day. If she couldn't bring herself to select a detail of nurses, what else could it mean other than there was a good chance the hospital would be overrun by Germans, that in all likelihood the nurses who remained behind would be killed or captured.

Annie looked around. The Malmedy massacre was fresh in everyone's mind. She could see it in their eyes. There was no reason for any of them to think the Germans would be any kinder to nurses.

"A show of hands, then," Captain Elliott said.

Annie started to raise her hand. Nina caught it and pulled it down.

"What are you doing?" she hissed.

"Volunteering."

"Oh no, you're not!"

"She's right," Mouse said. "You're a married woman now. You have to think of Keith."

Annie looked at her two friends. They were determined not to let her volunteer.

All around the room, hands went up bravely.

"I'll stay!"

"Count me in."

Captain Elliott's eyes glazed with tears as she looked proudly at her nurses.

Nina was holding down Annie's arm to keep her from doing anything foolish.

"All right, then," Elliott said. She pointed to them as she called their names. "Ethel Phibbs, Rebecca Newell . . . and Annie Rawlings makes three."

"But Annie didn't raise her hand!" Nina cried.

"Doesn't matter," Captain Elliott replied. "Dr. Skoglund is staying behind. He'll be in charge and he requested her."

Nina started to object again. Annie stopped her.

"Thanks for trying," she said.

"If Annie's staying, then I'm staying," Mouse said.

"We already have three," Elliott replied.

"Now we have four," Mouse said.

Captain Elliott stared at her.

"Very well," she said. "Rebecca, you're off the hook. Hanson is taking your place."

Rebecca Newell didn't object.

Captain Elliott wrote the names of the volunteers on a clipboard. She said, "Let's go, ladies. You have fifteen minutes."

The room erupted with noise as everyone jammed to get out the door that led to their sleeping quarters.

Still holding Annie's arm, Nina looked at her forlornly. Her voice trembled. "I . . . I'm sorry, Annie. But I . . . I can't . . . I can't stay."

Annie patted her hand. "One of us has to have the good sense to get out of harm's way," she said.

Nina smiled weakly. "But we've always been together . . . a trio."

"And we will be again," Annie said. "Save two cots for me and Mouse next to yours."

"Look on the bright side," Mouse said. "You only have fifteen minutes to pack. With Annie and me helping you, you'll be able to take three times as much as the other nurses!"

CHAPTER | 7

I loved your sister for volunteering like she did, Celia. Unless you've been in combat conditions, you can't begin to appreciate what she did back there. Put yourself in her place. She'd just been informed that the Germans would most certainly overrun the hospital, which meant she'd most likely be captured, possibly tortured, raped, and then killed. Your sister was given a "Get Out of Jail Free" card . . . and she turned it down! For me. She did it for me! I'll love her forever for it.

———————

The hospital was chaos as the evacuating nurses quickly tossed their personal belongings into their bedrolls and rolled them up. Fifteen minutes after the briefing, GIs were helping the nurses pile into the back of a large truck. Twenty minutes after the meeting, Annie and Mouse stood alone in the nurses' quarters. It looked as though it had been hit by a bomb.

Ethel Phibbs was in the ward checking on the seven patients who had been left behind.

Annie flopped onto her cot.

The building was eerily quiet.

Mouse began scrounging among the items Nina had left behind. "What are you doing?" Annie asked.

Mouse straightened up, holding a tin of fudge.

"Mouse! That belongs to Nina!"

"I know that!" Mouse said indignantly. "What? You think I'm stealing it? I'm going to hide it in a safe place."

Annie smiled. Mouse was up to something.

"Seriously!" Mouse said. "If you think I'm going to let the Germans eat all of our Christmas goodies, you've got another think coming!"

She had a point. There was a considerable stash of cookies, cake, candy, and fudge among the nurses' belongings, mostly packages from home. While they'd tapped the goodie stash for the party, they'd saved their best stuff for Christmas Day. The thought of Germans eating Christmas goodies made by American mothers for their daughters at war was simply unacceptable.

Phibbs entered the room just then, and she agreed. The three of them made a cot-to-cot search, looking for Christmas packages.

In no time they had a cot covered with Christmas goodies. Pulling the four corners of the blanket together so that it resembled a green version of Santa's bag, Mouse, Annie, and Phibbs went in search of a suitable hiding place.

Annie slipped one of her chocolate bars from home into the pocket of her coat, saving it for later. It had been a really bad day.

Blackout conditions were ordered, so the three nurses taped blankets over the windows. No one was allowed to go outside without an armed escort.

Annie didn't sleep a wink that night. The booming of distant shells gave the war a definite pulse. With every passing vehicle, every voice, every cough, every door closed, rumors of Germans in the vicinity became reality. Especially when Annie closed her eyes.

Phibbs had volunteered for the graveyard shift. Smart woman. If sleep wasn't possible, might as well do something useful. After being startled into a sitting position for the sixth or seventh time, Annie got up and sat with her. Phibbs welcomed her company.

What began as an endless night finally passed. As the sky grew lighter, Annie lifted one of the blackout blankets. The streets of Malmedy lay deathly quiet, as if the town were holding its breath.

Annie left Ethel to complete the last of the paper work for the shift. She could hear Mouse stirring in the nurses' quarters. Annie's stomach rumbled. Her thoughts turned to breakfast. With the hospital staff gone, who was going to fix it? And if the kitchen staff had raided the pantry like the nurses had raided their quarters, there was no telling what they'd left behind.

A jeep horn interrupted her thoughts. An engine coughed, sputtered, wheezed and died with a thud, followed by the horn again, only this time the horn let out a continuous wail.

Annie ran to the main doors. A wall of arctic air assaulted her as she pulled them open. An army jeep—American—had jumped the curb. A soldier was slumped against the wheel. The horn blared mercilessly until Annie pulled the soldier off of it.

The man was covered in mud and blood. At first glance Annie couldn't tell if the blood was his.

Mouse and Phibbs appeared at the door.

"Get a litter!" Annie yelled.

She felt the man's neck for a pulse. It was strong. Racing. His eyes fluttered. He gave a start, then grabbed her hand.

He didn't seem to comprehend where he was.

"It's all right," she said. "You're at the 67th Evac Hospital."

After several blinks, his eyes focused on her, shifted to the front of the hospital, then back to her. "Help . . ." he said.

"You're at the 67th Evac Hospital," Annie repeated. "We'll get you inside and take good care of you."

He licked his lips. "No . . . need help . . . need help . . . Gen . . . Gen'ral Max . . ."

His head slumped over.

"General Max . . . General Maxwell?" Annie's hand and heart raced to her throat. It was a tie. She fingered the necklace Keith had given her.

She tried slapping the soldier back to consciousness.

"General Maxwell? General Maxwell needs help?" she shouted at him.

The soldier's eyes flickered. His head lolled, but he didn't have the strength to lift it.

"Maxwell . . . send medic . . ."

Mouse and Phibbs appeared with a litter. Between the three of them they managed to ease the soldier out of the jeep and onto the litter.

Mouse and Phibbs started to lift him.

"Just a minute," Annie said. She bent over the litter. "General Maxwell needs a medic!" she shouted at the soldier. "Where? Where is he?"

"Tenm . . . ten . . . muh . . . emmwun . . ."

Annie looked up at Mouse and Phibbs. "I didn't get that. Did either of you get that? Say again! Where is General Maxwell?"

"Senmedic."

"Yes, we'll send a medic, but where?"

"Tenmuh . . . emmwun."

"Ten miles," Mouse said. "M1 road?"

"Are you sure?" Annie said to Mouse. She'd heard the same thing but got nothing.

Mouse shrugged. "That's what it sounded like to me."

"Road M1 leads into the forest, doesn't it?" Annie said.

All Annie got were shrugs.

"All right. Get him inside," she said.

Mouse looked at Phibbs.

"On three," Phibbs said. "One, two . . ."

"Buckle my shoe," Mouse said, straining.

While Mouse and Phibbs carried the soldier to the pre-op ward, Annie made a beeline for Dr. Skoglund. She found him and Dr. McKenzie packing.

McKenzie was a younger man, lean, with long elegant hands. He was the youngest surgeon on staff and he worshiped Skoglund.

"What was all that racket outside?" Skoglund asked before Annie could say anything.

"A wounded soldier," Annie said breathlessly. "He's in pre-op. He says General Maxwell needs medical help."

Skoglund scrunched his face. "Hmm. Bad timing. Where is the general now?"

Annie didn't know for sure. All she had to go on was an incoherent soldier and Mouse's guess as to what he said.

"He's in the forest, on route M1."

Skoglund stopped packing. He looked up. "How far?"

Annie grimaced. She'd stretched the truth as far as she could. Anything more would be a lie.

"Maybe ten miles. We don't know," she said, "but he can't be too far. The soldier in the jeep is in pretty bad shape. He couldn't have driven very far in his condition."

She sounded desperate. She was trying to maintain a professional tone, but even she didn't think she was doing a very good job of it.

Skoglund shook his head and resumed packing. "We don't do house calls," he said.

McKenzie laughed.

"Doctor . . ."

Skoglund didn't look at her. He kept packing. "That's what medics are for, Miss Rawlings," he said. "Surgeons don't go charging into the field searching for patients. They come to us."

McKenzie smiled appreciatively.

"Besides," Skoglund continued, "we just got new orders. We're joining up with the rest of the hospital. With any luck, we'll be there in time for breakfast. I suggest you and the other nurses start packing."

"Orders? But what about the patients?"

"The army has upgraded their status. We're moving out."

"And the soldier in pre-op?"

Skoglund looked up at McKenzie. "Take a look at him, will you? But make it snappy. I want to get out of here."

"Yes, sir," McKenzie said.

McKenzie gave Annie an amused grin as he passed by, which made her wonder how much Skoglund had told him about her.

Now it was just she and Eugene Skoglund.

"Doctor, the soldier in pre-op is acting under orders from General Maxwell. He was sent to get help. We should send someone to check it out."

Annie was overstating her case, yet she didn't care. Skoglund's actions were not only unprofessional, they were bordering on cowardly.

Skoglund stood and faced her. "Nurse, we don't have the personnel to respond. What we do have are orders to retreat. At this moment your concern is threefold: one, to prepare the patients for transport; two, to pack your personal belongings; and three, to get out of my quarters! Dismissed."

"Dr. Skoglund . . . Eugene. Keith is with General Maxwell."

Icy blue eyes stared at her through wire-rimmed eyeglasses. "This is war, Miss Rawlings," he said. "In war soldiers die."

Annie glared at him, her anger building to volcanic proportions. "My name is Mrs. Mitchell," she said through clenched teeth.

CHAPTER 8

*A*nnie pulled on her heavy coat and was reaching for her helmet when Mouse came in.

"What are you doing?" Mouse asked.

"I'm going after Keith."

"What are you talking about?"

"I saw Keith driving General Maxwell yesterday. They were going into the Ardennes."

"Keith is with General Maxwell? Oh, Annie!"

Annie buttoned her coat.

"Who's taking you?" Mouse asked. "I'm amazed Skoglund approved it. McKenzie said we were shipping out."

Annie didn't reply. She started to leave.

"Annie . . . Skoglund did approve it, didn't he?"

Still Annie didn't say anything. Mouse's eyes grew wide.

"You didn't ask him!"

"He refuses to send anyone," Annie explained.

Mouse grabbed Annie's arm. "Who's taking you?"

"Don't try to stop me," Annie said.

Mouse's grip tightened.

"Mouse, it's Keith. I have to go."

"I know," Mouse said. "But I can't let you go . . ."

"Mouse!"

". . . without me."

"Marcy, no. It's too dangerous."

But Mouse had grabbed her coat and helmet and was heading for the door. "I knew there was a reason God wanted me to stay behind with you," she said.

Mouse was big on God. She saw God's hand in everything. There was a time when Annie was like her, but two years of war had pummeled her faith senseless. Annie feared it would never fully recover.

"And where do you get off calling me Marcy?" Mouse said. "No one calls me Marcy except my mother."

Since the jeep in front of the hospital was DOA, they made their way around to the back of the hospital hoping to find something at the loading dock. They were in luck. There were two vehicles. A flatbed truck and an ambulance.

It began to snow.

Mouse jumped behind the wheel of the ambulance.

"Do you know how to drive that thing?" Annie asked.

"How much different can it be from my dad's Buick? You check the supplies in the back and I'll crank this baby up."

Annie climbed into the back. It had been cleaned out except for a couple of litters, two packages of bandages, some gauze, and half a tube of antibiotic salve. The state of supplies came as no surprise as the engine cranked but without firing. It sounded like someone groaning from a stomachache.

"Maybe we should try the truck!" Annie shouted.

She climbed back up front.

The truck made another round of groans, followed by a banging sound.

"What's that?" Annie asked.

Mouse cocked her head. "There it is again. It doesn't sound like anything I've ever . . ."

Annie looked through the windshield. The banging sound wasn't coming from the engine. It was coming from a second-floor window.

Holding back the blackout curtain with one hand, Eugene Sko-glund banged the windowpane with the other. He was shouting something. Annie couldn't make out what he was saying, but it didn't take a genius to guess.

She made eye contact with him.

"Mouse, get this thing going," Annie said.

Furious that she was ignoring him, Skoglund began fumbling with the window latch.

"We're running out of time, Mouse."

Mouse was leaning forward, her head bobbing with each turn of the engine, urging the engine to come alive. "I think . . . I can . . . get this . . . to . . ."

Skoglund looked like a crazed animal trying to break out of its cage.

"We're dead, oh, we're dead!" Annie cried.

The hospital window flew open, and Skoglund stuck his head out. "Rawlings! Get out of that vehicle! I order you to—"

The roar of the ambulance engine cut him off.

Mouse looked up triumphantly. "Like I said. Just like my dad's Buick!"

Annie looked at Skoglund. She cupped her ear and shouted, "I can't hear you! We're going to get General Maxwell! Okay? If you approve, shake your fist at me!"

Skoglund couldn't have heard her, but at that moment he reached an arm out the window and shook his fist at them.

With a grinding of gears, a laughing Mouse backed the ambu-lance out of the bay. Another grinding and they were in first gear, jostling onto the streets of Malmedy, heading toward route M1.

"I hope we have enough gas," Mouse said.

They'd been traveling for twenty minutes. Once they left the city and Mouse found fourth gear, the ride had been rather smooth. Annie kept checking the side mirror, expecting to see military police closing in on them. The view in the mirror was as empty as the countryside.

It was snowing heavily now. The windshield wipers whisked aside the flakes.

The lack of vehicles or any kind of military presence was eerie. While she hadn't given it much thought until now, she'd assumed they would pass some troops, possibly even tell them what had happened and enlist their help. But they hadn't seen a soul since leaving Malmedy. The phrase *No Man's Land* kept coming to mind. She had no idea where the two opposing armies were at this moment, so she couldn't say for sure whether they were actually in No Man's Land. But it sure felt like it. And the last thing they needed right now was to run out of gas.

Already Annie's hands were frozen and she couldn't feel her toes. However, she was feeling the weight of what they were doing.

She and Mouse were in big trouble. They'd left their post without permission and stolen an ambulance. And that was just the tip of their iceberg of trouble. As the ambulance rumbled down M1 road, Annie had time to think about it. Even if they found General Maxwell and Keith, who knew if the hospital would still be in Malmedy when they returned? Skoglund said they'd received orders to retreat, only Annie hadn't stuck around long enough to find out when. An hour? Two? Fifteen minutes? She had no idea.

"Oh, Mouse, what have I gotten us into?" Annie said, staring at a flat expanse of white on her side of the ambulance. About a hundred yards off the road, the edge of the Ardennes Forest swept by.

"What are you talking about?" Mouse said. "We're doing the right thing."

"Are we?"

"Are you kidding? Keith needs you!"

"General Maxwell, too."

"Yeah. Him, too. We bring him back and they'll give us medals."

Annie sighed. "Right now I'd swap a medal for the assurance that Keith is all right. How far have we traveled?"

"About nine miles."

The wounded soldier had said ten miles. At least they thought he had said ten miles. Annie fidgeted in her seat. The snow had erased any signs of tracks from the road. Was it ten miles down the road, or a total of ten miles? Maxwell could have left the road at any point and gone into the forest.

"Nine miles," Mouse said.

Time and gas were running out.

"Looks like Lower Slobbovia," Annie said.

"What?"

"Nothing. Just something Keith said."

Annie strained to see beyond the streaked windshield, through the snow, past the trees, for any sign of men and a jeep. As she searched, her mind envisioned all manner of scenarios, most of them not good.

She saw them finding an overturned jeep with Keith and General Maxwell lying next to it, half covered with snow. Dead.

She saw them coming upon an overturned jeep with Keith and General Maxwell surrounded by Germans.

In one scenario the Germans opened fire on Keith as they'd done to the prisoners at the Baugnez crossroads.

She saw them blindly driving past an overturned jeep covered with snow with Keith having enough strength to lift his head and see her, but not enough to call to her.

She saw them never finding Keith, but driving until they ran out of gas. She saw her and Mouse stranded in the snow, walking unarmed through enemy territory.

She saw her and Mouse captured by Germans. Held at gunpoint. Leered at. Groped. Raped.

What had she gotten them into? If anything happened to Mouse, it would be all her fault.

"Ten miles," Mouse said.

Still nothing but tree limbs heavy with snow, white mounds, and a road with a fresh layer of snow that made it appear they were the first vehicle ever to travel this way.

"How much farther do we go?" Mouse asked. She spoke with her best *I'm just doing my job* voice. She appeared calm.

"Just a couple of minutes more."

Mouse nodded. Annie was looking to see if she would check the gas tank, and she did.

They continued on.

"Eleven miles," Mouse said.

They'd run out of time. Would one more mile make a difference, or would it just be one mile more they'd have to trudge back in the snow? The next words out of Annie's mouth were the hardest words she had ever spoken.

"Let's turn around," she said.

"You sure?"

"Yeah."

But she wasn't sure. She wasn't sure of anything. For all she knew, a hundred yards farther down the road they'd spot Keith's jeep. Annie bit her lower lip as the ambulance slowed.

Mouse pulled hard on the wheel. She had to jockey back and forth three times in order to maneuver the ambulance in the opposite direction. After a succession of gears the ambulance began picking up speed again, like a horse heading for the barn.

"Mouse, stop! I think I see something!"

Annie stared hard three-trees-deep into the woods. She saw what amounted to a black half-moon rising over a snowbank. Beyond it were splintered half trees, their trunks black.

The ambulance brakes squealed as they slid to a stop. Mouse rolled down her window to get a better look.

"Do you want me to drive over there?" she asked.

That would mean leaving the road, and while it looked level enough, there was no way of knowing what kinds of ruts or axle-breaking obstacles the snow was concealing. Annie opened the door.

"Stay here," she said. "If I need you, I'll signal."

"Annie . . . I don't feel good about you going into the forest alone."

"Just to the edge," Annie said, opening her door.

Her boots crunched frozen gravel as she stepped out of the ambulance. Two steps off the road and she was up to her knees.

It was rough going, with the distance to the trees being about a hundred yards. Annie had to swing her arms to maintain her momentum, and by the time she'd covered a third of the distance, the icy air began burning her throat. She'd never been much of an athlete. The farthest she'd ever run in her life was from the batter's box to first base during Fourth of July church softball games.

And never in the snow, she thought.

The next step, her foot plunged into a hole and she fell.

"Are you all right?" Mouse called from the ambulance.

Floundering to stand up, Annie managed a wave. "Yeah, just a ditch or something," she said.

She was halfway to the trees. The ground beneath her began to rise. She got a better look at the half-moon. It was what she thought it was—a tire!

Annie pressed on with renewed hope, then sudden fear. She had no assurance it was an American tire. What if it belonged to a German vehicle? And what if its German occupants were still in the vicinity? In her enthusiasm to find Keith's jeep, had she been lured to the enemy?

A recurring nightmare flashed in her mind, one in which she was trying to run, but her legs felt extremely heavy, as though she were trying to run in sand or . . .

"Or knee-deep snow," Annie muttered to herself.

Her gaze darted through the trees, looking for movement or any sign of a German uniform. She strained to hear past her labored breathing and the pounding of her heart in her ears.

She pressed forward.

The vehicle was pitched forward at an awkward angle. As she got closer she saw that the tire was actually the spare, which was attached to the back of a jeep.

Her heart beat faster. It was a jeep! But was it Keith's jeep?

Before going any farther, she surveyed the woods again for any sign of movement. Seeing none, she circled the jeep. It tilted to the driver's side. On the front, stiff and frozen, was a flag with a single yellow star.

A general's star!

"Keith? Keith!" she shouted.

She took another step, steadying herself against the jeep. Her hand slipped. When she looked at it, snow was mixed with blood.

"Keith! Keith!"

"Annie?"

His voice was weak but recognizable. She'd married that voice.

"Keith?"

"Annie! Over here!"

She still couldn't see him. His voice was coming from deeper in the forest. She turned to shout at Mouse.

"They're here!" she yelled, waving an arm.

Mouse had climbed out of the ambulance. She gave a little jump, clapping her hands before climbing back inside the cab. The ambulance engine revved and gears meshed as the front end plowed into the snowy field.

"Where are you?" Annie called to Keith.

"I can see you. Follow my voice, and watch your step!"

Annie could see why the warning. Splintered tree stumps, sharp as daggers, jutted up from the ground.

"This way . . . this way . . . keep coming forward . . ."

She could see the vague outline of his form. He was sitting up beneath a large fir tree. There were others stretched out on the ground beside him.

Annie lifted a branch. A diffused light fell on her husband's face. At that moment it was all she could do to keep from losing control.

"Thank God!" she cried, crawling on her hands and knees to him. She fell on top of him, her hands grabbing his jacket, his arms, his face, as though she expected him to disappear at any moment. She covered his face with kisses.

"Ow. Ow! Watch the leg!"

"Oh, sorry," Annie said, rolling to one side yet still holding on. "Better?"

He started to answer, then couldn't, because her lips were covering his.

"I thought I'd lost you," she said.

Keith cradled her head in his gloved hands. His face was wet with her kisses. "I kept telling myself that if I could just hold on long enough to get to Annie's hospital, everything would be all right. I never dreamed you would . . ." He pulled back. "What are you doing here? You shouldn't be here! What nitwit sent you out here?"

"We don't have time for that now," Annie said. "We need to get you and the others back to the hospital."

"No hurry on the others."

Annie hadn't realized it until now, but none of the other men had spoken a word, or moved.

"Walker was the last," Keith said. "He died about an hour ago."

As the ambulance roared toward them, Annie checked the other men. Keith was right. They were all dead.

"What happened?"

"A bullheaded general, that's what happened. Everyone kept telling him to turn back, that we were headed straight into the Germans. He wouldn't listen. Called us cowards. That's when the shelling started. He ordered us into the trees for cover. Said it wasn't safe on the road. Either the guy was the unluckiest general ever to wear the uniform or a magnet for artillery shells, but somehow he managed to park us under a couple of them."

He shook his head.

"Paddock was killed instantly; the general didn't last much longer."

Annie clicked into nurse mode. "How bad is your leg? It looks like you've lost a lot of blood. Your color's not good. Did you drag these men under here with you?"

"Harris! He made it back, didn't he? That's how you knew to come. How is he? Is he all right?"

"He was alive when we left," Annie shouted, examining his leg.

She had to shout because of the roar of the ambulance that had pulled within a dozen or so feet of them. Mouse jumped out.

"Another woman?" Keith said. "They sent two women? Tell me you have an armed escort in the back of the ambulance."

Annie didn't look at him directly. "We're not exactly here under orders," she said.

He didn't respond. When she looked up, he was grinning at her. Not at all what she'd expected.

"Now that's a story I want to hear," he said.

"Annie? Where are you?" Mouse cried.

Before Annie could answer, Keith pulled her close to him. He kissed her. "I've never seen you in your helmet before," he whispered. "You look adorable."

CHAPTER 9

*A*nnie and Mouse fit Keith's leg with a splint and gave him crackers to eat while they prepared to load the bodies into the back of the ambulance. Mouse had insisted on taking the bodies back.

"If we leave them, the animals will get them," she'd said. "Their families deserve better than that."

They loaded the general first, pulling him from under the tree by his feet next to a litter.

"On three," Annie said. "One, two . . ."

"Buckle my shoe," Mouse said.

Keith was propped against a tree on his good leg, eating crackers. At best, he could hobble. Lifting was out of the question. He stopped mid-chew, amused at Mouse. Annie and he exchanged glances. She grinned and shrugged.

Loading dead weight into the ambulance proved to be more difficult than either of the women had expected, though it helped that the snow wasn't deep beneath the tree cover. Having slipped and slid, alternately propping the litter and climbing their way into the ambulance, Annie and Mouse returned, huffing and puffing, for the next body.

Annie stopped. "Do you hear that?" she said.

Keith heard it, too. With cracker paused just shy of his open mouth, he'd cocked his head at the deep rumble.

"What?" Mouse said, busily rubbing her hands to get them warm.

The branches of the trees trembled, knocking bits of snow to the ground.

"We have to get out of here," Keith said. He tossed his cracker aside and pushed off from the tree. One step, a grimace, and he fell back against it.

Mouse heard the rumble now. Undaunted, she bent low to get the next body. "I'm not leaving until we—"

"We're all leaving!" Keith barked. "Now! Annie, help me get to the ambulance."

Panic charged his voice. It was a side of Keith that Annie had never seen before. She'd seen him take the lead, but never like this. On the football field, he was known for his calmness under pressure. The Keith who called to her now had a no-nonsense set to his jaw, and—what twisted her stomach into a knot—a fearful glint in his eyes.

"Mouse, we'd better do as he says."

On her knees, Mouse reached under the tree for the feet of the next soldier. "I'm not leaving them here," she insisted, "not with Christmas coming."

"Then you'd better prepare to join them," Keith shouted, "because that's what's going to happen if we don't get out of here right now!"

Maybe it was the desperation in his voice, but something got through to her. Mouse got to her feet and climbed into the ambulance. Annie helped Keith into the passenger's side, then followed after him.

The rumbling grew louder.

With Keith shouting instructions at Mouse, they managed to turn the ambulance toward the road. The hood brushed aside tree limbs as they emerged from the forest.

"Stop! Stop! Stop!" Keith shouted.

Mouse slammed on the brakes. The ambulance skid a short distance, its nose poking out from among the trees.

Annie saw what Keith saw, and it made her heart sink.

A column of German tanks was clanking down route M1, heading for Malmedy.

"Back it up! Back it up!" Keith screamed.

Mouse struggled with the gearshift. There was a horrible grinding sound. She couldn't get it into reverse.

"Double clutch!" Keith shouted.

Mouse looked flustered. "What? I don't know how—"

"Let the clutch out, then put it back in!"

"Oh! Why didn't you say—"

"Just do it!"

Beyond the windshield they had a panoramic view of the infamous Third Reich in full attack mode. It was a fearsome sight. Now if they could just make it disappear before the Third Reich saw them.

Mouse managed to ram the gearshift into reverse, and the ambulance lurched. With a cough, the engine died.

Keith started to shout something.

"I'm on it," Mouse shouted first.

The engine cranked but didn't turn over.

"Too much gas!" Keith shouted.

There was a ping, then another. These were not engine sounds.

"They're shooting at us!" Annie cried.

The windshield shattered.

"Get down!" Keith shouted.

He pushed Annie to the floorboard and fell on top of her. Mouse slipped down behind the wheel.

The ambulance took another couple of hits.

"What did you do with my rifle?" Keith said.

"We loaded all the weapons in the back," said Annie.

"Great. Just great."

Another hit. A steam geyser erupted under the hood.

"We're sitting ducks! We have to get out of here," Keith said.

"But your leg . . ." Annie said.

"We're going to have to risk it," Keith said. "Stay down. I'm going to take a look."

He began to rise up, but Annie pulled him back down. "Be careful," she said.

He gave her a weak smile.

Keith rose up slowly until he could see through what was left of the windshield. From the floorboard Annie could see the bottom of his chin. Keith had always had a strong chin; it gave his face a look of confidence. Now, however, it dropped.

"We have to get out! Now!" Keith shouted.

"What did—"

"NOW!"

He reached over her and punched open the passenger door. Annie looked over at Mouse, who was fumbling with the door latch. The next thing Annie knew, she was on the ground. Keith had pushed her out of the ambulance and was going to land on top of her if she didn't move. She rolled over and ended up facing the road.

Now she understood the urgency. Two of the German tanks had stopped. Their guns were pointed directly at the ambulance.

"Go, go, go!" Keith shouted.

Annie scurried on all fours as fast as she could away from the ambulance. Keith limped down the side of the ambulance toward the back. He opened the back doors.

"What are you doing?" Annie cried.

He didn't answer. His top half disappeared, then reappeared, holding two rifles.

Annie heard the tank fire—a sickening sound when at the wrong end of the barrel. Earth and tree and snow exploded, knocking Keith to the ground, sending the general's jeep high into the air in a graceful tumble. But there was nothing graceful about its fall. Metal crunched as it rolled twice and then slammed into a tree.

Keith got up and scrambled toward her, wincing in pain, his face covered with mud and sweat and blood.

"Mouse?" Annie shouted.

She hadn't seen Mouse get out of the ambulance.

"Mouse!"

Annie couldn't see the driver's side of the ambulance. She ran to get a better angle while still staying clear of the vehicle.

"No! No!" she cried as she cleared the driver's side.

The door was still closed. Mouse hadn't made it out. The engine turned over with a grinding sound.

What was Mouse doing?

"Mouse! No!" she shouted. "Get out! Mouse . . . Marcy . . ."

She could see Mouse's face in the side mirror. Mouse was looking at the Germans as the engine cranked. She was crying.

"Mouse! Get out! Get out!"

Mouse heard her. Their eyes met in the mirror.

Mouse mouthed Annie's name.

Now Annie was crying. "Get out, Mouse! Get out!" she whimpered.

Mouse looked down for the door handle. Her shoulder hit the door to open it.

It didn't open.

She shouldered it again. Harder.

It still didn't open.

"The other side!" Annie shouted. "The other side!"

Mouse must have heard her. With a frantic glance at the Germans, she disappeared from the mirror.

Annie slid to the passenger's side just in time to see Mouse tumble out of the door. She rolled, crouched, got to her feet and ran.

The ambulance reared, its side doors lamely open, like a wounded bird attempting to take flight. It rolled midair and slammed to the ground on its side.

Mouse stumbled and fell at Annie's feet. She looked up from the ground. "I made it!" she said breathlessly.

Keith stared at the ambulance, the one bearing the general's body, which was now engulfed in flames.

"The guy was an artillery shell magnet," he said.

Another shell whistled overhead, missing both vehicles and sailing into the woods, felling several trees.

"Stay down!" Keith shouted as he hopped toward Annie. Unable to stop his momentum, he fell into her arms. She staggered backward.

"We need to get out of here," he said. "Here, take this."

Keith handed Annie one of the rifles.

"What am I supposed to do with this?" she asked.

"Carry it. We need to put some distance between us and these vehicles. They'll send some men to mop up."

Annie glanced toward the road. Through the smoke of the burning ambulance she saw he was right. A half dozen Germans with rifles were knee-deep in snow, heading their direction.

"Where to?" she said.

"Anywhere but here," Keith said. He was already hobbling into the woods.

"To think that a few hours ago my biggest concern was Skoglund," Annie said to Mouse. "Come on, let's go."

"You may have to go on without me," Mouse said.

"What are you talking about?"

Mouse rolled onto her side. The snow and pine needles beneath her were stained with blood.

"Oh no! Marcy! No!" Annie cried.

CHAPTER | *10*

"Come on, ladies, we don't have time to dawdle," Keith said, looking back.

On her knees, Annie knelt over Mouse, peeling back layers of clothing. She looked up long enough to say, "Mouse has been hit."

"How bad is it?"

Mouse's belly and left leg were a mess of blood and clothes and twigs. Annie's heart was in her throat. She was having trouble focusing. She'd treated hundreds of wounds like this before. But none of them had been Mouse.

Annie looked up helplessly at Keith.

"Can she walk?"

"She's losing blood fast," Annie said.

"We can't stay here."

"I'm not going to leave her."

Mouse grabbed Annie's arm. "Go," she said weakly.

"That's not an option, dear heart," Annie replied.

German bullets whizzed overhead.

Keith spotted a litter nearby, the one Annie and Mouse were going to use to load Paddock into the ambulance. He hobbled toward it.

"Get her on this," he said, dragging it back.

"We need two to carry her," Annie said. "Your leg won't hold up."

"We can drag her. You know, the way the Indians used to do it, like a cart without wheels."

Bits of tree sprinkled down on them, cut free from bullets.

Mouse needed attention now, but staying would endanger them all.

"Hang tight, Mouse," Annie said.

She and Keith positioned the litter beside Mouse. Annie took an anxious glance at the approaching Germans. She could see the sweat on their faces.

"You take her feet," Annie said.

Keith was on one knee.

Grabbing Mouse's shoulders, Annie said, "On three. One, two . . ."

"Buckle my shoe," Mouse mumbled softly.

They managed to drag her onto the cot. Annie sprang to her feet, lifting her end.

"I'll help," Keith said.

"I've got it," Annie replied. "You carry the rifles and lead the way."

"Annie . . ."

But Annie was done talking. She was angry and scared and sick to her stomach over Mouse's condition. With all her might, she pulled Mouse away from the approaching Germans.

"I think they found enough bodies to satisfy them," Keith said, peering through branches. "I don't see anyone."

Annie knelt beside Mouse, holding her hand. Mouse stared past the treetops at the sky. She was pale.

"She needs blood," Annie said.

Keith's attention was behind them. "They're soldiers, not trackers. With all the equipment and felled trees and bodies, I doubt if they'll notice the track the litter made. Besides, they'll see we're no threat to them. They're not going to want to extend their perimeter too far into the woods. They're going to want to keep those tanks moving."

"Keith, Mouse needs medical attention now. Is there a base nearby? Or a farmhouse?"

With the difficulty of a man who can't bend his leg, Keith sat next to her.

"Everything's fluid right now," he said. "There could be a unit nearby, or we could be behind enemy lines." His eyes—alert and jumpy—scanned the trees. "We can't stay here."

"Annie?" Mouse said weakly.

"What is it, dear?"

"I'm thirsty."

Annie looked around helplessly. They'd fled in such haste, there wasn't time to grab any supplies. Keith had removed his ammunition belt and canteen under the tree. For all Annie knew, it was still there. They had nothing but two rifles, a litter, and the clothes on their backs.

"I'll get you some water," Annie said.

She removed her gloves and scooped up a handful of snow, passing it from hand to hand, melting it with her body heat. Cupping the water in her palm, she lifted Marcy's head and did her best to pour the water onto her lips.

"More?" Annie asked.

"No, thank you," Mouse said.

Annie felt so helpless. Her best friend in the world was fading and there was nothing she could do about it.

"I knew God had a plan," Mouse said. "Why He wanted me to stay behind with you. We found him, didn't we, Annie? We found him."

"Yeah, we found him," Annie said. "And I couldn't have done it without your help."

"Promise me something?" Mouse said.

Annie squeezed her friend's hand. "Anything, dear."

"Bring me back something from Paris?"

Annie laughed. She kissed Mouse's hand. "Is there something in particular you want?"

"Perfume would be nice. Something real sophisticated. I need all the help I can get to trap me a man."

"Any man would be lucky to have you."

Mouse smiled. "Yeah, well, they haven't exactly been lining up at the door, have they?"

She shivered violently.

"I guess the sun sets early in the forest," she said.

Annie shot a worried glance at Keith. It was midday.

Mouse began to shake.

Annie took off her overcoat to cover her. It was cold, but Mouse needed the coat more than she did. "Better?" Annie asked.

"A lot better, thanks. I'm not cold anymore."

The shivering stopped.

Mouse's eyes were fixed on the tops of the trees. She was still. Too still.

"Mouse?"

Annie shook her.

"Mouse?" Louder this time, and harder.

Keith crawled to Annie's side.

"Marcy?" Annie cried. "Marcy?"

"She's gone, Annie," Keith said. He put an arm around her. Annie shook him off.

"No!" Annie cried. "No . . . no . . . please, God . . . no!"

Her tears fell on Mouse's cheeks and nose.

Annie was shivering. She felt Keith's arm around her again. This time she didn't resist.

"When all the other nurses evacuated, Mouse stayed for me. I should have made her go with Nina. And when she caught me coming to find you, she insisted on coming, too. She jumped behind the wheel to drive."

"She was a good friend," Keith said.

"Yeah. And what did it get her?" Annie curled a lock of Mouse's hair. "You deserved better than this," she said. "Oh, God, of all people she deserved better than this."

Keith reached down and closed Mouse's eyes. Then he reached for Annie's coat.

"No," Annie said, staying his hand. "She needs it."

"Annie . . ." His voice was soft. Firm.

He took the coat and draped it over Annie's shoulders.

Annie's face was buried against Keith's side. He had tucked her securely against him, his arm snug around her shoulders. They lay next to each other against a fallen log. An outcrop of rocks sheltered them from the wind; the large branches of a fir tree stretched over them like protective arms.

Her eyes closed, Annie tried to shut out the world. She didn't want to think. Didn't want to feel. But her sadistic mind didn't need visual light to torture her. Image after image of Mouse played in her head—laughing in a tent at Anzio, the night they made hot chocolate and knew they'd be friends forever; a drenched Mouse, bobbing in the sea the night the *St. David* was shot out from under them; wheeling the German patient into the Christmas party because it was the Christian thing to do; lying on her back, looking up at the sky with lifeless eyes.

Annie grimaced, trying to squeeze the memories out of her head. If she didn't admit Mouse was dead, then Mouse wasn't dead.

"It's not your fault," Keith said.

His words sounded distant.

"I'm telling you, it isn't your fault."

Annie said nothing. If she spoke, she'd cry.

"The enemy killed her," Keith said. "Look, I know what I'm talking about. You think I don't know what it's like to watch a friend die? Johnny Rivers bought it in the Rhone Valley. You remember me writing about Johnny. He was my best pal in basic, the one who could fit an entire apple in his mouth. Then there was Hut Wheeler. Took a bullet in the head at Toulon. I was the one who gave him the all-clear signal to cross the street. But I didn't shoot him. The Germans did."

Annie looked up at him. She knew he was trying to help, but there was nothing he could say that could make a difference right now.

"You were her friend. It was the enemy who killed her," Keith insisted.

"Yeah, I guess you're right," she said, in hopes that if she agreed, he would stop talking.

"I know I'm right! If your places were reversed and you were the one killed and Mousey . . ."

"Just Mouse."

". . . and Mouse was blaming herself. What would you say to her?"

"I'd tell her it wasn't her fault."

"That's right. And it would be the truth, too."

Annie closed her eyes. She saw Mouse laughing. The time and place wasn't clear, but the image of Mouse was, and it wrenched Annie's heart. She opened her eyes and wondered if she'd ever be able to close them again without seeing Mouse.

Keith stretched, then groaned in pain. "We'd better get a move on," he said. "If we don't find some friendlies before nightfall . . . well, I don't want to think about the alternative."

"We need to bury Mouse," Annie said.

"Sorry. Can't."

Annie dug in her heels. "It's important to Mouse. She wasn't going to leave those men back there exposed in the forest. It's the least we can do for her."

Using the fallen log to push himself up, Keith said, "Not possible."

"Keith! I'm doing this! You go ahead if you want to, I'll catch up. But I'm going to bury my friend."

"The ground's frozen."

Annie stared at the earth. She fought back tears. Everything in the forest was against her.

"But I can't just leave her lying out in the open like this!"

With effort, Keith bent over Mouse. He removed her jacket and draped it over her face, anchoring the sides down with rocks. Then, with Annie's help, they covered Mouse with tree limbs and twigs. Keith fashioned a cross of wood and, unable to stick it into the ground despite repeated effort, placed it on top of the limb pile.

He said, "When we get back, we'll inform the authorities where to locate—"

He bit off the end of the sentence. His head snapped to one side. Eyes alert.

"What?" Annie whispered, the suddenness of his actions scaring her. "What do you—"

Keith cut her off with a hand signal. The next thing Annie knew he grabbed her by the jacket and pulled her to the ground behind the log.

A moment later she knew why. She heard voices, voices speaking German.

CHAPTER 11

*T*here were two of them. One tall and lanky, the other shorter, more compact. They moved quietly, bent over with their rifles in hand. The swastikas on their uniforms visually screamed "Heil! Hitler!"

They appeared to be searching for something. They spoke to each other in whispers.

"They're looking for us!" Annie whispered.

Keith shushed her.

Together they peered over the log. Keith readied his rifle. Annie stopped him, her eyes questioning the wisdom of firing with the odds being two soldiers to one.

Keith scowled at her. He whispered, "I can get both of them before they know what hit them."

"But won't it alert others to our presence?"

"It's just the two of them."

"Are you sure?"

Keith wasn't sure, because he didn't shoot. But neither did he lower his rifle. They watched as the Germans' searching led them farther and farther away until finally they were gone.

Annie flopped against the tree trunk, her heart hammering in her chest.

"I don't like it here," she said.

"We'll give them time to put some distance between us," Keith said.

"What will they do to us if they capture us?"

"They're not going to capture us."

He spoke as if he were quoting an indisputable fact. But it was little comfort to Annie. Did he mean the Germans would kill them just so they wouldn't have to bother with captives? Or did Keith mean he'd die in a shootout before letting Germans capture them? Annie didn't like either alternative.

She sighed. She wasn't cut out for this. She was a nurse, not an infantryman. She regretted leaving the hospital in the first place, but didn't regret coming after Keith. If that made sense.

A whisper-shout in German broke into her thoughts and sent her adrenaline pump into full production mode again. The voices had circled back. Louder this time.

Such a hard, unfriendly language, she thought. *Fitting for such a cruel and savage race.*

"It's just the two of them," Keith said, taking a quick glance around. "I can take them both out before they have time to blink."

"Are you sure?"

Annie just wanted this to end.

Keith grinned. "It's what I've been trained to do."

The German soldiers were occupied with their search, heads down, fingers gripping and re-gripping their rifles.

From beneath the cover of the tree, Keith rested the barrel of his rifle on a log. He took aim, waiting for the right moment.

Annie held her breath for what seemed an eternity. Her eyes bounced from Keith to the Germans, the Germans to Keith. What was he waiting for? Why didn't he shoot?

The tall German toed something on the ground. He turned his back to them.

Keith fired. The squat German crumpled and hit the ground like a dropped duffle bag.

"That's for Johnny Rivers," Keith said.

The tall German swung around. Too late. Keith fired again. And again. The first round doubled the German over, the second spun him a full three hundred sixty degrees. He collapsed into an outgrowth of bushes.

"And that's for Hut Wheeler," Keith said.

"And Marcy Hanson," Annie added.

Keith nodded. "And Marcy Hanson."

Annie started to get up. Keith held her back.

"Give it a few minutes," he said. "Just in case."

Lying next to her husband, Annie scanned the forest. No one came running. There were no shouts. The only movements were the swaying and cracking of trees, birdsong and flight, a rabbit scampering past them, which drew Keith's aim by its sudden appearance but not his fire. As they waited, Annie felt a warmth she hadn't felt before, a satisfaction that they'd done something for Marcy, something to avenge the wrong done to her.

Finally, Keith said, "Are you ready to go?"

"How's your leg?"

"Stiff. But I can manage."

He set his rifle aside in order to use both hands against the log to hoist himself up.

"Wait, I'll help you," Annie said.

Easier said than done. The cold had stiffened her knees. They complained as she pressed them into service. Like Keith, she used the log as leverage.

Keith was already standing, looking down at her.

"We should frisk the Jerries before we leave," he said. "They may have matches or something we can—"

He never finished his sentence.

A loud crack shattered the forest, similar to the sound his rifle made when he shot the Germans.

Keith pitched forward, face to the ground.

He didn't move.

Annie's mouth gaped open. She couldn't catch her breath. Her arms refused to move. Her legs were dead. Her eyes were fixed helplessly on her husband's back with the red wound.

She collapsed to her hands and knees beside her husband, a soundless scream caught in her mouth. Her hands, regaining some mobility, reached out to him like two logs. The dexterity with which they had served Dr. Skoglund in the operating room all this time now abandoned her.

A whimper escaped her throat.

This wasn't happening. It couldn't . . . God wouldn't . . . Keith looked so still, so . . . so . . . still. Her hand fell on his back. There was none of the rising and falling of a breathing person, no beating from within, no stirring, not even a moan.

"Keith? Keith! Oh . . . Keith!"

She shook him. Then she laid her head on his back, too numb to cry, too devastated not to cry. With her cheek against Keith, her eyes fell on the lump of tree limbs beneath which Mouse lay.

This couldn't be happening. She refused to believe this was happening! Not both of them! No. That wasn't possible. She refused to believe a world could exist that didn't have Keith and Mouse in it.

But Keith wasn't moving, and a part of her—a minority voice she wished she could silence—knew she would never hear him speak her name again; she would never hear his laughter, never feel his arms around her, or his lips against her. She would never again snuggle under his arm and smell the warm scent of his body.

Such knowledge was a wound so painful, no physical pain could compare to it. Most definitely a fatal wound. One that would be her undoing. Consumed by the pain, she would close her eyes and when she opened them, she would be with Marcy and Keith in heaven, where nothing would ever separate them again.

A twig snapped.

No. She refused to hear it. There were no snapping twigs in heaven. It was an earth sound, an unwanted reminder that she was still chained to a world of pain and discord and misery. Her senses— the ones she wanted so desperately to shrug off like an old coat— prickled, alert and alive.

Someone was coming. Keith's killer was coming to finish the job.

Let him. She wanted to die. A bullet would be her ticket to heaven and Keith and Marcy.

Footsteps drew near. Frozen leaves and ice crackled beneath army boots.

Annie closed her eyes, eager for a rifle report. She didn't want to live in this world a minute longer.

The world grew silent.

She waited and nothing came. No life-ending stab of pain. No flash of light. No floating out of her body. She could still smell the damp mustiness of the forest. She could still feel the gnawing teeth of grief in her belly.

She looked up.

The first thing she saw was the deadly end of a rifle pointed at her. She traced the barrel to the stock, to his gloved hands, coated arms. The tall German glared down at her, his face plastered with leaves and twigs and dirt, glued in place by beads of sweat. A darkening red streak ripped his cheek, and his eyes were charged with anger.

"Go ahead," Annie shouted. "Finish it!"

She laid her head again on Keith's back. That was where she wanted to die, embracing her fallen husband.

Nothing happened.

She looked up again.

The German took a step back. He forced a blink as though he couldn't believe what he was seeing. He lowered his gun but kept it pointed in her direction.

Making his way to the log, he sat down, wincing as he did, favoring his left side. It was then Annie noticed the red stain on his jacket where he'd been hit.

"What are you waiting for?" Annie shouted. "Shoot me!"

The German said nothing. He just stared at her, his eyes hard, his mouth a pensive line.

What was he waiting for? Why didn't he shoot her and get it over with?

She saw something in his eyes. Something of a clue as to what he was thinking, why he hadn't shot her.

Surprise.

He hadn't expected to find a woman.

That changed everything, didn't it? The stories of what Germans did to captured women were legion.

Annie glared at her captor.

The German stared at her for so long that Annie lost track of time. Her legs, which she had folded under her, fell asleep. A couple of times the German repositioned himself on the log. Each time he did, his free hand was drawn to the bloodstain.

Annie took pleasure in his pain.

She passed the time feeding on thoughts of revenge. Images played out in her mind of her kicking his wound, disarming him, leveling a rifle at him, watching his eyes grow wide with fright as he pled for his miserable life; of her shooting him and standing over his lifeless body. Each time she played out this scenario, her heart and limbs surged with strength.

All she needed was a moment of inattention, a careless lowering of his guard, possibly a distraction. Keith's rifle was within reach; his pale hand rested on it. All Annie had to do was to reach across his body, snatch up the weapon, turn it on the German and fire. It would take just a second or two.

He stared at her, and she at him.

What was he waiting for?

Maybe his wound was serious. Maybe he was bleeding to death internally. She hoped so. As he bled, he'd find it increasingly difficult to keep his eyes open, to maintain consciousness.

She watched his eyes. They would tell. But so far he was an owl, perched on the log, eyes alert, head swiveling at forest noises, but never so far that she was ever out of his field of vision.

It didn't matter. He was injured, which meant that time was on Annie's side.

The snow had stopped falling. The forest grew darker with the approaching twilight. The frozen ground had seeped through

Annie's pants, numbing her legs and backside. Birds chirped. Leaves and limbs rustled in the wind.

The German stared.

Annie waited for her chance.

CHAPTER 12

I couldn't die fast enough, Celia. My world had come to an end.
I entertained thoughts of lunging for Keith's rifle for no other rea-
son than to force the German to kill me. I don't know why I didn't.
Well . . . I know now why I didn't. God's loving hand restrained
me. He's so good to us, isn't He? Can you imagine what our lives
would be like if He automatically answered all our prayers, espe-
cially those prayed in anger?

The death of your sister and my husband was the first time I'd
been touched directly by the war. As a nurse I dealt with death
every day, but I was never emotionally close to the soldiers who
died. In the back of my mind, I hoped God would think that was
enough, that the sheer quantity of deaths I witnessed would spare
me from losing someone close.

Those first hours with the German, my emotions went from
being despondent and wanting to die to disbelief that it had really
happened, to being angry enough that if I knew we had the H-
bomb then, I would've personally volunteered to drop it on Berlin.
And I'd place the German who'd killed Keith at ground zero.

The German communicated with grunts. He had Annie drag
Keith's body out of the way, next to Mouse. He forced her to collect
dead branches and leaves. He followed her at a safe distance. Unable

to bend over, he kicked Keith's rifles out of reach. Even then, pain registered on his face, and there was a moment when Annie hoped he was going to pass out, but he didn't.

When the wood had been collected, the German tossed her a box of matches. Annie knew what to do. She pretended otherwise. Over the last two years she and the other nurses had become self-sufficient at building fires, lighting lanterns in heavy winds, repairing tears during thunderstorms, and finding ways to keep warm in drafty canvas tents. But the German didn't know this, so Annie fumbled with the leaves and branches and matches as though she didn't even know which end of the match to strike.

A couple of times he groaned, or rolled his eyes, or shouted something she couldn't understand, until finally he ordered her away. Kneeling brought pain, so much that he fell forward and landed on all fours.

Annie saw her chance. She stepped toward him. He shot her a wounded-animal look that backed her away.

Working himself into a kneeling position, his brow beaded with sweat, he struck a match. His hand shook as he touched the flame to kindling. The blaze took hold, sheltered from the wind by the rock outcropping and canopy of fir branches. With the fire lit, the German slumped against the fallen tree trunk, exhausted.

Good, Annie thought. *He can't hold out much longer. And he certainly isn't in any condition to do any ravaging, though you could never discount what a man is capable of doing in that category when he has a mind to. Keep up your guard. Bide your time. Wait for him to fall asleep, and then . . .*

She couldn't bring herself to form the words, but she knew what she had to do.

As the forest behind him grew darker, the German reached into his pocket and pulled out a piece of dried meat. He bit it in half. While he chewed, he offered her the other half.

At the sight of food, Annie's stomach grumbled greedily. She hadn't eaten all day. She'd been on her way to breakfast when . . .

Tears filled her eyes at the thought of how the day had unfolded. She glanced at the bodies of her husband and friend lying side by side. Night's canopy was descending upon them. Never before had Annie faced a day like this. She'd lived a lifetime of sorrow within the span of a few hours. A fresh wave of grief threatened to wash over her. She fended it off. It would only weaken her, and she needed her strength to kill this German.

When she made no effort to take his offering, the German tossed the dried meat into her lap. He reached again into his pocket and brought out what looked like a cracker. He broke it and tossed her half.

Annie picked up the meat and cracker. She looked at them, then threw them at the German, hitting him in the face. The food pelting startled him, but to Annie's surprise he didn't get angry. He shrugged, chewed, and stared at the fire.

When he was finished chewing, with a painful grunt he got up and pointed his rifle at her. He barked guttural words at her, which she didn't understand. What she understood was the upward jerk of the rifle.

She stood. She was getting good at reading his rifle barrel.

He motioned for her to start walking.

Fear clutched her throat with an iron fist as she walked past the tab of meat and half cracker on the ground. Had she turned down her last meal?

From behind he pushed her in the direction he wanted her to go. She stumbled forward.

He made no effort to put out the fire, nor was he taking Keith's rifles, so they were probably coming back. Or at least he was coming back.

Her mind raced with possible scenarios. Two were prominent. Either the bit of sustenance had given him the strength he needed for a little after-dinner romance under the stars, or he didn't want to mess up his campsite with blood when he shot her.

Annie's eyes darted in a desperate search for escape routes. If she ran, how far would she get?

He pushed her again, changing directions. A few steps and he shoved her against a tree, pinning her with his hand on her throat.

With his rifle he warned her to stay put.

Annie figured his next movement would indicate his intentions. Would he press himself against her? Or would he step back and shoot her?

She looked him in the eye to try to convince him she wasn't afraid of him. It was a lie. She was terrified. He stared back, unblinking.

Then he made his choice. He stepped back.

That was when Annie saw the body on the ground. The other German. The squat one. Now it made sense. He was going to shoot her in the presence of his friend, his buddy, in some sort of sick revenge.

This one's for you, Jerry.

The German made his way to his buddy without turning around. Slowly, in pain, he knelt down and rummaged through the dead man's pockets, transferring whatever was there into his own pockets. Then, placing a hand on the man's chest, he said something.

In a similar circumstance Annie might have interpreted his actions as tenderness or sorrow, only she knew German soldiers were incapable of such emotions. It was more likely his actions were one vulture paying respect to his own kind just before picking the dead vulture's bones clean.

The German spoke to her, motioning her to come closer. Annie hesitated. He motioned again, this time barking an order. Reaching down, the German undid the other man's belt. He motioned to her that he wanted her to pull the man's pants off.

Annie was horrified. She refused.

He barked again, and when she shook her head, he stood with unexpected agility, pointed the rifle at her, and shouted.

Annie grabbed the man's pant legs and pulled. She couldn't get them over his boots, so she had to unlace the dead man's boots and remove them. Once that was done, the man's pants slipped off easily. His bare legs plopped onto the frozen ground, and Annie felt the chill, even though she knew he couldn't.

The German made a rolling motion with his hand. Annie rolled up the pants. Then he motioned her back to the fire.

It was with several shaky exhales of relief that she returned to the place where she'd been sitting beneath the tree limbs. The German returned to his place against the log. He motioned for her to throw him the wadded-up pair of pants. She did. He produced a knife and cut the bottom seam of the pant leg, then ripped it the length of the inseam. He made another cut and ripped again, producing a strip two inches wide.

He tossed the pants and the knife to Annie, indicating he wanted her to do the same thing. She did. He motioned for her to repeat the process until both pant legs had been reduced to long strips. He had her tie them end to end. Annie had the distinct feeling she was fashioning the bonds that would tie her hands and feet.

He wanted his knife back. It was a six-inch blade, double-sided with a sheath. The black handle had a swastika on it. Annie studied the knife, wishing that at some point in her upbringing she had learned how to throw a knife. She slipped it in its sheath and tossed it back to him.

Setting his rifle to one side, he unfastened his jacket and then began fumbling with the buttons of his shirt. With his chest exposed to the elements, he unsheathed the knife and motioned for her to come to him.

Annie's eyes were on the knife. He had to repeat his command. From the expression on his face, she seemed to have two choices: either she could go to him, or he would come to her. At present, he was reclined against the log. She decided to go to him.

She crawled toward him, stopping just out of arm's reach. He said something and motioned her closer. She inched closer. Another command and she was right next to him.

And so it begins, she thought. *And at knifepoint*.

"I'll slit your throat before I let you touch me," she said to him.

His eyes never left hers. He unbuckled his belt and his pants. He reached toward her.

She pulled back.

He said something. And reached again. In his other hand, the knife's blade flashed fiery reflections. His fingers touched her collar and tapped the caduceus emblem with the superimposed N.

"*Krankenschwester,*" he said.

He leaned back, pointing to the place where he'd been shot— the abdomen, just below the belt line. Then he pointed to the emblem on her collar again.

"*Krankenschwester.*"

"You want me to tend your wounds," she said with a shaky voice. "I'd rather not. You see, I'm hoping you bleed to death."

He looked at her, his expression unchanged.

"*Krankenschwester.*"

"Yeah, I know. *Kranken* . . . whatever you said. Just give me a chance and I'll *kranken* you."

She reached behind herself for the long strip of cloth. She held it up, loops dangling between her fingers.

"What good is this without. . . ?"

But he'd already produced a canteen and two handkerchiefs. She assumed one of them came from the pocket of the dead German.

"I see you've thought this out. Very clever," she said.

She soaked one of the handkerchiefs with water. He leaned back against the log and pulled his pants down over his hip, away from the wound.

Annie examined the wound. "It's a shame it didn't hit any vital organs," she said. Before applying the wet handkerchief, she caught his eye. "I hope this hurts."

He nodded and gave her a half smile.

Once the wound was cleaned it didn't look too bad. The bullet had passed in and out. She positioned the second handkerchief over the wound.

"About the best we can hope for is that infection will set in," she said calmly.

The worst of the procedure came when she wrapped the bandage strip around him. To do so, she had to put both arms around him while he raised his hips. She tied it off.

"There," she said. "If it's too tight, let me know and I'll tighten it some more."

She turned to crawl back to her spot. He caught her by the wrist. Her eyes flashed.

He pointed to his cheek. Keith's second shot. The one that had spun the German around.

She doused the handkerchief again and cleaned the wound.

"It's going to leave a scar," she said. "But then you'll fit in with all the rest of the jack-booted, goose-stepping morons of your country, won't you?"

She'd said this softly and sweetly, using her professional nurse's voice.

The good news was that he was shivering and felt feverish. Finished, Annie returned to her spot while the German buttoned his pants and shirt.

"*Danke schön*," he said.

"Tell it to Hitler."

CHAPTER 13

nnie fought to keep from drifting off. If she fell asleep, she'd be vulnerable. Defenseless. At the mercy of the German. She had to stay awake. But the fire wasn't making it easy for her. The smoke stung her eyes. The crackle lulled her.

Darkness had engulfed the forest, reducing her world to a small circle of light. Beyond the circumference of the fire were sounds only: the whistle of the wind, the creaking and popping of trees, the occasional rustle or howl of an animal.

The German sat at the edge of the light, sometimes staring at her, sometimes staring into the night, or up at the stars. About an hour ago he took a small book and a pencil from his back pocket. Mostly he turned pages and read; occasionally he wrote in it. After a half hour he started closing his eyes for intervals. Not to sleep, for he'd check on her every so often, and when he did, his eyes were alert.

The book was important to him. Annie could tell by the way he wrote in it. He would ponder for the longest time before making a mark or two, just a few spare strokes, and then set to pondering again. Annie guessed it to be a code book of some sort. Possibly a timetable, or a record of troop strengths. The longer he pored over it, the more convinced Annie was of its importance.

A reckless fantasy formed in her mind, one in which she not only escaped but somehow managed to get her hands on his little book. If she could deliver it to the authorities, the information might significantly alter the course of the war, and that would give some meaning to Keith's and Marcy's deaths.

The German bent over the book and wrote something. There was an intensity to the way . . .

He looked up and caught her watching him. Saw her staring at the book. Annie looked away. She tried to appear casual, though she knew she wasn't doing a very good job of it.

Keeping his eyes on her, he snapped shut the book and slid it and the pencil into the side pocket of his overcoat. With a grimace he repositioned himself. His side was hurting him. His brow glistened with sweat. Annie, on the other hand, was freezing.

She lay down on her side—a ploy to get him to relax by getting him to think she'd fallen asleep. She positioned herself so that he had to stare through the flames to see her face. The ground was pungent with the smell of pine needles and decomposed leaves. These became her bedding.

Once her eyes were closed, her mind forced her to relive the day's events. The injured herald arriving at the hospital. Skoglund smugly denying her permission to leave. Mouse insisting on accompanying her. The joy of finding Keith alive, followed by the horror of watching Mouse and Keith die. Tears mixed with the smoke to sting her eyes.

She opened them to check on the German. He was wide-awake, staring into the darkness.

The fire danced.

She waited for what she estimated was an hour before checking again. The German hadn't moved. Nor did he look tired. He had to sleep sometime, didn't he?

Another hour. He was still awake.

The next time Annie opened her eyes, it was morning.

The fire had been reduced to smoldering embers.

She chastised herself for falling asleep. She glanced at the German. His eyes were closed, his head tilted to one side. He was asleep!

It was early. The light in the forest was soft.

Annie stirred, gauging the German's reaction. He didn't move. Quietly she sat up, her hips complaining. She ignored them, more intent on how her heart was racing and how her adrenaline had put her senses and muscles on high alert.

Annie pulled her legs under her. She stood. So far, so good. The German didn't stir.

He was reclining against the log, his legs stretched out. His arms were folded across his chest, embracing his rifle. Annie looked around for Keith's rifles. To her dismay, she found that the German had tucked them under the log beneath him. There was no way she could get them without waking him.

Annie hesitated. She really wanted one of those weapons. She also wanted the code book in his pocket. But any attempt to get either of these would risk waking the German.

She looked around for a log or a branch, something heavy enough to knock him unconscious. There wasn't anything suitable nearby. Her gaze fell upon Keith and Mouse. Just as she'd left them.

Grief hung heavy around her neck. It made her legs sluggish. Silently she bid them good-bye. If they could speak to her, she was certain they'd tell her to run, to escape, to forget the code book, to forget trying to disable her captor, but just to get out of here as fast as she could.

With one last glace she turned to leave.

The German's eyes were open. He was looking at her. Startled. He struggled to sit up, to swing his weapon into firing position.

Annie acted instinctively, knowing that if he succeeded in pointing the rifle at her, it was over. She couldn't let that happen. Instead of running away, she ran toward him, managing to grab the rifle with both hands before he could swing it around. She forced it to one side, acutely aware that the moment she let it point at her, she was dead.

The German was stronger, but she had position over him. He struggled to sit up, to get leverage. She fought to keep him off-balance. His eyes bulged with the effort and—to Annie's immense satisfaction—she saw not only pain, but fear in them.

He shouted at her, wriggling and squirming to get up. Annie

stood over him, determined not to let him sit up, determined not to surrender her end of the rifle.

It was a standoff. Neither could gain the advantage. Neither was willing to give up.

Annie grunted with exertion. She couldn't hold out much longer. If she didn't do something soon . . .

She kicked the German's wounded side. He screamed but didn't let go. She kicked it again. And again. He let go of the rifle. She kicked it again and he rolled over, clutching his side.

Annie had the rifle. She pointed it at him. The tables were turned. All she had to do was pull the trigger and he was no longer a threat to her. Pull the trigger and Keith and Marcy would be avenged.

The German was curled up on the ground, grimacing, glancing up at her out of the corners of his eyes.

Never before in her life had Annie wanted to inflict harm on someone. Never before had she killed anything, or wanted to. Until now. With all of her heart and soul she wanted to pull the trigger. She wanted to kill a German. She wanted to kill *this* German.

The German looked up at her, his chest heaving. He knew he was dead. She could see it in his eyes. Defeated. In pain. At her mercy.

But Annie was feeling no mercy. She wanted revenge. This wasn't a man; it was her enemy. He was one cell of the larger Nazi cancer that had plagued Europe and Russia, leaving death and destruction in its wake. If Keith were alive, he would not hesitate to kill this man. If Keith were alive, he'd urge Annie to pull the trigger.

So why couldn't she?

Annie took fresh aim. Determined to push past her hesitation, to force herself to do it.

But she couldn't do it. She couldn't pull the trigger.

Angry with herself for her weakness, she kicked the German one more time. When he curled up tighter, blinded by pain, she reached down and pulled the black book from his pocket. Then, before leaving, she kicked him one last time for good measure.

CHAPTER | 14

I was free. And I was determined to stay free. While I had no idea where I was or where I was going, I knew two places I was running from—the German's campsite, and road M1 with the German tanks. That left heading deeper into the forest.

I don't mind telling you, I'd never been so scared in my life. And yet, at the same time, because of losing both Keith and Mouse, I had a cavalier attitude about living and dying. I know it sounds strange, but that's the way I felt. The code book drove me. I was determined to get it into the hands of the American authorities.

———

Overhead, the sky grew dark and threatening. Annie ran on rubber legs. Her lungs were on fire. She wasn't used to this level of physical exertion. Though the snow wasn't as deep beneath the trees, it was still rough going. She was wheezing and her calves were cramping. Still, she didn't let up.

She kept looking behind her, fearing that each time she looked over her shoulder she'd see the German coming after her. He would come after it, wouldn't he? If not for her, for the code book.

The trees began to thin. Annie saw a clearing. She slowed as she approached it, then collapsed against a tree, exhausted. While a clearing may mean a farmhouse or a road, it would also leave her exposed. Annie moved from tree to tree to get a better look.

She heard laughter—male laughter—and froze. Her luck. She probably stumbled onto the entire German army. She took a few cautious steps and saw a road.

M1? It couldn't be M1. At least she didn't think it could be. But then, how many stories were told of people lost, getting turned around, and wandering in circles? Enough to make Annie doubt herself.

One direction, the road was clear. The other direction was blocked by a thick crop of bushes—the direction from which the voices came. Gripping the rifle, ready to defend herself if necessary, she bent low, stepped forward, and poked her head around the bushes.

What she saw nearly sent her into a bout of laughter.

Three American soldiers and a jeep!

They were stopped next to a telephone pole, smoking. Annie stepped into the clearing—not too suddenly, for she didn't want to startle them and draw their fire—waving one arm over her head.

The man facing her looked up. Startled, he reached for his weapon, alerting the other two, who swung around with their weapons drawn.

"Don't shoot!" Annie cried, continuing toward them. "I'm an American!"

When they took note of her uniform and her voice, they appeared amused, though not so amused that they lowered their weapons.

The snow was deeper in the clearing. Annie trudged toward them with difficulty. If her legs and lungs were complaining, she didn't hear them. She was safe. She'd escaped, and she was safe.

"Lookee what we have here," one of the soldiers said, tossing his cigarette aside.

Now that Annie was closer, she could see that one of them was a lieutenant, the other two privates. All three men were grinning, and why wouldn't they be? She must be a sight—an American nurse, armed with a rifle, emerging alone from the forest. She imagined they'd be telling stories about her to their grandchildren about the crazy nurse who walked out of the Ardennes Forest. That was all right with Annie because she had a story to tell, too.

"Boy, am I glad to see you guys!" she said breathlessly.

She took the last steps out of the restraints of the snowdrift and onto the road. Her feet now moved easily, as if invisible shackles had fallen from her ankles.

"I'm Lieutenant Annie Mitchell," she said, "from the 67th Evacuation Hospital at Malmedy."

"You're a long way from home, darlin'," said the lieutenant. He was hollow-cheeked and bony, with the bluest eyes Annie had ever seen. The two privates were shorter. One had two or three days' growth of stubble; the other had a round face with wide, staring eyes, and an infectious grin.

The grin nearly disarmed her. Now that her ordeal was over, her emotions rushed to the surface and threatened to spill over. She fought them back. There would be time for all that later. For now, report and get back to the hospital.

"Yeah, long way from home," she said, smiling back at them. "I was part of an ambulance team. We were fired on by a German tank unit. A few of us managed to escape, only to be set upon by a couple of Krauts. I was the only one to survive. I was captured and managed to escape this morning."

She offered them the rifle as proof. "This is the Kraut's weapon."

The lieutenant accepted it and examined it.

"You killed him?" Private Stubble asked.

Annie shrugged, remembering how she'd had a chance to kill the German but didn't. These men shot Germans every day. They'd laugh at her inability to pull the trigger. "I . . . I left him as good as dead," she said.

The lieutenant handed the rifle to Smiley with a stern look that wiped the grin from the man's face.

He said, "It must have been someone important to summon an ambulance all this way from Malmedy."

"General Maxwell," Annie replied.

She started to say more, to tell them about Keith, but then held her tongue. Now that she was safely in American hands, she began thinking like an army nurse again. And while it was true she'd managed to escape a life-threatening situation, she still had to answer for the decisions that brought her to the forest in the first place. After all, she'd disobeyed orders and stolen an army ambulance, and as a result, Army Nurse Marcy Hanson was dead, as were all the people she'd hoped to rescue. Being in love with her husband was sounding less and less like a worthy defense.

"Maxwell, eh?" said the lieutenant. "And his condition?"

"He was dead when we arrived."

The lieutenant's eyebrows rose appreciably.

"And the others?"

"I already told you. I'm the only one who survived."

The three men exchanged glances.

"Oh, one thing more," Annie said. She reached into her coat pocket. "I managed to take this from the German soldier that captured me. I believe it's some sort of military code book."

The lieutenant took the book from her and examined it. The two privates leaned into him to get a glimpse.

"It's definitely code of some kind," the lieutenant confirmed. "Have you looked at it?"

"There wasn't time," Annie said.

"So what made you suspect it was a code book?"

"The way he treated it, and studied it."

The lieutenant flipped page after page, his brow knotted in a perplexed frown.

"Sir!" Private Stubble said, raising his rifle.

Something in the direction of the forest alarmed him. Annie joined the other two men in looking to see what it was. She couldn't believe her eyes.

The German, her captor, had emerged from the woods and was trudging through knee-deep snow toward them with the two American rifles held over his head. He was having a rough go of it with an exaggerated limp on his wounded side.

"That's him!" Annie shouted.

The two American privates had their weapons trained on him. They were shouting at him to keep his hands raised. They were also looking past him into the forest, afraid it might be some kind of trap. They bounded into the snow, shouting as they went. The German stopped halfway and let them come to him.

"That's the man who captured you?" the lieutenant asked.

"Yes."

"And you took this book from him?"

"Yes."

Annie kept her eyes on the German. Obviously he was surrendering, but why?

"Stay here," the lieutenant said to her.

He followed the two privates into the snow. The Americans had flanked the German, keeping him covered.

Annie watched in disbelief. This was the last thing she'd expected of the German.

They were far enough away that, while she could hear their voices, she couldn't make out what they were saying. The lieutenant stopped in front of the German, the two privates on either side of him, angled in such a way that they kept glancing into the forest.

What a strange turn of events this is, Annie thought. Had she hurt him that badly? Why else would he surrender other than to get medical attention?

The interrogation took longer than Annie thought necessary. The back of the lieutenant's head would wobble from side to side and then the German would say something in reply.

Annie shifted uneasily at the thought that she'd be sharing a jeep ride back to Malmedy with the German.

Laughter disrupted her thoughts.

She refocused on the scene. They were laughing. Laughing! All four of them! The two privates had lowered their weapons. The German had lowered his arms. And they were laughing!

Annie couldn't believe what she was seeing.

The lieutenant held out the black book to the German, pointing to a page. The German cocked his head to get a good look. He said something, then reached out and turned a couple of pages, said something else, and they laughed. The private with the goofy grin shot a glance at Annie.

This whole scene was beyond weird.

The lieutenant turned and called to her, motioning for her to join them.

Dread gripped Annie's insides. She didn't want to join them. There was no reason for her to join them.

She looked around. For what? An answer? An explanation? For someone to tell her she didn't have to join them if she didn't want to?

A fleeting thought crossed her mind: get into the jeep and drive away, which would mean a second stolen vehicle she would have to account for. She looked at the jeep, then back at the lieutenant.

The lieutenant took note of her hesitation. He sent Private Stubble to get her.

If she ran now, they'd think she was the one who had something to hide. Would they fire at her?

Afraid to obey, afraid to run, Annie's training made the decision for her. Just because she'd disobeyed orders once didn't give her license to do it whenever she didn't understand her orders.

She stepped away from the jeep, into the snowdrift.

Private Stubble met her halfway. He took her by the arm, which was totally unnecessary.

As she got closer the conversation became clearer. Sounds became words. German words!

As disturbing as that was, it wasn't alarming. Obviously, the lieutenant had studied German. A man with linguistic skills was valuable in the army. The alarming part of the conversation was its jovial tone.

The lieutenant turned, and both he and the German grinned at her. Stubble must have felt her reaction, because he tightened his grip on her arm. A sick feeling swirled in Annie's stomach.

Nothing was said to her. She watched in horror as the German handed the lieutenant both American rifles, and in return was handed his own rifle and the black book.

The next thing Annie knew, Stubble shoved her at the German's feet. The lieutenant looked down at her, laughing. He winked, then returned to the jeep. The two privates trailed behind him, casting occasional looks over their shoulders.

Moments later the three American soldiers climbed into the jeep and tore off, leaving Annie behind, once again staring down the barrel of a German rifle.

CHAPTER 15

The German marched Annie out of the snowdrift and back into the woods. Stunned by what had just happened, she was unaware her feet and legs were moving. It didn't make sense. One minute she was free and pondering the consequences awaiting her at Malmedy, and the next minute she was right back where she was before escaping as if it had never happened.

Snow filtered through the treetops. Behind her, the German spoke only when necessary to get her to change course, which usually entailed a one-word command and a shove in the back. Gone was the joviality he displayed with the American lieutenant.

The pace was slow due to the German's injury. Annie knew, given the chance, she could outrun him. But she couldn't outrun a bullet.

They walked all morning. Annie's feet were frozen, her legs weary, her mind exhausted from trying to figure out what had happened. She didn't have the energy to conjure up fear over what would happen to her now. She'd do that later.

With the cloud ceiling low and dark, it was difficult to keep track of the time. When they finally stopped beside a frozen stream, Annie stole a glance at her watch. It was after one o'clock in the afternoon.

After planting Annie beside a tree, the German broke the ice on the stream and refilled his canteen. As he did the first night, he fished in his pocket, found a piece of dried meat and a cracker. Halving them, he tossed her a portion. This time, feeling light-headed from hunger, Annie chose to eat them rather than throw them back in his face.

"What do you want from me?" she asked.

The German stared at her and chewed.

"You got your book back. Let me go."

He sipped water from the canteen, then offered it to her. She didn't want to take it, but her throat was hot and sore, so she did. She handed the canteen back without thanking him.

"What did you say to that lieutenant to convince him to hand me over to you? Did you tell them I was a spy? Your sister? Your wife? Or was it a straight swap, guns for woman?"

He stared at her and chewed.

"What I really don't get is why would they do you any favors in the first place? Who are you? And why are we wandering around the forest? Don't you have a unit?"

The way he stared at her was maddening.

"You know, given the chance, I'll kill you next time," she said.

Her emotions swelled with the threat. Without the physical exertion as an outlet for her rage, they came on suddenly, uncontrollably. She began to cry, then got angry with herself that she was crying. The last thing she wanted was for this Third Reich monster to have the satisfaction of knowing he was getting to her.

When he saw her tears, he said something she didn't understand and once again they were on the move.

Twenty minutes farther into the forest he grabbed her around the waist and threw her to the ground behind a bush, knocking the wind from her. She didn't see it coming.

On her back, gasping for air, she stared up at him as he straddled her. In the back of her mind she'd never dismissed the idea that he might eventually force himself on her.

Pinned down as she was, he had the advantage. But she was not going to let him have an easy time of it. She tried to buck him off, but he was too heavy. He crouched down over her. His hand went to her mouth, and she saw her chance.

Lunging upward, she bit it. Got it good, too. She got the side, at least two knuckles deep, and shook it like a dog. She tasted dirt, then blood.

He stifled a scream and fell down on top of her.

Annie launched her second offensive. She kicked and clawed, bit and scratched, and did her best to knee him in the wound or groin, though it seemed he'd anticipated attacks on the lower targets, because he'd twisted his body to shield them.

Despite her attempts, the German proved to be much stronger and heavier. He survived the assault and managed to maneuver himself so that his legs pinned her arms. He covered her nose and mouth so she couldn't breathe. When she tried, he freed his hand from her mouth, then quickly cupped it over her mouth so she couldn't scream.

That was when she realized they weren't alone. She heard snow crunching, the sound it makes when compacted by boots.

Soldiers.

The German warned her with his eyes not to make a sound. She saw in his gaze an intensity that was greater than urgency. She saw fear.

The soldiers were passing close by. But how close? Annie's mind raced. One scream and she could alert them. But could they respond quickly enough? She remembered the German's knife, the one she'd used to cut bandages. It was certainly capable of silencing a scream before it had half a chance to escape her lips.

Annie's eyes strained in the direction of the footfalls. If she could somehow determine the distance, and if they were close enough, she might risk it.

Through the branches of the bush Annie could see the boots and pant legs of the soldiers. They were closer than she'd originally thought. Close enough to risk screaming.

Decision made. Take a breath. Try to wriggle free. Scream as though her life depended on it.

Which it did.

She took a deep breath.

The German kneed her in the stomach, and the scream dissolved into a forced exhale. He'd anticipated her attempt.

Fighting to breathe, fighting to scream, Annie shook her head side to side, trying to break free from the hand that held her down. The German pressed harder to keep her silent.

Then, all at once, she went limp, her eyes wide. Confused.

Through the branches of the bushes she'd caught a glimpse of the soldiers, more than just their boots and pant legs, but their faces. Their uniforms.

They were German.

Her captor was hiding her from his own kind.

———

"You're a deserter, aren't you?" she asked him later that night as they sat facing the fire.

She didn't expect an answer. She was thinking out loud.

"Or you're an American. Undercover, of course. That would explain why the American lieutenant gave me back to you—I think. It doesn't really explain that, does it? But if you're an American . . . no, that doesn't make sense, either."

She sighed.

"You didn't want them to find me, because they'd take me away from you. That's it, isn't it? They wouldn't let you keep me. Which means you still have designs on me. You degenerate."

The German didn't seem to mind her talking. She wondered if he'd let her talk like this if he understood what she was saying.

"You haven't reported to anyone for two days, and we don't seem to be headed anyplace in particular. We keep doubling back, at least as far as I can tell. Yet that may just be a ruse to confuse me. We eat stale pocket food. You're friendly with Americans and hide from Germans. You're not French, are you? No, you don't look French.

You look German. You sound German. You stink like a German."

She gauged his reaction. He sniffed and pulled out his little book.

"And what's with that book? The Americans obviously could make no sense of it. It's obviously some kind of code. And they handed it back to you without blinking an eye."

With the book open in his hands, the German closed his eyes and rocked back and forth. A pleasant expression came over his face.

Annie made a sudden movement.

Alarmed, the German's eyes flew open. He reached for his rifle beside him.

Annie grinned. "Just testing."

The German scowled at her.

CHAPTER *16*

*T*he German was awake when Annie fell asleep. He was awake when she woke up.

"Got your second wind, did you?" she said, stretching. As she did, she took a quick look at his bandaged side, hoping to see an enlarged bloodstain. She was disappointed.

Minutes later they were up and walking. It took a good half hour for Annie to work the cold out of her joints. She felt a mess. There were pine needles in her hair, and she hadn't bathed or changed clothes or brushed her teeth in three days. While it made her miserable, it also brought a smile to her face. If the German waited any longer for his strength to return before taking advantage of her, he would have to attack her with a clothespin on his nose.

By midmorning the snow had stopped falling. The temperature took a nosedive so that walking was no longer enough to keep her warm.

They came upon a road that cut through the trees and led to a farmhouse. Annie slowed when she saw it. The German pushed her in the back, his way of telling her to keep going.

She saw no activity in or around the house. Likewise, the barn and fields looked deserted. Still, the structure looked inviting. Annie hadn't seen shelter for days. Four walls that blocked the wind and the promise of a fireplace seemed like paradise. But it also had its frightening side. A little privacy. A little warmth. Was this the German's intended destination all along; here, where he could take his time with her?

Apparently she'd slowed at the thought, because she got another shove in the back. She managed to catch a glimpse of her captor. His eyes were fixed on the house.

When they reached the walkway leading to the front porch, Annie slowed to turn up it.

"Nein!"

The German pushed her past the walkway.

Beyond the house was a barn. They passed it, too. Annie saw no animals. No sign of life at all. They came upon an area that had been marked off by a wooden fence. Headstones made for easy identification. A graveyard.

At the German's urging, Annie stepped into the colorless scene. Grave markers—some gray tablets, others white crosses—were topped with snow within a white field. Like a monochromatic watercolor, the forest provided a textured background with streaks of jagged gray limbs and black shadows. Lining one side of the cemetery was a single row of trees, their limbs looking like roots growing into a steel gray sky. What Annie saw next made her gasp.

Bodies dangled from the branches like overripe fruit. There must have been a dozen of them, stretching lifeless and somber. A memorial to mankind at his worst.

The display of death reminded her of Keith and Mouse. Her mind still refused to concede to reality. Something deep within her kept assuring her that all she had to do was get back to Malmedy. Once there, Mouse would reappear and be full of life, Keith would show up at the front door to take her to Paris, and Nina would be furious with them until she and Mouse explained that they didn't eat her Christmas fudge but were hiding it from the Germans.

A shove brought her back to the present moment. They passed through the cemetery's open gate, which wouldn't close again until spring when the snow had melted. Another shove propelled Annie toward the trees from which dangled the fruit of war and hate.

A word flashed in Annie's mind—a chilling, horrible, disgusting thought. She didn't know what sparked it; she didn't want to know. It was the kind of thought that would never cross the mind of a person living in a sane world. But then, that wouldn't be this world, would it?

The word that flashed in her mind was *collection.*

The people hanging from the trees looked like someone's collection. That made the man shoving her the collector, and like a charm added to a bracelet, she was about to be his next acquisition.

He ordered her to stand aside while he searched for something at the base of one of the trees. With his boot he kicked the snow, never once turning his back on her, never once lowering his guard.

His boot hit something. He bent over and brushed away snow, only to find a tree root. He continued the search, expanding it in wider circles around the tree. Again his boot hit something and again he bent over. A grunt of satisfaction indicated he'd found what he was looking for.

He pulled up. The wooden handle of a shovel appeared. The German carried it to Annie and thrust it at her. She had no choice but to take the shovel. He pointed to one of the graves and said something. Using his rifle as a prop, he made digging motions.

"You want me to dig up a grave?" she said, though it was obvious what he wanted her to do.

He pointed at the shovel. At her. And made digging motions again.

The color drained from Annie's face until it felt as gray as the people hanging from the trees.

She glared at him, then tossed the shovel to the ground.

His response was quick. The rifle came up. His jaw set in anger. He shouted at her, pointing the rifle alternately at her and the shovel.

Annie felt curiously hostile. Either way she was dead. If he wanted a grave dug, he'd have to do it himself.

JACK CAVANAUGH

The German shouted again, this time taking a threatening step toward her.

For some reason, self-preservation kicked in. Annie couldn't explain it; nor did she embrace it. But she yielded to it. She picked up the shovel.

The German pointed again at the grave, as though in the last few seconds she might have forgotten which one it was he wanted dug.

Halfheartedly, Annie struck the ground with the shovel blade. It plunged effortlessly through the snow. What Annie felt next made her heart sing.

"Impossible," she said. She banged the point of the blade against the ground. "Frozen. The ground's frozen. There's no way I can dig up frozen ground."

The German looked at the ground.

"Look all you want. It doesn't make it less frozen."

Cradling the rifle in one arm, he grabbed the shovel from her and tested it himself.

"See? Frozen. I told you."

He tested it again in a different spot and got the same result. He tested it in a third spot. This time the blade didn't sound like it was hitting rock. The tip sunk into the earth.

Again the shovel was shoved at Annie. The German stepped back and ordered her to dig in the new location.

To her horror Annie found that the ground here had been recently turned. She scooped out a shovel's worth of snow and dirt and looked up at the German. He nodded for her to keep going.

Within twenty minutes she had cleared a hole in the ground nearly three feet square. The frozen ground made it easy to find the edges. The hole was nearly a foot deep. Ten minutes later it was another half a foot deep when the blade thudded against something hard, but not as hard as frozen ground.

She tested it with the blade. The German nodded, motioning with his hands that he wanted her to keep digging. Annie began uncovering a wood surface the same size as the hole. On one side she'd uncovered an iron handle; on the other, hinges.

"Makes sense now, doesn't it?" she muttered. "Buried treasure. Nazi booty. Guess Keith did you a favor, huh? Now you don't have to share any of it with your buddy."

With his rifle he indicated he wanted her to open the hatch. Dropping the shovel, Annie got down on her knees, grabbed the handle, and tugged. Nothing moved. She tugged again, harder, but still couldn't budge it.

The German pushed her aside. He fell to his knees. Laying his rifle beside him, he pulled at the handle. He couldn't open it either, and that frustrated him. He pulled harder. When that didn't work, he feverishly began running his hands around the edges, clearing dirt away.

Seated in the snow where she'd landed when he pushed her, Annie backed away. Whatever was in there, it had the German's full attention. She looked around. Running was out of the question. She wouldn't get far. Neither would she be able to get to his rifle. She'd have to go through him to get to it.

She could kick him in his wound again, but that would mean standing up and getting close to him. He'd see her coming out of the corner of his eye. That left the shovel.

The German had cleared the edges and was trying the door again. It creaked and gave a little. It appeared the wood had swollen. He pulled again, grunting this time. Progress. An inch of darkness showed. He was going to have to fight the door all the way open.

Annie's hand inched through the snow toward the shovel.

The German grunted and succeeded in gaining another inch.

Annie's hand gripped the wooden handle. She realized then she was going to need two hands on it to get a good swing from her knees.

The German jumped up. Had he seen what she was up to?

He bent down like a weight lifter, curling his fingers under the edge of the door. He pulled. The door yielded to him. He managed to lift it up enough to get in and out of the hole.

Annie was running out of time.

The German dropped to his knees, then to his stomach, and crawled toward the hole, looking as though he was going to crawl inside it headfirst. He stopped at the edge and reached in.

Annie wouldn't get a better moment than this. She lunged for the shovel, gripped it like a baseball bat, and swung with all her might. It made a wide, graceful arc, tossing snow as it flew, and landed with a sickening clang as the flat of the shovel made contact with the back of the German's head. He convulsed as if hit by lightning.

The blow didn't knock him out.

He struggled to get up, managing to get to his knees.

Annie swung again. This time the flat of the shovel blade smacked him on the back, knocking him to the ground.

To Annie's dismay, he began moving again.

She gripped the handle for a third swing when the German looked over at her with pain in his eyes and shouted, "In the name of all that's holy, woman! Can't you see I'm trying to do something here!"

CHAPTER 17

$\mathcal{A}$nnie gaped at the German, shovel poised in hand, as though he had just grown a second head.

He rubbed the back of his neck and, after giving her a warning glance not to hit him with the shovel again, bent low and peered into the hole.

Rising up, he motioned to Annie and said, *"Kommen!"* Then, realizing he was speaking German, he said, "Come here!"

He moved to one side, indicating for her to look inside the hole. Still wary, Annie inched toward him, the shovel still in her hand. She got down on her knees, and seeing how vulnerable she was in this position, she turned and shot him a doubting glance. He backed away. He made no attempt to reach for the rifle.

Her senses on full alert, Annie looked inside the hole.

"I don't believe it!" she cried, dropping the shovel.

She fell to her belly and scooted forward so her head was inside the hole. She stretched out her arms.

"It's all right," she said soothingly. "Come here. That's right. Come to me."

She emerged from the hole with a mud-covered boy in her arms. He must have been three, maybe four years old. His clothes were so soiled she couldn't tell what color they were.

"Here."

She attempted to hand the boy to the German. The boy screamed and fought hysterically to keep from being handed over, and wouldn't calm down until Annie assured him she wouldn't try handing him over again.

"How will I get the other one?" Annie said.

"They won't come to me," the German said. "Their mother? Can she help?"

"There's a mother down there?" With the little boy in one arm, she knelt into the hole. "Hello? Hello?" she called. "Can you lift your child up to me?"

"They probably don't speak English," the German said.

Annie looked at him with thoughts whirling in her mind like a tornado. One thought surfaced. Get them out of there.

"We have to get this door open," she said.

The German jumped up so fast it scared her. He grabbed his rifle—they exchanged glances—and he tossed it aside. This time he approached the door from the side. Since it was already raised about a third of the way, he bent low and put his shoulder into it. His feet slipped in the snow. That didn't deter him. He set them again, slipped again, but kept at it until the door began to give way. It was halfway open now. He repositioned himself so that his left leg dangled over the pit. Annie saw what he was doing and nodded her approval. He was using the front edge of the opening for leverage.

She shifted the child in her arms to one side and took a position on the opposite side of the hole. She grabbed the corner of the wooden door, and together they managed to push the door open. It wasn't all the way open, but it was enough.

Muted sunlight illuminated the square-shaped grave. A little girl cowered in the corner, squinting up at them. She was on the far side of the wall, as far away from the German as she could get, obviously terrified of him. Annie reached out to her with one hand. The girl was hesitant, but Annie—and the sight of her brother being safe—convinced her. With difficulty, Annie managed to pull her out, but only because the little girl was bone thin. At one point Annie slipped and the German reached out to help her. It was the worst thing he could do. The girl flew into hysterics and nearly pulled Annie into the pit.

"The mother," Annie said.

She needn't have bothered. The German had already dropped into the pit and was bending over a woman slumped against the side of the wall.

Annie thought of the rifle. She couldn't help it. Now would be the perfect time. She edged toward it, all the while keeping an eye on the German.

His shoulders slumped. He looked up.

"She's dead," he said.

There was nothing military about the way he said it. The lines across his forehead were deep. Genuine. He looked forlornly at the children in Annie's arms. Bending over, with tender hands he scooped up the dead woman into his arms and held her, standing in the middle of the pit, looking around, stymied as to how he was going to climb out. It seemed a real dilemma for him. He stared up at Annie with a hangdog expression on his face. His eyes filled with tears.

Annie couldn't help but be moved.

"Maybe . . ." she offered, "maybe it's best to leave her there. It's not like we can give her a proper burial. The ground's frozen, remember?"

The German didn't set her down immediately. Still holding her, he said, "It just seems wrong to leave her here."

A revelation struck Annie hard. Was that what they'd been doing all this time? Coming here to rescue a mother and her two children?

The German lowered the grown woman as carefully as he would a baby, laying her body corner to corner, positioning her arms serenely at her sides. She was a young woman, and pretty from what Annie could see beneath all the dirt. The German fussed over her for a while, straightening her dress. Then he climbed out of the pit.

The children began to whimper when they saw him. It was he they feared, not the fact he was leaving their mother in the pit. They seemed to have already come to terms with her death, though Annie was certain they'd be feeling the scars of it well into adulthood.

Annie hushed them. They laid their heads on her shoulders. The German brushed himself off and went straight for his rifle.

"Take them to the house," he said. "See if you can find food." He handed her the rifle. Their eyes met. "Just in case," he said.

"What are you going to do?" Annie asked.

"Bury their mother," he replied.

Inside the house, Annie found crackers and a box of raisins. She also found pillows and blankets and made the children a little place to rest in the corner of the kitchen. The rooms were cold. As she bundled them up tightly, neither child said a word.

Annie went to the window and pulled back the curtains. From here she could see the graveyard. The German had managed to close the wooden door and had covered it up. For a long time he stood over the woman's grave. Maybe Annie was mistaken, but it looked as if he was praying.

CHAPTER 18

You have to understand, the children changed everything. First of all, they forced me to see a side of my German captor that profoundly disturbed me. There was no room in my world for a compassionate German.

Secondly, the children took the focus off me. My attention turned to their needs, their safety, and getting them food and medical attention. In a way, they complicated things. Any thoughts of escape now had to involve them. And make no mistake, my thoughts were still on escaping. After seeing the German holding that dear, dead mother, I didn't fear him as much as before, but that didn't mean I trusted him or his kind.

———

"You speak English," Annie said.

"*Ja.* I don't do too badly for a scar-faced, goose-stepping, jack-booted moron, don't you think?"

Annie flushed at the thought that all this time he'd understood what she'd been saying to him.

They were sitting on the floor of the kitchen, their backs against the wall. The inside of the house was a shambles. Someone had destroyed all the furniture, ripped wallpaper from the walls, peppered the ceiling with gunshot, and apparently set fires in several of the rooms. From the looks of things it was amazing the house was still standing. Annie had found the crackers and raisins by rummaging around the well-trashed larder, which was messy work with broken bottles of preserves coating everything. Her gloves were sticky.

The German had returned from the cemetery with an armload of dead branches, which he used to start a fire in the wood-burning stove. The children had been moved closer to the stove and were now bundled up on the floor sleeping. It was night.

"Where's my rifle?" the German asked.

"I hid it."

He pondered this for a moment.

"We may need it," he said.

"I like it where it is."

The German got up. He walked into the next room. She thought he went to look for his weapon. Instead, he stared out the window of what had once been the parlor, squinting and straining to see into the night. He didn't say what he was looking for, or whom. After a few minutes he returned and sat down.

"What do you plan to do with us?" Annie asked.

The quickness with which the German answered gave evidence that he'd already thought this through.

"There's a farmhouse a couple kilometers north of here. As far as I know, it's still occupied. In the morning, I'll take you and the children to it. The people there can hide you until you can get back to your unit."

Annie stared at him. Was this some sort of German interrogation ploy? Offer them hope. Make them think you're a friend. Get them to relax, then after they've confided in you, throw them in prison camp or kill them.

"I don't believe you," she said.

"It doesn't matter."

A fatalistic tone tinged his voice. She'd heard it before in patients who'd given up hope.

Annie said, "If what you say is true, then you won't mind us leav-

ing right now. The sooner we get the children to safety, the better."
She started to get up.

"Sit down," he said.

"If it's all the same to you—"

"SIT DOWN!" he shouted.

He startled the children. They began to cry. Annie went to them and cuddled and soothed them back to sleep.

"That's what I thought," she said.

After the children were asleep again, the German said quietly, "It would be foolish for us to leave now. There are German troops all around us. If they capture you, they'll take the children from you and make you a prisoner of war."

"Prisoners. And what are we now?"

The German didn't answer her question. He said, "Besides, you don't know where you are and you don't know where you're going. I'll take you in the morning."

"Said the wolf to Little Red Riding Hood."

The German glared at her. He got up and moved into the parlor, where he slumped against a wall and pulled out his little book, reading it by the moonlight that streamed through the window.

Hours passed. Annie fought sleep, which was harder to do tonight because of the slumbering bundles just a few feet from her. The German did what he'd done every night. With the open book held in front of him, he read a portion, then closed his eyes and swayed back and forth.

The fire crackled. Annie could barely keep her eyes open, so she got up to stretch her legs and get her circulation going. She walked into the parlor. The German heard her coming and looked up.

"You came back for them, I'll give you that," she said.

He looked down at his book and closed it, marking his place with a finger.

"How long were they down there?" Annie asked.

"Several days."

Annie folded her arms, bracing herself against the chilling thought of a mother and children being buried alive, and then of the children huddled against their dead mother.

"Are you the ones who . . ."

"We tried to prevent it. Hans and me."

She didn't know if she believed him. She knew the atrocities of which the Germans were capable. Never before had she heard that they were ever sorry for what they did. Shuffling her feet, she turned to head back into the kitchen.

"The pit was a hiding place," said the German, "dug by the man who owned this house."

"Is he one of the men hanging in those trees?"

The German nodded solemnly.

"My *Unterfeldwebel* . . . um, sergeant—that is correct?"

"Sergeant is a rank, yes."

"My sergeant is not a sane man. There is no other way to describe him. He is cruel. He loves to inflict pain. To kill."

"Naturally. He's a German soldier."

The German studied her, absorbing the sarcasm. His eyes grew sad, weary.

"Why did he hang them? What did they do?"

The German swallowed hard. He stared at his feet. "Nothing. They did nothing. My sergeant was angry because supply would not requisition him new boots."

"That's it?" Annie shouted. "He was angry over boots, so he murdered all those people?"

"I told you. He is not a sane man. Our assignment was to scout the perimeter. The farmer saw us coming. He had dug a hiding place for his family in the graveyard with a rather ingenious method of covering it up once they were all inside. Only, they didn't hide fast enough. Kleist saw them. He pulled them out. We found more of them hiding in the barn."

"And he killed them for sport?"

"He claimed they were collaborators. There was no evidence to support that fact. He hanged the men, but not before raping the woman in front of them and burying her in the pit with the children. Kleist watered the wood to make it swell, then replaced the false covering with dirt. He then hung the men in sight of the grave so the last thought they would have would be of the woman and children buried alive."

Annie's anger flared. Her heart burned with thoughts of revenge. "Did you report him to your superiors?" she cried.

The German sighed heavily. "Kleist—that is my sergeant's name—is well connected. He comes from a prominent military family. My superiors are more concerned about advancing their careers than they are over the deaths of a few civilians."

"A few civilians?" Annie thundered. "A family! A husband, a wife—"

"Their reasoning, not mine," the German interrupted her.

"What about the other men in your unit? Why don't you all stop him?"

"Kleist is wealthy. He buys protectors of the body."

"Bodyguards."

"Ja."

"But surely someone . . ."

"Hans and I tried to stop him. Kleist set Dietle and Jaeger on us."

"His bodyguards."

"Hans and I managed to escape. That may have been Kleist's plan all along."

"What do you mean?"

"For the hunt. Now he can shoot us on sight. Now that we are deserters. Only, Hans . . ."

". . . was killed."

"Ja. Killed."

"We thought you were searching for us."

"We were hungry. Hans saw a rabbit. We were beating the bushes when your quick-on-the-draw cowboy friend ambushed us."

"Ambushed?" Annie shouted. "Keith was protecting us!"

"We were hunting a rabbit!" the German shouted back at her. "We didn't know you were there!"

"Well, we didn't know you didn't know!"

"How could you not have known? My back was turned to you!

Your cowboy friend shot me in the back!"

"There . . . there were two of you . . . and only one of him! And quit calling him a cowboy. Keith was . . ."

"Keith, is that his name? The name of the American coward who murdered my best friend in all the world?"

Annie was trembling with rage. Through clenched teeth, she said, "No, Keith is the name of my husband, whom *you* killed!"

Her words slapped him hard. For a long moment he said nothing; then he stood up and walked outside.

Annie didn't see him again until morning.

CHAPTER 19

The sound of his footsteps startled her. Having fallen asleep next to the children, Annie jumped up, her head still swimming in sleep. The German entered the kitchen carrying a bucket of water.

"I thought we could heat this up and wash the children before we go," he said.

"That was considerate. Thank you."

He set the bucket near the stove without looking at her. In fact, he was clearly making a conscious effort not to look at her as he stoked the fire.

The little boy opened his eyes and became frightened.

"I'll get more wood for the stove," the German said.

Annie found clothes for the children in the rubble upstairs. The children went with her, sticking close to her sides.

When they returned to the kitchen the fire was blazing and the German absent. Annie bathed and clothed the children. The boy's ribs were pronounced; the girl had a wine-stain birthmark on her thigh. And they both had bruises that were tender to the touch. Annie did all the talking. After a time, she stopped asking questions. They wouldn't tell her their names. She fell into a running commentary of what she would do next: "I'm going to slip this shirt over your head and then put this arm through the sleeve just like that, and now the other."

It felt as though she were dressing life-size dolls. They stood, letting her wash their faces and comb their hair as their gaze wandered about the kitchen. The look in their eyes gave the impression they saw it as a dream, where it was their kitchen and yet it wasn't at the same time.

Annie hugged them every thirty seconds. She couldn't help herself.

Outside, the sky was clear. Ordinarily it would be a glorious day, but the presence of two shivering war orphans sapped all the glory from it. Annie tried not to dwell on the hand life had dealt them. She focused instead on getting the children to friendly surroundings as quickly as possible so the healing could begin.

The German returned.

The children flew to Annie, nearly knocking her over.

"It's all right," she assured them, though her voice rang hollow in her own ears.

"My rifle," the German said.

Annie was ready for him. "Take us to the farmhouse, and once I'm convinced the children and I are safe, I'll tell you where it is."

He looked at her as if she were joking. When he realized she wasn't, he got angry. "We're not leaving here without the rifle," he said. "It's not safe."

"Not safe?" She straightened herself defiantly. "Speaking from experience, as one who has been shoved through a forest for two days at gunpoint, I can tell you for a fact that I feel a lot safer with the rifle right where it is!"

"Tell me where my rifle is!" he shouted.

The children began to cry.

"No!" Annie shouted back.

The German glared at her. He muttered something she didn't understand and began clamoring around the house looking for the rifle, while Annie and the children stood in the center of the kitchen watching him. Failing to find the weapon, frustrated and even more furious, he stormed toward her.

"Tell me where it is!"

Annie flinched but held her ground. "When the children and I are safe."

He walked in circles muttering in German.

"You're scaring the children!" Annie said.

He looked at them, at her, then bounded toward the door, shouting over his shoulder, "Let's go!"

Annie and the children followed him out the door into bright sunlight.

They didn't get far.

Three armed German soldiers stood side by side in front of the door, blocking their way.

"Kleist," Annie's German muttered.

The soldier in the middle stepped forward with a grin, more evil than friendly. Of the three, he was tallest. Malevolent eyes flashed like a knife in sunlight.

He addressed Annie's German with familiarity. And while Annie couldn't understand what he was saying, his tongue seemed well oiled, reminding her of a door-to-door salesman. Mockery in any language grates on the nerves just the same.

Kleist motioned to Annie and the children, who were hiding behind her and whimpering. He said something with a smarmy smile, then held up his hands as though to take a picture with an invisible camera.

The two goons on either side of him laughed. Kleist's body-guards. Thick in the neck and—if the brute-animal expressions on their faces were any indication—thick in the head as well. They were jovial now, but Annie needed no reminder that this was the trio that had hanged the civilians in the graveyard and buried a mother and her two children alive.

Kleist ambled closer. He made an inquiry. Annie recognized the word *Hans*.

The German motioned toward Annie. He made two statements.

The first one with a sneer, while the second brought a trio of lusty grins and appraising looks at Annie.

Another inquiry from Kleist and Annie's German raised empty hands with a sheepish shrug. He said something that Kleist repeated to the thugs, prompting another round of guffaws.

Kleist turned his attention to Annie, making no attempt to disguise his intent. He stepped to within inches of her, then moved closer, leaning so close that Annie could feel his breath on her cheek. He brushed her cheek with his nose. Annie felt a shiver of revulsion, as though she'd just been nuzzled by death.

He stepped back and ordered everyone into the house, shoving her toward the door and reaching for the children, who screamed and recoiled. Annie slapped his hand away.

In a flash her arm was caught in a vise grip, which Kleist viciously twisted, bending Annie sideways, forcing her to bend backward to keep it from breaking. A vein pulsed on Kleist's forehead, his eyes bulged, and flecks of spittle flew at her as he leaned close to her face and spat guttural words.

The German who had captured her said something appeasing to Kleist. He let her go.

Rubbing her wrist, Annie herded the children into the house.

Kleist strutted into the house as if he owned it, studying the destruction of the place with an appraising eye. The warm kitchen stove drew the soldiers to it. Kleist pulled off his gloves and took advantage of the heat. His two goons—Dietle and Jaeger, if Annie remembered correctly—followed his example, setting their rifles to one side.

Annie glanced at her German and saw that he was looking at her with pensive, fearful eyes, which did little to calm her. He knew better than she what Kleist was capable of.

A couple of minutes of small talk identified which goon was which. Dietle had a smashed potato for a nose. It looked as though it had been broken more than once. Jaeger had a box jaw that jutted forward with attitude. They took turns rubbing their hands to get them warm and leering at Annie.

With a clap, Kleist signaled hand-warming time had concluded, and now it was time to get down to business. He asked Annie's captor a question.

The German looked at her with a rakish grin. His reply to Kleist was suggestive in its tone, and it prompted laughter from the other three. Annie's stomach flip-flopped.

Kleist snapped his fingers and barked an order.

Dietle and Jaeger peeled screaming, crying kids away from Annie. Her protests and clawing was ineffective to stop them. They dragged the children to the larder.

"No! Don't put them in there!" Annie cried. "Not in the dark again!"

She made a lunge for them. The German, the one who shot Keith, grabbed her by the arm, swung her back around to him, and slapped her so hard that, had he not been holding her up, the blow would have knocked her off her feet.

Dietle and Jaeger threw the children into the larder and slammed the door shut. Because there was no lock on it, Dietle put his back against it to keep the children from escaping. Fitful screams and whimpering came from the other side.

Annie's German pulled her roughly to him.

"We have one chance of staying alive," he hissed in English, "and that's if you cooperate. You must do everything I tell you to do or we're dead. Understand, woman?"

Annie glared at him with fury in her eyes.

Amused, Kleist and the goons looked on.

The German slapped her, snapping her head to the side so hard it made her eyes water. Her cheek burned and her head swam.

"Take that look off your face or we're both dead!" he shouted. "Act submissive! It must appear I have broken your will! Now get on your knees and keep your eyes to the floor."

He forced Annie to her knees. She started to look up at him. He raised his hand. She lowered her head.

Her captor stood over her. He said something to the other three. They laughed.

Annie had seen men behave like this before when they were drunk. Cruel and crude. What made this scene more horrifying was that these men weren't drunk, their judgment not impaired by alcohol. These were the kind of men who found pleasure in inflicting pain.

"I have violated you repeatedly," her captor shouted to her. "And now, because I say so, you are going to submit to my three friends. Keep your head down and tell me you understand."

Annie understood. Of course she understood. The question was whether she would go along with him. Why should she trust him? This was the man who'd killed her husband and led her through the forest at gunpoint. For all she knew, he was sacrificing her to save his own skin. He was, after all, a German.

"I said, do you understand?"

"Yes," Annie whimpered.

There were four of them. What could she do? How was she going to get out of this?

Kleist chuckled appreciatively.

"I want you to look up at Kleist, and in your most seductive voice I want you to tell him where you have hidden my rifle!"

She glanced up.

He raised his hand. But this time he didn't hit her.

She turned slowly toward Kleist. The roguish twist of his lips was the most repulsive thing she'd ever seen in her life. In a low voice—sultry was impossible, given her fear—she said, "It's on top of the cabinet over the counter, you pig."

Kleist liked it, made a grunt, and then began unbuttoning his coat.

"Take your clothes off!" Annie's captor shouted.

Annie hesitated. How far was this going to go? Looking the German in the eyes, she began working on the buttons of her coat.

Kleist barked something that startled her. Dietle and Jaeger grabbed their rifles. With Dietle guarding the door, Jaeger guarded Annie's German. Feeling that his back was covered now, Kleist turned his attention to Annie. He oozed words that sent a chill down Annie's spine.

"He told you to lie down on the floor," the German translated. "He wants you to appear willing."

Her hands shaking, Annie reclined on the floor. She had to fight every instinct within her to do it. She wanted to scream. To kick. To bite. To gouge. Reclining onto the floor felt as if she were lowering herself into a grave.

The German saw her hesitancy. He shouted, "Do as he says! If you resist, we're dead!"

Her coat unbuttoned, Annie lay back.

Kleist straddled her. He worked feverishly at getting his pants unbuttoned. When it took too long, he fell down on top of her, his face buried against her neck.

Annie fought the urge to wretch. The man's weight on top of her was suffocating, his breath nauseating.

Out of the corner of her eye, she could see the German grinning, bending over to get a better look, pointing and saying something obscene to Jaeger, who was ogling her and grinning like a buffoon. The German stepped aside so Jaeger could get a better look. A show of black teeth indicated he liked what he was seeing.

Kleist started ripping at Annie's clothes. His breathing against her neck was growing labored. She closed her eyes to fight the urge to vomit.

Just then she heard a shout. Then stumbling. Heavy boots pounded the hardwood floor. Annie's eyes flew open in time to see Jaeger's arms flailing as he attempted to keep his balance. He couldn't. He went crashing into Dietle, sending them both to the floor.

Alarmed, Kleist tried to push himself up. Annie grabbed his shirt and pulled him back down.

On the far side of the kitchen, the German was frantically feeling on top of the cabinet, searching for his rifle. He couldn't find it! A look of terror swept over him.

"Toward the back!" Annie yelled.

He jumped and felt, repeatedly.

With each jump, Annie's heart sank. It had to be there. She'd put it there. She knew she did!

Finally, a look of relief on his face told Annie he'd found it.

Again Kleist tried to get up. Annie held on to his shirt with all her might to keep him from getting any leverage. She couldn't let him get into the fray; it would be three against one.

But this time, Kleist retaliated. He bit her neck. Annie screamed with pain.

Dietle and Jaeger were fumbling to get to their feet, clamoring to untangle their rifles.

The German had his rifle in hand, ready to fire, just as Jaeger swung toward him. The blast from the German's gun sent Jaeger reeling backward into Dietle. There was a second blast as Dietle's rifle discharged. The bullet hit Jaeger in the back, reversing his direction. Jaeger collapsed to the floor, dead.

The German got off a second shot. Dietle slumped against the wall.

Two down.

His bodyguards dead, Kleist quickly came up with a plan. To Annie's horror, he'd managed to grab his sidearm and roll over, pulling Annie on top of him. The cold barrel of the pistol pressed against Annie's cheek.

Annie didn't have to understand the language to know what Kleist said to the German. Lower the rifle, or he'd blow her head off.

The German stared at Kleist helplessly. His rifle was aimed at Kleist's head. He made no attempt to lower it.

Kleist pressed the barrel harder into Annie's cheek, so hard it felt as if he was going to push out a tooth.

With that, the German started lowering his rifle.

"No!" Annie screamed, then winced as the barrel was rammed even harder against her cheek.

Transferring the rifle to one hand, the German raised his other hand in surrender. He bent his knees to set the rifle down.

Kleist chuckled. The pressure against Annie's cheek eased as he rolled her to one side so he could get up.

Annie saw her chance. She lunged for the side of his face and bit his ear, chomping down on it with everything she had.

Kleist screamed.

It was a short scream, cut off by the sound of a rifle shot. Kleist went limp. Annie let go of his ear. The German stood over them, his rifle aimed at Kleist's chest in case another shot was needed.

It wasn't.

Annie shoved Kleist away. The German reached down and helped her to her feet. For a long time they stood there in disbelief, neither of them speaking.

The German collected the rifles and Kleist's pistol and put them all out of reach on top of the cabinet. He dragged the three bodies into the parlor—Kleist first, then Jaeger, then Dietle—unblocking the larder door.

Annie had to coax the children to come out. They wouldn't come until the only surviving German stood at the far end of the kitchen. Annie sat on the floor, holding them, rocking them, telling them everything was all right now.

At first, her voice and her hands shook as she consoled them, but she finally succeeded in convincing not only them but herself, too.

The German slumped to the floor, watching from a distance. He motioned to Annie that one of her shirt buttons needed buttoning. Her arms were filled with children, and she couldn't reach it.

"I'll get it later," she said.

"By the way," said the German. "My name is Karl."

"I'm Annie."

CHAPTER 20

Karl. Just like that. He said his name like we were at a church social. All of a sudden my captor had a name.

Numb doesn't begin to describe how I felt at that moment in the kitchen. It was the culmination of every fear I'd ever had about the war.

When the war started and Keith joined up, I thought I'd never survive if I heard that he was killed. I never imagined I'd witness it. Then it was Mouse and Nina. I didn't know what I'd do if something happened to either of them. Now Mouse lay dead in the forest.

On some of the longer nights, when sleep wouldn't come and the shells were so close they shook my molars, I wondered how I'd react if our position was overrun and I was captured. What I would do if a Kraut tried to rape me. Now I knew.

Violated. Vulnerable. Shaken. Numb. Choose a word. It'll be inadequate to describe how I felt.

It's not like I was a stranger to hardship or danger. I had four battle stars on my uniform.

At Anzio when the Germans forced us off the beachhead, taking potshots at the transports as we loaded the wounded on hospital ships, I'd felt like one of those tin ducks at a carnival booth.

In southern France, while I was changing a shoulder-wound dressing on a soldier who was sitting on the edge of his cot, a .50-

caliber machine-gun burst from two planes in a dogfight ripped through the canvas wall of the hospital tent, missed me, and killed my patient.

I'd been soaked to the bone in rain, and so hungry it felt my stomach was turning inside out, so scared the slightest sound made me jump out of my skin. I'd been knee-deep in mud and blood and death to the point that I wondered what would give out first, my knees or my will. I knew fear and discouragement and homesickness to such an extent that I'd buried my head so deep in the bedding I didn't think I'd ever find the strength to get back up.

But never had I felt more shaken than what I felt in that blood-stained kitchen holding those two orphans.

Comforted comforter. That was how Annie thought of herself as she sat on the floor clutching the two children against her. She didn't know if she was comforting them or they were comforting her. All she knew was that she didn't want to let go.

The German—Karl—had not moved. His head lay back against the wall. His eyes were closed. But he wasn't relaxed. His fists were clenched, and every so often he shuddered.

If she got up and moved toward the door, would he stop her? All Annie wanted was to get to the neighboring farmhouse. They could help her get the children to safety, and help her get back to the 67th Evac, a haven compared to where she was right now.

Tears filled her eyes as she trembled. She tried to stop them. Both the tears and the shakes. Couldn't. She found herself doing something she hadn't done in months. She prayed.

As a young girl, Annie believed that God watched over her. Her family attended church every Sunday. She was baptized following a statement of faith when she was eight years old. In her teens, her closest friends were those in the church youth group. If she were asked to recount key rites of passage in her life, she would include several spiritual moments among them.

The war had changed all that. It hadn't made her an atheist. God existed, of that she was certain. It was just that she couldn't say with conviction she saw any evidence He was in the neighborhood. She didn't know why He would absent himself. Maybe He'd grown so sick of what human beings were doing to each other, He'd washed his hands of the whole lot and walked away. Annie hadn't prayed since Anzio. It didn't make sense to pray to an absent God.

Now she felt compelled to pray. There came a point when thinking about what God was doing or why just didn't matter anymore. Her life had been reduced to a wordless heart cry to God.

Annie's tears and trembling were her prayer.

"Anytime you're ready," Karl said from the far side of the room.

Annie fortified herself with a deep breath. "Let's go," she said.

Despite what the German had done to save them, Annie still didn't trust him. Had he really rescued them, or had he just settled a score with an old adversary? Had he saved them, or was he saving himself and they just happened to be on the winning side?

Annie coaxed reluctant children and her own wobbly knees to stand. She spoke soothing, encouraging words to them, even though they'd never given any indication they understood English. But despite her coaxing, she couldn't get either of them to take a step. The German stood between them and the door.

"You'd better lead the way," Annie said.

The German looked at the children. He seemed to understand. He made a few loping strides to the parlor and the front door.

"Wait!" Annie said. "What about the rifles?"

"You said you didn't feel comfortable with me carrying one," Karl replied.

That was before Kleist and his thugs. For all Annie knew, there were a thousand more Kleists between here and the neighboring farmhouse.

Annie blinked, surprised at what she would say next. "I . . . I think I'd feel safer if you took one."

The German appeared relieved. He retrieved a rifle from on top of the cabinet.

"Shield the eyes of the children as you pass through the parlor," Karl said. "They've seen enough death."

There had never been a more homey sight than the old stone Belgian farmhouse situated a short distance from the road. They came upon it suddenly. The forest thinned, and there it was. A lazy river of smoke rose from the chimney promising a cozy hearth.

When the road first came into view, the German stepped aside. "You'll continue from here alone," he said.

Until now he'd been leading the way by fifteen or twenty paces to keep from scaring the children. He never once looked over his shoulder to see if they were following.

"It's best if no one in the house sees me," he said, plucking at his uniform.

A wary Annie ushered the children past him. This was the moment of truth. He had told her he'd deliver them to the farmhouse, but now that they'd arrived, she found it difficult to believe he was really going to let them go.

Several paces past him, she couldn't resist looking over her shoulder. It wouldn't have surprised her to see him pointing his rifle at them, ordering them to come back. Nor would it surprise her to reach the house only to discover that it had been commandeered as some sort of German outpost.

At the moment everything was as he said it would be. His rifle at his side, the German had stepped back and was partially hidden by a tree.

The craziest thing nearly happened then. Annie almost thanked him! The words were on her lips. Habit, she guessed. Luckily she stopped them before they got out.

Quickening her steps, she and the children made their way across the snowy terrain to the farmhouse. As they approached, a back door opened.

Annie pulled up. The children saw it, too. They drew close to her.

An elderly man emerged. From his clothing, a civilian. And from the expression on his weathered face, he wasn't expecting to see anyone.

Hardened blue eyes went from Annie to the children, and for a long moment he seemed to assess his find. Then, turning his head toward the house, he shouted, "Elthia! You'd better get out here!"

A moment later a small, thin woman appeared, her gray hair pulled back. She was wiping her hands on a dish towel. "What is it?" she said. And then seeing Annie and the children, she cried, "Justine! Niels! What are you doing here?"

The children stared at her blankly. Their reaction perplexed the woman, but only for a moment. "No!" she cried, rushing toward the children.

When she reached them, she bent down and addressed the children individually. They gave no indication they recognized her, yet neither were they afraid of her.

The woman looked up at Annie. "Their parents?"

Annie shook her head. It was enough. She didn't have to say anything. The woman understood.

"Justine, Niels, let's get you inside," she said. "You must be freezing. Are you hungry? I just made biscuits."

Annie followed the woman and the children into the house. The man held the door open for her and, as he did, peered past her at the forest. At the threshold of the door Annie turned to look, too. The German was gone.

CHAPTER 21

$\mathscr{S}$ tepping into that Belgian country kitchen was like stepping into another world. There was color here. Warmth. The heavenly odor of fresh-baked biscuits. And a sense of domestic order. The war had not touched this room. Had she not seen it for herself, Annie wouldn't have thought such a thing was possible in all of Europe.

The first order of business was taking care of the children. While they should have been ravenous, Justine and Niels merely pecked at the biscuit and jam that was set before them. After a while, they were taken to a bedroom, where they quickly fell asleep even though it was early afternoon.

Annie, on the other hand, devoured her biscuit and stared hungrily at the children's uneaten biscuits. She learned that she was in the home of Armand and Elthia Billaud—both in their early seventies, both with white hair. Towering over his wife by nearly a foot, Armand had the broad shoulders and leathery skin that came from a lifetime of work in the fields, including the largest hands Annie had ever seen, although they moved with slow grace.

Elthia was thin, almost to the point of appearing frail, but from the way she bustled the children around, she was a hearty soul. It was easy to see why the children were comfortable with her. Her eyes were quick, intelligent, and she treated them like relatives who'd come for a visit. Armand did not exude the same warmth. While cordial, his mouth had been set in a grim line since they'd arrived. He kept staring at Annie's American uniform.

"I can't tell you how glad I am that you speak English," Annie said when Elthia returned.

"I *am* English," Elthia said. "I have a twin sister who lives in Bridge, a little town between Canterbury and Dover. Armand is French. All of his family live in Reims—those still alive, that is."

"It's not necessary to bore the woman with details of our lives," Armand said brusquely. It was the first he had spoken since announcing Annie's arrival.

"I'm just trying to be sociable, dear," Elthia said. To Annie she said, "We don't get too many visitors nowadays, as you might expect."

Annie sipped her coffee. It was ersatz, not the real stuff, but it was hot, and at the moment had never been so flavorful.

Elthia reached across the table and touched Annie's arm. "Tell us what happened, dear," she said.

Even though Annie knew she would have to tell them eventually, the telling was difficult. Partly because it was painful to relive, and partly because it seemed a shame to spoil such a delightful setting with talk of war. The small kitchen with its dented pots and pans, freshly laundered tablecloth, and frilly curtains all had the warmth and security she so missed. She didn't want to spoil it.

Elthia had removed the children before requesting an explanation, and Armand had lingered to hear it. Beginning with the arrival of the jeep at the 67th Evacuation Hospital, Annie sketched the events that had deposited an American nurse and two children on their doorstep. She didn't tell them the whole story, nor was all of it the truth. She told them they escaped from their German captor this morning while he slept. The truth about him escorting them to the house didn't make any sense. It raised questions for which she had no answers.

When she told them the part about Keith and Mouse dying,

Elthia squeezed her arm in sympathy. Annie had to compose herself before continuing. It was the first sympathy she had been shown over their deaths, and she found she wasn't ready for it.

Armand listened stoically, his expression never changing. Annie got the impression he didn't like her being in his house.

"We could take the children to Pastor Cuvier," Elthia said. "He'll know how to contact the proper authorities."

"Do the children have relatives?" Annie asked.

"Claire came from the Anjou region," Elthia said. "That's all I know. Maybe the pastor will know more."

Claire. It was the first time Annie had heard the name of the woman who had died in the earthen pit. Giving her a name somehow made her human, her death even more tragic. Annie fought back a fresh round of tears.

"I'll take them when they wake up," Armand said. He stood abruptly, put on his hat and coat, and walked out the back door.

"You have to forgive him, dear," Elthia said. "It's not you. It's your uniform. It will go bad for us if the Germans learn we've harbored an American."

Annie had been so relieved about being warm and safe, she hadn't realized she might be putting them in danger.

"I should leave," she said.

"Nonsense, dear!" Elthia said. "However, it wouldn't hurt to get you out of that uniform. Let's see what we can find."

She led Annie to a back bedroom, where she opened an old chest and began pulling out neatly folded clothes. Men's clothes.

"These belonged to my son," Elthia said. "Of course he was bigger than you, so we might have to cinch things up with a belt."

"Where is your son?"

Elthia pulled out a pair of jeans, set them aside as unsuitable, then pulled out another pair. "He left shortly before the war broke out. That's all you need to know. There. These should fit you. You're used to wearing men's clothes, aren't you?"

Annie blushed. The comment seemed innocent enough, but for her it brought back unpleasant memories.

Having to wear trousers like a man was one of the things her mother used as an argument to keep her from enlisting in the Army Nurse Corps. Prevailing public opinion was that women of good character did not wear trousers, and they did not become nurses. Nursing necessitated an unwholesome mingling of the sexes, exposing young, unmarried women to men in various stages of undress and—because it was the military—treating men with diseases that were sometimes of a sexual nature.

Patriotism, however, out-argued her mother's objections, and Annie enlisted. In the States she always wore her army-issue skirt, which was suitable for training but not practical in war conditions.

"Here. Try these on," Elthia said, handing Annie a pair of jeans and a long-sleeved shirt. "And you'd probably better remove your dog tags."

"I don't know if that's a good idea," Annie said.

"It's a very good idea. The tags identify you as an American soldier. If the Germans catch you in civilian clothes they'll shoot you as a spy. This way, we can pass you off as my English niece."

Annie slipped the tags over her head. It felt wrong, but she was in uncharted waters here.

As Annie changed clothes, her hostess took each article of military clothing as it was removed, folded it, and stacked it on a wooden chair beside the bed. Placing the dog tags on top, Elthia scooped up the bundle.

"Why don't you lie down and rest," she said. "I'll hide these for now. We'll figure out how we're going to get you back to your hospital when you get up."

Elthia closed the door. Annie stood at the foot of the bed in clothes that were roomy but comfortable. She thought her waist looked like a sack of potatoes the way the belt gathered up the excess inches, but then she doubted she would be attending many social gatherings while she was here, so what did it matter?

She lay down on the bed, weary yet not sleepy. The last time she'd slept on a bed was on her honeymoon night, a thought she dismissed quickly before it could inflict emotional damage. Now was not the time to deal with such things.

As she stared at the ceiling, she told herself she'd just lie down for a little while and rest.

Two hours later, she awoke.

CHAPTER 22

*A*nnie entered the kitchen to the sound of swishing water and the aroma of soap. She was still a little groggy from her nap. Elthia stood over the kitchen sink, her hands in dishwater.

"Good, you're up," the older woman said. "You can help me with the dishes."

"I'm surprised I slept," Annie said.

"Not surprising, considering all you've been through."

Annie took up a dish towel and reached for a plate in the drainer. It was a comfortable feeling. Drying the dishes was her first household chore when she was growing up. Somehow, in this whirlwind of chaos and uncertainty, returning to the actions of a simpler time felt therapeutic.

A glance outside the window in front of the sink revealed lengthy shadows. It would be twilight soon.

"The children are gone," Elthia said matter-of-factly. "Armand has taken them to a place where they'll be cared for."

"I wish I could have said good-bye to them," Annie said.

"Wishes are the first casualty of war," Elthia said. She spoke as a woman who had a good deal of experience in the matter.

Annie dried a saucer with a green-and-yellow floral design, then reached for a matching cup. Disappointed she wouldn't see the children again, she wasn't disappointed Armand was gone. The house felt friendlier in his absence.

As Annie helped Elthia, contentment warmed her like an old sweater. The kitchen smells. Womanly chores. The civilian clothes. For the first time in as long as Annie could remember, she felt safe.

"I'm going out to the barn," Elthia said after the dishes were all put away. "We have a secret cellar where we store things. Hide them from the Germans, you know."

Annie knew. One of the last things she and Mouse had done together was hide Christmas goodies so the Germans wouldn't get them.

"Can I help you?" Annie asked.

"Thank you, dear. How thoughtful."

Elthia found a coat and an old hunter's hat for Annie. She felt ridiculous in the hat, but it was fur-lined and they were just going out to the barn and back.

Two steps out the door and the winter wind greeted Annie by biting her cheeks. Elthia led the way at a no-nonsense pace that reminded Annie of how much she admired the older woman's generation. They'd seen so much, endured so much. It had toughened them. Annie drew strength from her.

The barn was cavernous with all the usual barnyard tools and smells. It was dark inside.

"Over here," Elthia said. "We use a meat hook to work the latch. It's right over there beneath that canvas." She pointed to the end of a workbench.

Annie recognized a command when she heard one. She went to the workbench and pulled back the canvas a little. Only there was no meat hook beneath it. What she saw made her heart skip a beat.

"Pick them up," Elthia said behind her.

Annie looked over her shoulder. The old woman stood a discreet distance away with a pistol pointed at Annie.

"Elthia . . ."

"I'm not afraid to use this," Elthia said. "Now pick them up."

Perplexed, Annie folded back the canvas the rest of the way.

Beneath it was her uniform and coat with the dog tags lying on top. She picked them up.

"I don't understand," she said.

"Of course you don't, dear. You seem like a nice enough girl. If you understood, you never would have come to our house in the first place."

"You're a collaborator," Annie said.

"Don't be ridiculous," Elthia replied. "The Germans lured my son into the Reich with their silly rhetoric and then marched him off to Russia, where he was slaughtered. I'd kill every last one of them if I could."

"Then why. . . ?"

"Quite simply, you're a threat. If the Germans learn you've been here, they'll do to us what they did to Justine and Niels's family. I won't have that. Armand and I have survived this long, I'm not about to let an empty-headed American ruin it for us now."

"I'll leave," Annie said. "I'll walk away. No one need know I was ever here."

Elthia shook her head. "You'd be picked up within the hour and you'd tell them about us."

"I won't!" Annie insisted.

"You would. They'd force it out of you. I'm sorry, dear, but you were dead the minute you stepped into my kitchen. Now put your uniform on and be quick about it."

It made sense that the change of clothes was temporary, just in case someone happened by and saw her in the house. It would be easier to explain a woman in civilian clothes than it would an American army nurse.

Elthia, still holding the pistol, folded her son's jeans and shirt as Annie took them off.

It was twilight now. The sun was setting on the day and, Annie couldn't help but think, on her life. Her own clothes were cold from being out in the barn and she was freezing. Her jaw ached from trying to keep her teeth from chattering.

With a jerk of the gun, Elthia steered her out of the barn and into the woods.

Annie was beginning to hate the Ardennes Forest. Every time she entered it, she did so convinced she was going to die.

"Where are we going?" she asked.

"To the creek. Whoever finds your body will think you were lost while following it. There will be no ties to our house."

"What about our footprints?"

"By the time anyone finds you, they will have been covered over."

The terrain began to slope. Annie's time was running out.

"That's far enough," Elthia said.

Annie turned. "You're going to have to look me in the face when you shoot me, and I don't think you can do that. I think Armand put you up to this and left you to do his dirty work."

Elthia laughed. It was a cold laugh, colder than the whipping wind.

"Armand couldn't kill you, dear. If I left it to him, he would risk both our lives to save you. I just can't see it. Why should our lives be put in danger because an American girl happened upon our doorstep? If anyone's to blame for your death, dear, it's you. We don't want you here—not the Germans, not the Americans, not the English. Why can't you all just leave us alone?"

Annie didn't know what else to say. The woman was as emotional about killing her as she would be disposing a rat from a trap.

Elthia pointed the pistol at Annie's face.

"Put the gun down!"

The voice came from behind Elthia. She jumped at the sound.

"Put the gun down, Elthia."

The woman turned to see her husband. It was the first time Annie had seen her flustered.

"Armand, you know I have to kill her."

"Put the gun down, Elthia."

"You said it yourself. If anyone were to discover she's been in our house—"

"You're too good of a woman, Elthia," Armand said. "Put the gun down."

Elthia's back stiffened. With the shock of her husband's sudden appearance wearing off, she regained her resolve.

"Go back to the house, Armand," she said. "Let me take care of this."

"Put the gun down!"

This time the command didn't come from Armand. The German stepped from behind a tree, his rifle pointed at Elthia.

"I won't say it again," Karl said.

For the second time Elthia appeared stunned, but she recovered quickly. She kept her pistol trained on Annie.

"What is this?" Elthia said suspiciously. "A German soldier and his American whore? If you value your prize, lower your rifle and I'll let her go."

The German considered this. He swung his rifle around until it was pointing at Armand.

"I have no desire to harm you," he said. "You can walk away like this never happened, or you can walk away a widow. You have to the count of three. One."

Elthia wavered but didn't lower the gun.

"Two."

Armand walked toward his wife. He caught her eye, and once he had it he didn't let go. Slowly and without hesitation, he reached out and took the gun from her hand, lifted his coat, and stuck it in his waistband. Then he reached out and pulled his wife to him in an embrace. Elthia didn't resist. It was obvious she found herself in a familiar place.

"Do with us as you will," Armand said to the German.

"Like I said, I have no desire to harm you. Take your wife and go home."

Armand looked at Annie. "She's not a bad woman," he said.

With his arm around Elthia, Armand walked his wife in the

direction of their house. Annie and the German watched them until they were gone.

"Are you all right?" the German asked her.

"Who are you, and why are you so obsessed with me?" Annie said.

CHAPTER *23*

Where was the sense of it all? That's what angered me the most about the entire situation. The world of the forest made no sense.

The hospital at times could be hell on earth, but at least it made sense. Good and evil were well defined. Our boys were there to fight the evil that threatened Europe. To do that, they had to stand in harm's way. Some of them got hurt. Some were killed. The injustice of it all infuriated us at times, yet it made sense.

But in the forest, German tanks fired on ambulances. A sweet girl who had dedicated her life to helping others got killed in battle. My husband, an experienced soldier, shot and killed by a German hunting rabbits. Three American soldiers whom I thought were my saviors handed me back to my captor for a couple of rifles. Innocent children were buried alive, only to be rescued by one of the men who buried them. Germans killed Germans in a farmhouse kitchen over an American nurse. And a grandmotherly housewife plotted to murder me.

To top it all off, the only reason I was still alive was because my German captor was running around the forest acting like my guardian angel.

The world of the forest made no sense.

Stumbling back into the Ardennes, her German captor silent and at her arm, Annie walked until she couldn't take another step in Alice's twisted wonderland. The daily brush with death had taken its toll. Her legs buckled, and she collapsed in the middle of a hunter's trail, blinded by a flow of tears that tapped a seemingly endless supply of emotion.

Between sobs she could hear the German hovering over her. His feet shuffled, paused, then shuffled again, circling her. Then, without threat, without shouting, without prodding her in the back with his rifle, he sat against a tree and Annie soon forgot him. Her head ached.

Annie wanted to lie here until the angels came for her. Instead, the frozen ground seeped into her from beneath, and the penetrating night air hugged her from above. Chilled and chattering, Annie could take it no more. She urged her frozen joints to get up.

A hand assisted her.

She saw the German through blurry eyes. Given the surreal nature of this forest, she wouldn't have been surprised to see a white rabbit with a pocket watch.

"I have a camp not far from here," he said.

The stubble on his cheeks and chin was heavier than she remembered. Not enough to hide the red slice on his cheek, though. There was definitely going to be a scar.

"This way," he said, pointing with a hand.

Like an invitation. Not a prod. Not a command.

With nowhere else to go, Annie went with him.

He led her to an alcove of rock where there were remnants of a campfire. He hadn't gone far after delivering her and the children to Armand and Elthia's farmhouse.

After getting Annie situated, he told her he would collect wood for a fire. He handed Annie his rifle. "If anyone but me approaches, defend yourself," he said, then disappeared into the darkening twilight.

Before long a fire was blazing and Annie was warming her hands.

"How are your feet?" the German asked.

"Um . . . fine, I guess," she said.

"Here," he said, scooting close to her.

He reached for a boot. She pulled back.

"I'm not going to hurt you," he said, somewhat exasperated. "Don't you know that by now?"

She did know that by now. She just hadn't admitted it to herself. By admitting it, she would be denying the natural order of things, surrendering to this weird and bizarre world, and only a crazy person would do that.

He reached again for her boot.

This time—her only excuse being that she wearied of the fight—she didn't resist.

The German unlaced her boot and set it close to the fire. He then removed her sock and draped it over a pile of kindling stacked near the fire.

"Move closer to the fire," he said.

He pulled on her leg, giving her little choice, nearly knocking her off-balance.

The German took her foot in his hands, which had begun to be warmed by the fire, and started massaging her foot.

"We learned this on the Russian front," the German said. "We would massage each other's feet to restore circulation."

After several minutes, he fitted her foot with a now-toasty sock and boot.

When he reached for her other boot, Annie didn't resist. Despite the fact he was a Nazi killing machine, his warm hands massaging her frozen feet felt heavenly.

Moments later, observing him guardedly, she asked, "What made you come back for me?"

"I never left," he said.

He finished massaging and warming her foot, then got up and stoked the fire while she put her sock and boot back on.

"Oh? What would make you stay?"

Settling close by, facing her, he answered, "I couldn't leave until I knew you and the children were safe."

"What did it matter to you whether we were safe or not?" Annie said.

"It mattered," the German said. "Isn't that enough?"

"No. No, that's not enough."

The question sprang from out of nowhere, like a door that had been locked suddenly cracking open. Who knew what lay behind it? Possibly some answers to this weird world of the forest.

For a long time the German stared at the fire, either refusing to answer or finding it difficult to answer.

Finally he said, "When Hans was shot, I didn't understand. I was angry. I'd promised him I would get him back to Riesa."

"Your home?"

"We grew up there. Classmates in school. Summers in the river. Thoughts of the river kept Hans going. He loved to swim. He was good at it. His goal was to swim in the Olympics once all this nonsense was over."

Nonsense, Annie thought. *What a strange word to describe a war they started.*

"Strange, isn't it?" the German continued. "The things we take for granted when we're at home are usually the things we miss most when we're away. The river was the first thing I thought of when I realized Hans was dead. How he would never swim again. Seeing him on the hard ground like that . . . a body that was most at home in the water . . . I was angry."

Annie shifted uneasily. This had been a mistake. Getting him to relive the death of his friend, to rekindle his anger at Americans, at the American who shot him . . .

"Mostly I was angry that Hans was dead and a man like Kleist was still alive. The injustice of it. I guess there are some things we'll never understand. And then there was you."

"We were defending ourselves," Annie protested.

The German looked at her. His eyes weren't angry. They were sad.

"For the longest time I couldn't figure out why God would bring an American nurse into my life."

Annie was taken aback by his words. It wasn't what she was expecting. Not from a German. Certainly not from the enemy.

"You were a real puzzle to me," he said. "It took me the longest time to piece it together. I mean, what was I going to do with you? I couldn't hand you over to my unit. I couldn't take you back to your unit without getting shot myself. I couldn't just walk away and leave you alone, not in the forest. That's when I remembered the children and I thought, of course! It made perfect sense! God knew exactly what He was doing. He brought you into my life to help rescue the children."

"Justine and Niels," Annie said.

The German smiled. "You learned their names! I watched as the farmer took them away. They're safe?"

Annie nodded. "He took them to a minister who will see they're cared for."

The news seemed to warm him in ways the fire never could.

His talk of God knocked Annie out of kilter and added to the topsy-turvy world of the forest. What could a German, born of a godless race of Germans, know of God? And she refused to concede that God had anything to do with bringing her into this forest to save the lives of two children at the cost of Mouse's and Keith's lives.

The German didn't notice her struggle.

"I expected the farmer would take you next," he continued. "Then I saw his wife lead you at gunpoint into the woods, just as her husband was returning. I apologize for not acting sooner, but I had to assume he was in on the plan and that he was armed. It took me a while to get into position. As it turned out, it was just her."

Even with her boots on, Annie could still feel the German's warm hands on her feet. This Nazi deserter. This unlikely guardian.

"I still don't understand why you stuck around," Annie said. "There was no indication I was in any kind of danger."

"Stuck around," the German repeated. He smiled. "I've not heard that phrase before. Stuck around. It was my decision to stay stuck there. I just wanted to make sure you were safe, that's all."

"I was safe once," Annie protested. "Only you stole me back from those three American soldiers for your own purposes."

"They weren't Americans."

"They most certainly were!"

"They were German soldiers in American uniforms."

"But they spoke perfect English. One of them kept calling me darlin'."

"Didn't you notice the telephone line was down?"

"They were repairing it."

"They were the ones who cut it."

"How did you know?"

"We were briefed to be on the lookout for squads of Germans in American disguise. They were dropped ahead of the invasion to pass along disinformation and disrupt communications. Had I left you with them, they would have killed you."

"But from a distance you couldn't have known for certain. They could have been Americans."

"Yes."

"And yet you walked out of the forest with your hands up."

"Call it a hunch."

"You exposed yourself on a hunch?"

"I prayed first."

Annie laughed. She couldn't help herself. "You prayed first?"

"Not for myself. The worst that could have happened to me would be that I would be captured or killed. I've been prepared for that eventuality for years. I prayed for the children. If I was wrong, they would die."

Annie stared at him. Either the man was telling her the truth or he was an incredibly gifted liar. She hadn't ruled out the latter possibility. Her head was swimming.

He sat staring at the fire. From the looks of it, he was reliving a portion of their shared experience.

"Karl?"

He looked up. Surprised to hear his name.

"Thank you for coming back for me," she said.

CHAPTER 24

$\mathcal{M}$orning came early and loud. They were awakened by ratcheting, clanking, diesel-belching tanks in retreat. A line of armor-plated vehicles flanked by German soldiers snaked its way through the forest. Overhead, against clear skies, Allied planes streaked to targets. Ground-thumping explosions could be heard in the distance.

Startled, Annie scrambled to get to her feet. She was pulled back down to the ground by Karl and half dragged behind some nearby rocks. They lay low the entire morning as the tanks passed.

Neither of them spoke. Karl's head swiveled in constant lookout all around them. They were lucky. The German tank division moved rapidly and with purpose.

When the last of the machine noise died away, Annie and Karl emerged from their hiding place and set off on foot. Karl led, with Annie following close behind. She didn't ask him where they were going. Their meandering course suggested no specific destination other than to stay out of sight. Several times they heard German voices and would hug the ground behind a bush or tree until the voices faded away.

Midmorning they stopped to rest.

"Why didn't you speak English at first?"

A half smile curled Karl's mouth. "You did enough talking for the both of us."

Annie blushed.

"If I remember correctly, you threatened to slit my throat," he said.

"If you touched me!" Annie clarified. "I threatened to slit your throat if you touched me! I was scared."

"You also hoped I'd bleed to death, or that infection would set in, and you were disappointed the bullet didn't strike any vital organs."

"All right, all right! I get it. Had I known you understood English—"

"You would have said the same things."

"I would have *thought* the same things. There's a difference."

"Tell it to Hitler," Karl said.

That set them both to laughing. It felt good. Annie hadn't laughed in a long time.

It struck her as odd to see him laugh. She'd never thought of a Nazi as laughing. It didn't fit their image. Sneering, definitely. Evil, sadistic, derisive laughter, possibly. But humorous, good-natured laughing? Laughing the way Karl was laughing now? She never would have imagined it.

She liked the way his eyes sparkled when he laughed.

"Seriously," she said, "why didn't you speak English from the start?"

"I was afraid you would plead with me to release you, and then how would I rescue the children?"

"Would it have worked? Would you have released me?"

"It's hard to say now. Probably."

"And if I were to plead with you now?"

Karl looked at her. "You don't know?"

"Know what?"

"All day we have been working our way toward the American lines."

"You're taking me back?"

"Ja."

Annie cautioned herself not to get too excited. She remembered the Baugnez crossroads, where the assembled Germans captured American soldiers. The Americans were led to believe they were prisoners of war. The next thing they knew, they were being executed.

"Tell me more about Hans," she said, changing the topic to protect her heart. Given her situation, too much hope could prove unhealthy.

A surprised look flashed in Karl's eyes. He smiled at her request.

"Hans was an athlete," he said. "The fastest runner. The best swimmer. The best wrestler. All the girls adored him . . . until they talked to him."

"What do you mean?"

Karl laughed. "Hans never grew up. He was a boy in a man's body. He'd do and say silly things. He thought they were funny. Girls found them offensive."

Annie caught herself grinning. Hans sounded remarkably like her Keith.

"Oh! Here's something you'd know about," Karl said with a chuckle. "Hans collected American Burma Shave sign slogans. He thought they were hilarious."

The touch of home caught Annie off guard. "Burma Shave signs? How did he ever hear about them?"

"Hans had an uncle who lived in Ohio. His uncle used to end every one of his letters with a Burma Shave slogan. Hans was forever repeating them. Let me see if I can remember one. . . . Okay, I got it.

"'My job is
Keeping faces clean
And nobody knows
De stubble
I've seen
Burma Shave!'"

Annie found the familiar format in a German accent funny. "Keith loved Burma Shave signs!" she cried. "Here's one:

"'Dinah doesn't
Treat him right
But if he'd
Shave
Dyna-mite!
Burma Shave.'"

Karl guffawed. "How about this," he said.

"'He tried
To cross
As fast train neared
Death didn't draft him
He volunteered.
Burma Shave.'"

"This one is Keith's favorite:

"'The wolf
Is shaved
So neat and trim
Red Riding Hood
Is chasing him!
Burma Shave.'"

Karl slapped his knee repeatedly as he laughed harder than the slogans deserved. Annie held her side, fighting to take a breath.

"It sounds like my Hans and your Keith could have been . . ."

Karl didn't finish the sentence. He'd obviously started it before he'd thought it through.

The unfinished portion of the sentence hung uncomfortably between them.

. . . Hans and Keith could have been good friends.

Had Keith not shot Hans, and had Karl not killed Keith.

The laughter died a quick death.

"We'd best get moving," he said.

————————

At first Annie didn't recognize the area, and then she saw the fallen log and, beyond it, a body and a simple grave, both dusted with snow. She let out a whimper.

"I'm sorry," Karl said, seeing her reaction. "I figured you would want to pay your respects."

The next thing Annie knew, she was standing over the bodies, though she didn't know how she got here.

Keith and Mouse were just as she'd left them. Keith, facedown on the ground, and Mouse's body covered with tree limbs with the wooden cross Keith had fashioned lying on top.

Annie knelt beside her husband's body. She brushed the snow from Keith's hair. His head was hard, his neck stiff. Annie stifled a gasp.

She laid her hand on his back and wept silently.

The forest hushed.

CHAPTER | *25*

*W*hen Annie realized she hadn't heard any movement for a while, she looked up. Karl sat a short distance away, his hands folded in front of him, his head bowed, respecting her privacy.

Her gaze seemed to unnerve him.

"I'll start a fire," he said.

"Tell me about your husband," Karl said softly.

A small but lively fire crackled.

"How did you meet him?"

Annie's eyes burned from a combination of dried tears and smoke. Her voice was husky with grief.

"It seems like we've known each other forever," she said. "We grew up in the same neighborhood."

"You were classmates?"

"Since the second grade. North Park Elementary in San Diego."

"San Diego. That is a state?"

"A city. In California."

"Ah, California! I have heard of California. In the West."

"That's right."

"Palm trees. Bathing in the ocean waves."

"The beach."

"Your parents arranged this marriage from childhood?"

Annie laughed. "No. We attended the same school through high school, but we really didn't know each other."

"The schools are that large?"

"It wasn't that. We ran with different crowds. Keith was an athlete. Football was his sport, and there was a certain crowd that hung out together."

"Hung out, I don't understand."

"Stuck around together."

"Ah! Stuck around! That I understand!"

Annie laughed.

"And what crowd did you stick with?"

"The Choralaires. It's a girls' choir. I was also on the yearbook staff."

"So if you and Keith stuck around with different crowds, how did you fall in love?"

"During the summers," Annie said.

She hugged her knees. Her head cocked to one side as she remembered.

"The sun had just gone down on a really hot day. I was sitting in front of the house on the grass trying to catch a breeze. Keith walked up and said hi. He knew my name. That surprised me. I didn't think he knew me."

"Ah, he was attracted to you from afar!"

Annie smiled. "No, that's not how it was. He was just out walking. He used to do that to get out of the house. His father drank a lot, and when he did, he liked to hit people. It didn't take much to set him off—the mashed potatoes were cold, the newspaper wasn't where it was supposed to be, Keith's grades weren't high enough. That sort of thing.

"Sometimes it got so bad that Keith just had to get out of the house. As he got older, he was afraid his father would make him so angry, he'd hit back. The night we first talked, Keith's father was in rare form. Keith was out walking and trying to cool down. That's when I found out that Keith was a really nice guy. I'd always thought he was this stuck-up jerk."

"Stuck-up jerk. Not a nice guy, correct?"

"Yeah. Only he really was a nice guy. I found that out sitting on the lawn, just the two of us. Keith was a different person when he wasn't around his buddies. Kind. Sensitive. I saw a side of him other people didn't get to see. He started coming over every night that summer, and not just when his father was drunk. We'd sit on the grass and look at the stars and talk."

"And you fell in love."

"I did. He didn't. After that first summer, I thought we had something special between us. But then that fall, when we went back to school, he was a complete stranger again. He had his world. I had mine. He didn't even say hi to me when we passed in the halls. I figured we'd had a nice summer together and that was that."

"Your figures were incorrect."

"Yeah," Annie chuckled.

"The next summer, he came over again," Karl said.

Annie sat up, surprised. "How did you know that?"

"It's what I would have done. Your relationship was different after that?"

"No. It wasn't until the end of the third summer that I finally worked up the nerve to tell him off."

"Tell him off?"

"I yelled at him. I told him not to come around again if he didn't have the decency to act civilly to me in front of his friends."

"Weren't you afraid he would stay away for good?"

A sly grin stretched Annie's face. "No. By then, I knew him. I knew he felt something for me. After that we started going together and on the day of graduation he proposed to me. We were going to wait to get married until after the war, but then . . . well, we were both stationed here in Belgium and we thought, why not? We got married."

Up until now Karl had been all grins, enjoying the story. At this, his face drained of all good humor.

"How long have you been married?" he asked.

Annie looked over at her dead husband. "What day is today?" she asked.

"The day is Saturday, December twenty-third."

Annie began to weep. "Today is our one-week anniversary. We were in Bastogne, on our way to Paris for our honeymoon when our leaves were canceled. We had one night together."

Karl looked away. He stood. The pain he felt was obvious. He walked away. For an hour Annie couldn't see him, but she could hear snow crunching and twigs snapping as he paced.

When Karl returned, he stood over Mouse's makeshift grave.

"And this one?" he said. "Tell me about your friend."

Annie walked over to him. "Mouse? Oh, Mouse was great."

"Her parents named her after a rodent?"

"A nickname. Her parents named her Marcy."

"You have been friends a long time?"

"About two years. We met at our first assignment in Italy and have been together ever since."

"She died how?"

Guilt launched a fresh assault on Annie. She fended it off as best she could.

"Helping me," she said softly. "We'd received word that Keith's jeep had been hit. She drove the ambulance out here to pick him up."

"Your superiors sent two women onto a battlefield without armed support?"

"We didn't exactly have official approval."

Karl grinned a conspiratorial grin. "You stole an ambulance and are absent without leave?"

"Yeah. I'm officially AWOL."

"And I'm officially a deserter."

"Quite a pair, aren't we?"

"And your Mouse . . . she came along willingly?"

"That's the kind of person she was," Annie said.

"Everyone should have a friend like her," Karl replied.

"Yeah. Everyone."

A somber wave swept over Annie at the fresh realization that she'd lost both her Keith and Mouse.

"'For everything there is a season,'" Karl said.

Annie looked over at him. He'd removed his helmet. With his hair mussed up, he looked younger, like a regular guy. Take away the Nazi symbols and he looked just like any number of guys she saw every day at the hospital.

But if his appearance shocked her, what he was saying shocked her even more.

"'. . . and a time for every matter under heaven.'"

He was quoting Scripture.

"'A time to be born, and a time to die; a time to plant, and a time to pluck up what is planted; a time to . . .'"

He choked back emotion. It took him a moment before he could continue.

"'. . . a time to kill . . . and a time . . . a time to heal; a time to weep, and a time to laugh; a time to mourn . . .'"

Tears ran down Annie's cheeks.

Karl cleared his throat. "Now is a time to mourn," he said. "For Keith. For Mouse. For Hans, the best friend a man could have."

He paused.

"Almighty God, embrace them in your love until such time that we shall see them again. Amen."

"Amen," Annie echoed, both bewildered and touched.

CHAPTER 26

O ut of the question!" Karl shouted.

"I don't remember asking your permission!" Annie shouted back at him, pulling branches from Mouse's grave.

"In case you haven't noticed, we're in the middle of a war!" he said.

"I'm not going to leave my husband and best friend just lying here in the forest, this close to Christmas. Their families deserve better than that."

Mouse's words. A fact that was not lost on Annie.

"It'll slow us down," Karl argued. "It could get us killed."

Annie was no longer listening. The canvas tarp that covered Mouse's body was exposed. Now came the hard part, pulling it back and seeing Mouse again.

"Have it your way. Do what you will," Karl said. "But I'm moving out. You're on your own now."

Annie removed the tarp with her head turned aside. She couldn't bring herself to look. She knew how death could alter a person's appearance and she didn't want to have that picture of Mouse forever in her head.

The German gathered his things and stomped loudly into the forest.

Moving to Keith, Annie knelt at his head. She pondered the best way to pull him onto the litter. She grabbed his coat at the shoulders.

"I'll get the upper body, you get his feet," Karl said.

Annie knew he'd come back. The same way she knew Keith wouldn't dump her when she confronted him about the way he ignored her at school.

"I can work up a harness for the litter," he said, laying his rifle aside. "I saw Russian peasants carry heavy loads that way."

––––––––

Karl's craftsmanship abilities proved to be unequal to the task. He may have seen Russian peasants using a shoulder harness to pull a skid, but he didn't know how to rig one up. After a couple of failed attempts, we had to abandon the idea. We also had to abandon the idea of carrying the litter in traditional fashion. We tried that for a while but didn't get far. I just didn't have the strength. It was one thing to muscle a litter into pre-op; quite another to tote it for miles over rocky, uneven terrain. We had to resort to dragging the litter just as Keith and I had done with Mouse's body.

With both bodies on the litter, covered with tarp and strapped down, we set off in the direction of Malmedy, thinking that at some point we'd run into American troops. We just didn't know when, or how far. How many German troops were between us and the American lines? Which army controlled Malmedy? These were questions for which we had no answers. All we could do was set a course and keep our eyes and ears open.

While Karl dragged, I walked ahead, scouting the terrain and keeping a lookout for company. Since his hands were occupied, I carried the rifle, which I did with enthusiasm. Keeping your enemy unarmed is always a good thing, or so I thought at first. But then the more I thought about it, the uneasier I became with my role. What if we came across a squad of Germans suddenly? I didn't know how to shoot the thing.

Karl didn't seem all that concerned about it. So, with him pull-

ing the bodies of my best friend and my husband, I gripped the
Nazi rifle and led us in the direction of the American army.

———————

After thirty minutes of dragging the litter, Karl was sweating profusely. An occasional rock or branch snagged the litter, pulling him up short. He'd grunt, groan, utter something in German, and somehow manage to maneuver the litter past the obstacle. Progress was slow. Several times Annie found that she had distanced herself from Karl and the litter and so would either have to wait or double back.

"You need a rest," she said, after one particularly stubborn snag.

"I'm all right," Karl groused, trudging determinedly.

He still hadn't forgiven her for insisting they bring the bodies with them.

"Would it help if I helped you take your mind off the task? Sometimes we do that with patients during physical therapy."

"Hauling bodies through a war zone isn't physical therapy."

"I'm just trying to help," Annie said. "You don't have to snap my head off."

The litter snagged on a root. One frustrated cry and a yank by Karl and it was free again. Pressing his lips hard together, he trudged in silence for several minutes.

"What kind of things do you talk about?" he said.

Her back to him, Annie allowed herself a grin.

"Well, two subjects usually worked best." She thought a moment. "Let's try this one first: a good-looking guy like you, I imagine you have a girlfriend waiting for you back home, correct?"

When he didn't answer immediately, she glanced over her shoulder. He was grimacing. From exertion? Or had she chosen the wrong question?

"If the topic is too painful . . ."

"Ilse Leber," he said.

"So you do have a girl waiting for you."

"Had a girl."

Now she understood the wince. "A recent breakup?"

"Two months ago. More like a betrayal."

"I see. Do you mind telling me about it?"

"I probably deserved it. I should have known better. She was too beautiful for me. I should have known I wouldn't be able to keep her."

Already Annie didn't like the woman, even without hearing the story.

"How did you meet her?" she asked.

"She's Hans's cousin."

"How long were the two of you together?"

"Ten months. We met last Christmas. She had just ended it with a man who treated her like she was his pet animal. Do you have that type in America? He'd snap his fingers at her and belittle her in public."

"Yeah, we have that type."

"You're a woman. What is it about attractive women that they are drawn to the lowest, meanest form of mankind?"

Annie wanted to reply, *What is it about men that they are attracted to self-centered, eyelash-batting, slinky females?* But instead she held her tongue. This was his story.

"A month before their wedding, he began beating her. She fled to Riesa to get away from him."

"Where she found a sympathetic ear."

"Oh, it was more than that," Karl said. "Sure, I listened to her, and I wanted to hunt down the man and give him a thrashing, but there was also a definite streak of lust on my part."

Annie laughed, shocked by his candor.

"We became friends. It was agony for me, because I wanted so much more. She told me she'd never met a man as caring as me, and kept saying things like, 'Why can't I ever meet a man who's sweet, like you?' Finally I said, 'Are you blind? Can't you see you'll never meet a man more like me than me?'"

"You won her over."

Karl gave a shrug. "Not at first. I think more than anything, I wore her down."

The litter snagged another root. Karl tried to tug it free. When he couldn't, Annie circled back and managed to free it.

Once on the move again, she said, "It sounds like you did more than wear her down. Was it serious?"

"I thought it was. We talked about marriage. And then last October, on leave, I returned to Riesa, having worked up the courage to ask her to marry me."

"She turned you down."

"Oh, she very much liked the idea of marriage. She liked it so much she'd already gone ahead and gotten married without me."

"Ouch. To the man who abused her?"

"The same. It was the first news I received when I stepped off the train."

Annie's commiseration was cut off by the mechanical whine of an approaching engine. The sound bounced among the trees. She couldn't place it exactly, yet it was unmistakably coming their direction, and it was getting louder.

"Over here!" Karl shouted.

He jerked his head toward a ridge that fell away to a creek.

Annie's first thought was that the sound couldn't be coming from that direction. But when she saw him high-stepping toward the ridge, she realized he was telling her what direction to run.

At any other time the way he was churning his legs would have been humorous. He looked like Annie sometimes felt in her dreams—trying to run, but slowed by sand, or super thick air, or paralyzed muscles.

Despite his efforts, he wasn't moving fast enough. The whine of the engine grew louder. It wasn't a tank or a truck; the sound wasn't deep enough. More like a jeep, which meant faster, more maneuverable.

Annie caught up with him. She grabbed one side of the litter. They picked up speed as the litter bounced through patches of mud and snow.

Then it came to an abrupt halt, nearly pulling Annie's arm from its socket. She looked back. The litter had snagged on a root.

"I'll get it," Annie said.

Karl grabbed her handle while she dropped to her knees to pull up on the litter. It was snagged good this time. The root had ripped the canvas and entangled itself with the threads. Annie tried breaking the root, but it was too thick.

The engine's whine was close now. Almost on top of them.

Annie tried moving the litter sideways to free it that way. The snag held it down. She looked behind them. She could see movement through the trees.

"I can't get it!" she cried.

"What if I back up?"

"Yeah! I think that'll work."

Karl pushed instead of pulled. The two dragging handles gouged into the ground. The litter barely moved. The root held tight.

"You lift, I'll push!" Karl said, peering into the trees. From his expression, he too could see the approaching jeep.

Annie lifted. Karl pushed. They gained an inch. The snag held.

"Again!" Annie cried.

They tried it again. Another inch, but still not enough.

"One more time."

They were hitting something solid now, the litter barely moving, yet it was enough that Annie was able to reach under and pull the offending root from the canvas and free the litter.

She scrambled to her feet and grabbed the litter handle. Together they pulled it over the ridge and down the slope.

Two descending steps and the toe of Annie's boot caught on something. She went tumbling. Karl stumbled as the weight of the litter suddenly shifted. He went down, too. Both of them rolled through mud and snow and dead leaves. The litter skidded like a sled all the way down the slope, coming to a stop just short of the frozen creek.

"You all right?" Karl whispered.

"Nothing broken," Annie moaned.

From the sound of it the jeep was nearly on top of them. Annie scrambled for Karl's rifle that had come to rest a short distance away. She tossed it to Karl.

The jeep wasn't slowing down. Karl crawled up the incline to the ridge. Annie followed him. It passed just as they peeked over the crest of the ridge. Annie gasped. She didn't know why the jeep surprised her; it just did.

There were three soldiers in the jeep. One driving, two with rifles. They weren't patrolling. They were heading somewhere in a hurry.

They wore American uniforms and rode in an American jeep.

Call it intuition, but somehow Annie knew these three were the real thing. Americans. Not Germans masquerading as Americans like before.

Within moments, they had disappeared into the trees.

His chest still heaving from the race to get over the ridge, Karl went to check on the litter. Annie lay still, listening to the dimming sound of the jeep.

The whole thing had happened quickly, but not so quick that Annie couldn't have called out to them.

But she didn't.

Had she tried, would Karl have stopped her? She didn't know. And now she'd never know, would she?

Annie lay motionless on the ridge. It was a sobering experience for her, one that she doubted she'd get over quickly. She could have been rescued. One shout and right now she could be riding in the back of an American jeep and headed for Malmedy. Tonight she could have eaten in the hospital mess, slept on her cot, been reunited with Nina, been reinserted into the nursing schedule, surrounded by people with whom she was familiar.

Had only she shouted.

But she didn't shout.

Why?

CHAPTER 27

*N*ight covered the forest quickly. Stars twinkled between tree branches against an inky blue backdrop. The moon made an early appearance, bright enough to cast shadows.

Karl was eager to lay his burden down. Despite the drop in temperature, he leaned back against a rock and appeared in no hurry to build a fire. His arms were limp at his sides. Annie began gathering wood.

"I'll get that," he said without moving.

"You rest," she replied, the rifle still slung over her shoulder.

She didn't stray far in her search for firewood, and when she returned Karl was on his knees clearing the ground where the fire would be made. Before long they were holding their hands to flames.

"How much farther to Malmedy?" she asked.

"At the rate we traveled today? We could possibly reach the outskirts of town by nightfall tomorrow. More likely the next day."

She watched him for a while. His arms were so tired he couldn't hold his hands up to the fire for longer than thirty seconds at a time before they flopped back down to his sides.

"I've been thinking," she said. "Maybe we should leave the bodies here. We could maybe put them up someplace, off the ground, between branches or something. Or maybe cover them with rocks.

To keep the predators away. Then when I get back I can send some soldiers to retrieve them, or possibly come back with them in a jeep or a truck."

Karl studied her. "That's not what you want to do," he said.

"No, but . . ."

"We'll get a fresh start in the morning," Karl said.

"Those aren't going to heal by morning." She grabbed one of his hands, turning it palm up. A line of open blisters stretched from forefinger to pinky. "And I'd be willing to bet the strain on your wound is causing it to bleed again."

"We're going to finish what we started," he insisted. "I can heal after we get Keith and Mouse home."

He used their names.

Annie sat back. It didn't seem right for him to speak of them in the familiar.

The fire crackled.

Annie stretched out on the ground. She tried to get comfortable, but that was next to impossible. She kept thinking about how often she and the other nurses had complained about sleeping on cots. Right now a cot would be heaven.

She dozed.

A loud pop in the fire startled her awake. When her eyes focused she saw Karl sitting with his back partially to her. His black book was open. As before, his eyes were closed. With the fire illuminating the pages, she got a good look at what was on the pages.

They were the strangest markings. Slashes. Lines. An occasional pairing of numbers.

Annie propped herself up on one elbow to get a better look. Maybe she could detect a sequence. Three lines in a row began with a diagonal slash. Did that mean anything?

"Can't sleep?" Karl said.

He was looking at her. So intent was she on deciphering the writing in the book, she hadn't seen him turn his head toward her.

"Umm . . ." she stuttered.

It was pretty obvious what she was doing. He'd caught her. Yet he didn't seem angry. Nor had he slapped shut the book. Dare she risk ruining everything now by confronting him about the book?

"I . . . I couldn't help but notice . . . for several nights now you seem to have an attachment to that book. If it's not violating any military secrets, because I'm not trying to spy or anything, it's just that I'm . . . well, it's only natural, isn't it? . . . that I would be curious the way you sit off by yourself and stare at the pages and all?"

"This?" Karl held up the book. "It's the official Nazi guidebook. All German soldiers get a copy. It's written in code so that if it falls into enemy hands, the enemy won't be able to read it." He flipped the pages. "Standard stuff, really. Timetables for invasions. Locations of strategic headquarters and factories for every major city. An abbreviated version of *Mein Kampf* and select speeches by Der Führer. Hitler's personal phone number."

He had her going.

"You think I'm making this up?" he asked.

"I think I know when someone's poking fun."

"What else could it be but an official guidebook? After all, you stole it from me so that you could deliver it to Allied command for decoding."

"Can you blame me?" Annie cried. "If our roles were reversed, what would you think?"

Karl laughed. "I almost wish you'd succeeded. I would liked to have seen their faces when they broke the code."

"So it *is* in code!" Annie said. "You weren't kidding about that part?"

"More like personal shorthand. Something I developed to help me remember."

She waited. Remember what? Would he tell her? Was he waiting for her to ask? Should she ask?

He grinned at her obvious anxiety.

"You can be mean sometimes," she said.

"I like to think of it as playful," he said.

He let her twist in the wind awhile longer before letting her off the hook.

"It's my music."

Annie looked doubtful. Was he telling her the truth this time, or was he being playful again? The notations in the book didn't look like any music she'd ever seen.

"The truth!" Karl insisted. He held up the book for her to see. Pointing to the top of a page, he explained, "This is a Bach Fugue in D Major for organ." Moving his finger across the page from symbol to symbol, he began humming. His voice had a wonderful melodic quality to it. "My memory isn't good enough to remember the entire fugue, so I developed this system. Simple prompts that remind me of things like timing, modulations, and key changes. Just enough to be able to play back the piece in my head."

He spoke with an enthusiasm Annie had not seen in him before.

He turned a couple of pages and said, "For example . . . here, *Orpheus* by Franz Liszt. You'll recall him as the inventor of the symphonic poem."

Annie nodded, though she hadn't recalled that at all.

"It's a quiet piece. I play it at night mostly. It calms my soul just before I go to sleep. And here. Another Liszt. *Les Préludes*. You'll recognize this tune." Referring to his notes, he hummed a few measures.

Annie smiled. She did recognize it. "You have a lovely voice," she said.

"This little book has kept me sane throughout this despicable war. I can't imagine what it would have been like without regular music baths."

"Music baths?"

"That's what I call them. I close my eyes and let the music wash over me until I'm totally immersed in it. The sounds permeate the flesh and resonate in the soul."

He was speaking rapturously. Apparently realizing this, he paused and looked as if embarrassed.

Annie said, "So that's what you've been doing when you close your eyes—letting the music wash over you."

He shrugged. "I know it sounds silly. I guess it's not for everyone. Some people don't understand."

"I do," Annie said.

She did understand. She'd experienced exactly the phenomenon he was talking about, but had never discussed it with anyone. She tried telling Keith about it once. He'd looked at her as if she was crazy.

"You do?" he said.

"My first live symphony concert, actually. A high school friend—Cynthia Weber—had an extra ticket. Her father was wealthy. They lived in La Jolla."

"La Jolla?"

"A two-story home on the cliffs overlooking the Pacific Ocean. He was in real estate. Anyway, we drove up to Los Angeles. Cynthia's father was making her go, and she dragged me along for company. I went sort of as a favor to a friend. I hadn't heard a whole lot of classical music. A couple of things on records, but I'd never been able to listen to a whole record and didn't know how I was going to sit through a whole symphony concert."

Karl smiled at that. "You were surprised."

"Surprised? Surprise doesn't begin to describe what I experienced."

"What was the piece?"

"*Adagio for Strings* by Samuel Barber."

Karl's smile widened. "I know the piece."

"Do you?" Annie said, touching his arm, thrilled to be talking to someone about an experience she'd kept locked inside for years.

"Do this," Karl said. "Close your eyes. Go on. Close them. Now relive that moment. See the concert hall in your mind. Try to remember as many things about it as you can, even the feel of the seat."

He waited a moment.

"Are you there?" he asked.

Annie sat with eyes closed. "Okay. I'm there."

"Describe it to me."

"Well . . ." She opened her eyes.

"No! Keep them closed!" Karl insisted.

Annie giggled. "This feels weird. But . . . um, all right." She adjusted herself to get comfortable. "We're sitting third row, center. Cynthia is to my right, between her father and me. There's an old woman in a black sequined dress to my left. She is far too old to be wearing that type of dress."

"And the orchestra? Do you see the conductor?"

"He's coming on stage now. Applause. He turns to the orchestra and raises his baton."

Annie took a sharp inhale of breath.

"The music has begun," Karl said.

"Yes. It's lovely."

"You remember it."

Annie grinned. "I bought a recording. I must have listened to it a hundred times in my room."

"But the recording is nothing like the live performance."

"It doesn't begin to compare," Annie said.

"Describe it to me. What do you hear?"

For a moment Annie froze, unable to find the words to describe what she'd heard, what she was feeling.

"Take your time," Karl said.

"Well, it begins slowly, softly . . . a simple theme, but rather intimate, isn't it? Sad."

"What is the theme doing? Compare it to something."

"Like what?"

"Oh . . . something in nature. If you were taking a stroll and you came upon this music, what would it be?"

Her eyes closed, Annie said, "A river. A small one, a stream."

"And what is it doing?"

"Flowing lazily along, gracefully."

"Continue."

"Now there are two streams, similar to each other, both somber and haunting, intertwining." She sat up. "A third stream has joined them. It sent them spiraling, lifting them upward, twisting in the air, weaving in and around each other; bolder now, spiraling ever higher, blending together as one, combining forces; they're like a mighty river now, swelling with intensity, expanding, growing stronger and greater and . . . oh!" She caught her breath.

"What? What is it?" Karl asked.

Her eyes still closed, Annie said, "Elevating now to a climax of such magnitude and intensity and angst, it's . . . it's as though my heart wants to burst with longing."

Tears trickled down her cheeks.

She opened her eyes.

Karl's eyes were happy for her.

"You've just taken a music bath," he said.

CHAPTER 28

I don't mind telling you, Karl's music bath was an incredible experience, one that I never imagined I would share with anyone. When my eyes were closed and the music washed over me, for a few blissful moments, the Ardennes Forest, the winter cold, the war, the suffering, the anxiety—all of it ceased to exist.

And to think that such a beautiful experience was orchestrated by a stinkin' Kraut.

———

The next morning, as Karl pulled the litter and Annie scouted the trail, they talked mostly of music.

Annie learned that Karl Hausmann was a classically trained organist, so while Adolf Hitler urged the German nation to blame their economic woes on the Jews, the Czechs, the Poles, the Russians, and the French, Karl dreamed of performing in the great cathedrals of Europe. While the Hitler Youth organization counted his body among their numbers, Karl's mind belonged to Bach, Buxtehude, and Pachelbel.

Surely, he thought, his superiors would see the absurdity of putting him in uniform and would grant him his wish to perform the works of the great German organ masters.

"Wishes are the first casualties of war."

Isn't that what Elthia had said? The lady may have been crazy for wanting to kill her, Annie thought, but she was right about wishes and personal dreams.

"A few years back I was offered a chance to tour with a band," Annie said.

This excited Karl. "A big band? Jimmy Dorsey? Glenn Miller?"

The sound of Glenn Miller's name reminded Annie about the bandleader's recent tragedy. She started to tell Karl about it, then decided not to. They were having too good of a time to taint the conversation with the realities of war. The litter Karl dragged was reminder enough.

"They played big band music," Annie said, "but they weren't famous."

"But you sang with them?"

Annie grinned. "One song. 'Moonlight Serenade.'"

"Tell me about it!"

The weight of the litter on his shoulders, the blisters on his hands, the cramps in his legs didn't seem to bother him when he talked about music.

"Well, it was a place called the Rainbow Room, downtown San Diego. The band was called Matty Lawson and the Marauders. Keith and I had gone there on a date. He liked to dance, and was really good at it."

Keith's stiff, frozen legs beneath the canvas tarp came to mind. Legs that would never dance again.

A time to mourn.

Annie forced the image from her mind, concentrating on the night in the Rainbow Room.

"During the show Matty would invite someone from the audience to come onstage and sing with the band."

"And you volunteered?"

"Keith volunteered me. He told Matty I wanted to sing but was too shy to volunteer."

"He did that for you?"

Annie laughed. "No, he did that *to* me. You have to understand

Keith. He did it because he thought it would embarrass me. He never figured I'd go onstage."

"But you did go onstage."

"I didn't have a choice!" Annie cried. "Everyone in the room began shouting and whistling and chanting my name. Matty walked down into the audience and took me by the hand. Everybody was looking at me!"

Karl gave a sly grin. "Inside, you wanted to sing."

Annie blushed. "All right, yes. Deep down inside, a part of me wanted to sing."

"So you were onstage . . ."

"I was scared out of my wits! I'd never done anything like that before. Someone shoved a microphone in my face. There was an entire band behind me. The lights were so bright, I couldn't see the audience, but I could hear them and I knew they were all looking at me."

"And then the music started . . ." Karl prompted.

"Then the music started," Annie said.

Looking at him, she knew he understood! He understood the desire to make music, not just for yourself, but to perform it in such a way that it filled people with joy or moved them to dance or moved them to love when they heard it.

"The first couple of notes were shaky," she said, "but then . . . I don't know, something came over me. The music sort of took control of me."

"Everyone applauded."

"It was embarrassing how much they cheered! I thought I did all right, but I wasn't Helen O'Connell, or anything like that. Afterward, Matty came up to me. He said they were looking for someone to sing with the band and that he'd be willing to work with me, that with a little practice I could tour with them."

"He wanted you to be his canary."

Annie laughed. Why was she surprised he would know that term?

"Yeah, I guess so."

"So why didn't you?"

Annie sobered. "Keith got angry when I told him about it. He said Matty had more on his mind than just music, that Matty probably said the same thing to a hundred girls."

"He didn't like your singing?"

"He said it was all a big joke and I shouldn't take it seriously."

Annie fell silent.

"Keith said more than that," Karl said.

Annie looked at him. How did he know?

"He said, 'Why would you want to embarrass yourself like that again? Everyone was laughing at you.'"

"Were they?"

Annie shook her head. "You have to understand Keith. If he couldn't be the best at something, he didn't want to do it. If he thought I was good enough to sing with Jimmy Dorsey or Glenn Miller, he would have supported me."

"With music, you have to work your way to the top."

"See? That's what Keith didn't understand. He was always the best in sports."

"Do you still sing?"

"Hymns. Christmas caroling. That sort of thing. I've never performed on stage since then."

Karl mulled this over for a moment. "A shame," he said.

This angered Annie, though she didn't know why.

"In case you haven't noticed," she said, "there have been other things of greater importance that have occupied my time. Tending the sick and wounded is a far more important calling than singing in a band, wouldn't you say?"

"While I'm sure you're good at what you do, and the people you tend are grateful for your skills, you're missing the point," Karl said. "You gave up something you loved, something that brought you and others joy, all because one person was critical of your talent."

"That person you refer to became my husband."

"Let me ask you this: Who gave you a voice to sing?"

Because the answer was obvious, she didn't reply.

"God didn't give the gift of singing to everyone. So, it seems to me, you are accountable to God, not to Keith, for this gift. Besides, imagine if everyone who had a gift to sing refused to use it because they weren't the best in the world? We'd have only one singer. One organist. One pianist. And the world would be poorer for it."

Annie looked away.

"Someday you will stand before God, and He will require an accounting of the gift He blessed you with. What will you say to Him? Will you tell Him you stopped singing because Keith didn't think you were good? And how will you respond if God says, 'But I didn't give the gift to Keith'?"

Annie didn't like this conversation anymore. She pretended she saw movement in the trees.

For the next hour, neither of them spoke.

CHAPTER | *29*

I tried not to let it show that he got to me with all that talk about being accountable to God for my music. But he really struck a nerve. Music had always been important to me. I never felt more alive than I did when I was singing. And I loved being around people who loved to sing.

During my freshman year in high school, a touring choir sang at our church. College age. I don't remember the group all that much, but I remember distinctly Bobby Joe and Anna Marie. From the moment they stepped forward to sing, you knew they were meant to be together. So it came as no surprise that when they introduced themselves, we learned they were engaged.

Oh, Celia, they were amazing. The way their voices blended in perfect harmony, the way they handed phrases back and forth, the split-second syncopation, the way they looked into each other's eyes as they sang. They would reach out and take each other's hands—for me, it was the perfect union of two souls. Every word, every note was a declaration of their love to God and each other.

From that day on, whenever I fantasized about being in love, it involved singing. My soul and his soul blending in perfect harmony, the ultimate romantic experience.

Then I met Keith, and I fell in love. Only Keith didn't sing. So I set my singing on a shelf with my dolls and other girlish fantasies.

Midafternoon of their second day transporting the litter, they got caught in a firefight between a squad of retreating Germans and Americans on the attack.

It came upon them like a thunderous squall. Annie and Karl dove under an enormous fir tree and managed to pull the litter under with them.

For an hour the skirmish played out all around them. One minute, Annie would look up and see German uniforms, while the next minute she saw Americans. Mostly, however, she kept her head down. With the air heavy with bullets and projectiles, she hugged the ground so hard she was digging a hole. From overhead, branches severed from the tree trunk and fell on her; the sides of the trunk exploded in splinters as the tree took one hit after another.

Annie had the rifle, and she kept it pressed against her, on the side away from the German.

The storm finally passed, with the Germans and Americans disappearing deeper into the forest, leaving the area to the dead.

She had hoped for a lull, a time when she could call out to a passing American without getting shot. The opportunity never presented itself.

All was still. She and the German were alone again.

She started to get up.

"Wait," Karl said.

Annie looked around. The only thing moving was smoke high in the trees.

"I'm going to tend the wounded," she said.

"Not yet. It's not safe."

"It's my job," she said, getting to her knees.

She reached up to push a branch aside, and froze.

Not more than a dozen feet away, a fallen German soldier's eyes sprang open and locked on her. His grin led Annie to believe he wasn't as injured as he pretended to be, and the quickness with which he moved confirmed it.

Before she could move, he'd pushed himself up and was swinging his rifle in her direction.

Two shots rang out simultaneously. One from behind Annie.

The German in front of Annie spun and hit the ground, dead. His rifle clattered lifelessly next to him.

"Great shot, Jimmy! I thought for sure you'd miss him!"

Annie felt herself being pulled back beneath the tree as two American privates wandered cautiously onto the field of battle, wary of other surprises. They approached the fallen German, turning him over with the tip of a boot.

"You nailed him, Jimmy!"

The two soldiers gloated over their enemy, unaware that Karl's rifle was trained on them, the very rifle that had killed the German, regardless of what Jimmy's friend thought.

Karl was shaking, his breathing rapid. His eyes blinked with fear as he stared at the Americans down the barrel of his rifle. He followed them as they went from body to body, checking to see if any of the German soldiers were still alive.

BAM!

Karl and Annie jumped.

"That one was still breathin'," Jimmy said to his buddy with a smile. "Not anymore."

From beneath the branches of the giant pine tree, Annie watched as the two soldiers made their rounds, firing two more shots at bodies on the ground.

She didn't know what to do.

Call out and identify herself? But what if Jimmy or his buddy shot before they saw her uniform? They wouldn't, would they? But would they shoot Karl? Of course they would—he was the enemy!

What really confused her was that the enemy wasn't shooting them. He'd just killed one of his own who was about to shoot her, yet he hadn't fired on two of his enemy. Was it because there were two of them?

"I can take them both out before they have time to blink. It's what I've been trained to do."

Keith's words.

The situation was identical. Two enemy soldiers, their heads down searching the battlefield, oblivious to the fact that they were in the enemy's sights.

She knew she couldn't let Karl kill the two American soldiers. At the moment he seemed content just to watch. But that could change, and if it did, would she be able to stop him in time? And if she couldn't, how could she live with herself knowing that she lay next to a German soldier as he picked off an American, with her not doing anything to stop him?

The American privates continued to work their way through the forest, unaware of Annie's personal battle beneath the pine tree.

Jimmy cursed. Propping his rifle against a tree, he examined his hand, picking at a blister or splinter. His back was to them as he cursed at how much it hurt. His buddy came over to take a look.

Karl wouldn't have a better shot than right now.

"Why didn't you shoot them?"

Karl clearly didn't understand the question. "You wanted me to shoot them?" he asked.

The American soldiers had moved on. The sun had fallen below the tree line. It would be dark soon. Litter in hand, Karl was pressing to get another kilometer behind them before stopping for the night. They would reach the outskirts of Malmedy in the morning.

"They're your enemy. They would have shot you," Annie said.

Karl sighed heavily. "You think I'm a killer because I shot your husband."

"I think you're a Nazi."

His hands hurting, Karl stopped to get a better grip. He didn't like interrupting his momentum. It was always harder to get started again.

Once they were under way again, he said, "I'm a musician, not a soldier, Fraulein Annie. I wear the uniform of the Reich, but I don't embrace their philosophy or their politics. I am *not* a Nazi."

Annie had never heard of such a thing. A German who was not a Nazi? Was that possible?

Reading the expression on her face, Karl saw that further explanation was necessary. "I love my country. I am German. However, I don't respect our leaders or their ways of terror. I fight for my country because I have been ordered to do so, but they can't make me hate. I do not hate Americans. I do not wish to kill Americans."

Annie didn't know how to respond. She remembered Keith's eagerness to kill Germans, and her own for that matter.

"What about you?" Karl asked. "You wear the uniform of the American army. Do you wish to kill Germans?"

She had. She did. How could she not hate Germans after two years of patching up boys as a result of Hitler's grisly handiwork? After hearing report after report of German atrocities? How could she not hate the people who callously orchestrated the massacre at Malmedy, gunning down unarmed American prisoners of war?

Yet, at the same time, she didn't want to admit her feelings to Karl.

It didn't matter. Her lack of response confirmed his suspicions.

"In my country, the Nazi party rose to power by sowing seeds of fear and hatred. We were told repeatedly that the Jews were to blame for our economic troubles with posters, movies, official decrees. The government granted us license to hate them. At first I believed I could not be a good German if I didn't hate Jews."

Or a red-blooded American if you didn't hate Germans, Annie thought.

"Something changed your mind," she said.

"It was something my pastor said."

"Your pastor?"

The shock in her tone of voice amused him.

"It surprises you that I have a pastor? I am a Christian, Fraulein Annie. Is that so hard to believe?"

As a matter of fact, yes. Although he had prayed over Keith's and Mouse's bodies. Still, it wasn't possible to be a Christian and a German, was it?

"What did your pastor say to you?" she said.

"That each person chooses his own emotions. That hate is a choice. That no one can make you hate, or love, or feel sad, or happy."

"I don't agree. Keith made me happy. And there's a certain surgeon at the 67th Evac that has a knack for making me angry."

Karl shook his head. "People say and do things and we respond to them. Sometimes our responses are automatic, but that's because we've chosen to respond the same way so often. But the choice is still mine unless I let someone else dictate to me what I should feel.

"My superiors expect me to hate American soldiers, and Poles, and English, and Russian, and French. I choose not to. You expect me to hate Keith because he killed Hans. I do not hate your husband, Annie. I fired at him in self-defense. It grieves me that Keith killed Hans. It grieves me even more that I killed him, especially now, knowing that I have hurt you and taken from you something precious. I will never forgive myself for that. And I can't stop thinking that if you and Keith and Hans and I knew each other, we could have been friends, and no power in the world could have convinced us to shoot at each other."

CHAPTER | *30*

As night settled, the forest grew quiet.

All day long the mechanical sounds of war had echoed among the trees. Aircraft roaring overhead. The distant rumble of trucks and tanks and personnel carriers. Now the only sounds were the ones Annie and Karl made as they settled in for their last night together. Tomorrow morning they would reach Malmedy.

"I'll take you as far as the tree line," Karl told her. "In the open I'd be an easy target."

Annie found it hard to believe he'd taken her this far. Karl was definitely behind enemy lines now. She doubted there was another German within ten kilometers of them.

The forest seemed tired of war. It was in a reverent mood. Overhead, the stars shone bright in a crisp sky. Trees hushed. The animals, it seemed to Annie, had chosen to spend a quiet night at home.

"Did you know it's Christmas Eve?" Karl asked.

She didn't. With all that had happened, Annie had lost track of the days.

Christmas Eve. She and Keith were supposed to be in Paris on their honeymoon. Tonight was supposed to be the night of the Glenn Miller concert. They had tickets. She'd been dreaming of this night for months. The lights of Paris. The spirit of the holiday. She and Keith married, away from the hospital, a break from war and death. She'd imagined it would be a magical night, one of those nights she would relive over and over the rest of her life.

Instead, Keith lay nearby, strapped to a litter, a canvas tarp covering his face, stiff and cold. The concert hall in Paris that had been decked out for the occasion was undoubtedly dark and silent, in mourning for the popular bandleader who lay entombed in a plane at the bottom of the English Channel. And instead of spending a night of gaiety and laughter with her husband, enjoying a nonmilitary meal and feasting on famous French pastries, she was stuck in the Ardennes Forest, shivering next to a German soldier. Her stomach growled.

"I have something special," Karl said as he gathered tree branches for the fire.

It was difficult for him to grab things with his heavily blistered hands. Earlier in the day he'd used the bandages from his torso—the ones made with Hans's pants—to wrap around his hands. Pulling his gloves on over them made his hands look inflated, like the hands of a cartoon character. He had to use both hands to pick up a branch.

However, he wasn't thinking about his hands at the moment but about his surprise. He hummed happily as he built the fire, casting occasional smiles at Annie.

His smiles were not returned. Having been reminded of Paris, Annie's mood was anything but festive.

"I wish it could be more," Karl said, handing her a stale cracker after they'd settled next to the fire. "As it is, this is the last of them."

Annie took the cracker but didn't eat it, even though she was hungry.

Karl didn't seem to notice. "My family has a Christmas Eve tradition," he said cheerily. "Every year, after dinner, we hike to the top of a hill behind our house. It's a pretty good climb, but the view is worth it. All of Riesa lies at our feet. A golden glow from the lights of all the houses settles over the city. There's something special about Christmas Eve lights, don't you think? There's a fantasy quality to them. And the stars . . ."

He looked up, peering beyond the branches, past the treetops.

"On clear nights, the stars put on their best sparkle for the occasion. They know, don't they? After all, He is their creator, too."

"You mentioned family," Annie said.

"Mother, Father, Rikka. She's my little sister. Well, not so little anymore. She's fifteen years old."

"What does your father do for a living?"

"He's one of the best diamond cutters in Germany. I got my musical talent from my mother. She could have been a concert pianist."

"They don't sound like the hiking type to me."

Karl laughed. "The destination makes it worthwhile. Standing up there, looking out over all the lights with the Elbe River flowing peacefully in the background, sparkling with moonlight, breathing in the crisp air, singing Christmas carols to the city."

A far-off gaze—highlighted by the flickering firelight—indicated he was back there, in his hometown, standing on the hill overlooking the river, remembering what the voices of his family sounded like in the cold December night.

A moment later the spell was broken.

"How about you?" he asked. "What is Christmas Eve like in California?"

"Warmer," Annie said. "Definitely warmer."

"It doesn't snow in California?"

"Not near the coast where I live."

"How can you have Christmas without snow?"

"I used to think I was missing something," Annie said. "But I've seen enough snow since coming to Europe to last me several lifetimes. I can't wait to get back to San Diego, where it's warm."

"Any family traditions?"

Annie looked off into the darkness. She wasn't in the mood for this. "I'm an only child, so it's just been my mom and dad and me. We decorate the tree. Mom makes cinnamon rolls. Nothing special."

They stared silently at the fire for a few minutes. Annie's mood seemed to be dousing Karl's festive spirit. She felt guilty.

"You said you had something special," she said.

Karl grinned as he reached into his pocket. He paused for dramatic effect, and then with a flourish produced a single white candle.

CHAPTER *31*

I found it a month ago in an abandoned farmhouse," Karl said, holding his prize proudly. "Been saving it for tonight."

"A candle," Annie said.

His level of excitement baffled her. She'd told him about Paris, hadn't she? How tonight was supposed to be her honeymoon in the city of lights. How could a candle make up for that?

"This isn't just any candle," he said, seeing her expression. "It's a Christmas tree candle!"

Annie still couldn't believe he was getting this excited over a stick of wax with a wick.

"Come here," he said, leading her to a fir tree.

He told her to kneel next to a low branch, then he knelt opposite her. From his pocket he pulled a match, which was no small effort given his bandaged and gloved hands. He lit the candle and dripped wax onto a limb.

"The Christmas tree is a German tradition," he said as he worked. "The ancients believed evergreens were magical trees based on the fact that they survived the winter while all other trees appeared to be dead. Then one night Martin Luther, the great German reformer, was walking home. He looked up and saw the stars shining through tree branches, just like they are tonight. He was so struck by what he saw that he hurried home to describe it to his family, only words failed him. So, hurrying back into the woods, he cut down a small fir tree, brought it indoors and decorated it with candles to represent the stars."

While talking, Karl continued dripping wax onto the branch, He then pressed the base of the candle into the wax. When he let go, the limb bounced slightly, but the candle held.

"Of course it's only a single candle," he said, "but then that works, too, doesn't it? We can think of it as the star that hung over Bethlehem." He leaned back, giving the candle center stage. "What do you think? Our very own Christmas tree!"

Annie had to admit it looked lovely. The little candle did itself proud, illuminating the rich green pine needles and casting spiked shadows against nearby limbs. It flickered white and yellow like a beacon to two weary travelers. An unexpected lump of emotion rose in Annie's throat.

The candle had a reverential power to it, unmatched by the strings of colored lights she was accustomed to seeing on Christmas trees. It flickered hypnotically, gloriously. She could almost hear the angels . . .

> "O Tannenbaum, O Tannenbaum,
> Wie treu sind deine Blätter!
> Du grünst nicht nur zur Sommerzeit,
> Nein auch im Winter, wenn es schneit. . . ."

Karl's clear, melodic voice complemented the candle's glow. When he reached the end of the verse and fell silent, there was a tangible void. Even the trees seemed to notice. They rustled impatiently for more.

"That was lovely," Annie said in a whisper.

"Now you."

"No . . . no, I couldn't." Annie blushed, suddenly feeling very self-conscious.

"Why not? I know you like to sing."

She laughed. "I knew I shouldn't have told you that story."

"Are you telling me you'll sing for Matty and the Marauders, but not for me?"

He remembered the name of the band?

"That was different," she said. "Unless you have a big band in your pocket . . ."

"It would only distract from your voice."

Was he making fun of her? Annie looked for the upturned corners of a joker's grin. She saw no joker in him.

"A Christmas carol," he insisted. "Your choice. What song comes to your mind whenever you think of Christmas?"

"Well . . ." Annie began. He wasn't going to let her get out of this, was he? "I don't know, let's see . . . just off the top of my head, 'Hark! The Herald Angels Sing.'"

"A good German carol."

"It is not!" Annie protested.

"Sure it is. The tune was written by Felix Mendelssohn, 1840. Born in Hamburg, he grew up in Berlin, the son of a banking family. He studied piano with Ludwig Berger—"

"All right! You convinced me!" she cried. "How do you know that?"

Karl grinned. "Don't let this uniform fool you. I'm not the efficient, military fighting machine you mistake me for. I'm a musician, remember?"

He was joking, but he had a point. Since getting to know him, she decided he didn't belong in a Nazi uniform any more than she did.

"Do you want me to get you started?" he asked.

"No, I can do it myself. Just give me a minute."

Annie closed her eyes. She thought of Christmastime at church, of singing carols in the pew, and the crèche display in front. The next thing she knew, she was singing.

"Hark! The herald angels sing,
Glory to the newborn King;
Peace on earth, and mercy mild;

God and sinners reconciled. . . ."

She sang the entire first verse with her eyes closed. When she opened them, Karl was sitting opposite her with his eyes closed, listening with joy.

Without opening his eyes, he said, "You should have gone on tour with the Marauders."

Again Annie expected to see a glint of mirth, a hint of humor, something that indicated he wasn't being serious. What she saw in his eyes unnerved her. She saw respect, with a touch of affection.

"Now together," he said.

"Oh, I don't know . . ."

"How about this one? In the original German, of course."

"Another German Christmas carol?" Annie cried. "There are two of them?"

Karl sang:

"Stille Nacht! Heil'ge Nacht!
Alles schläft; einsam wacht
Nur das traute hoch heilige Paar.
Holder Knab' im lockigten Haar,
Schlafe in himmlischer Ruh!
Schlafe in himmlischer Ruh!"

"Of course," Annie said, nodding. "'Silent Night.'"

"Written by an Austrian in German," Karl replied. "Now together. You sing it in your language; I'll sing it in mine."

The idea intrigued Annie. They began.

She started out shaky at first, but then fell into the rhythm of it. It was beautiful. A perfect blending of song and voice and sentiment. Two enemies joined in worship.

With the second verse Karl eased into harmony. Annie's heart soared at the sound of it. Their voices entwined, blending in tone and pitch, complementing each other, growing stronger with each phrase.

The Christmas candle lit Karl's face. Its flame reflected in his eyes. The world and its war dimmed around them, the candle's glow fending it off, embracing them in a cocoon of light.

Never had Annie felt so caught up in song, so perfectly joined in heart and voice with another human being. It was just like Bobby Joe and . . .

Annie stopped singing. She cut it off midphrase.

"No . . . this is wrong," she said.

She began to cry.

"What's wrong?" Karl said. "Did we sound that bad?"

Tears blurred the Christmas candle.

She turned and ran away, though she didn't go far because they were in the Ardennes Forest and there was a war on.

CHAPTER | 32

hristmas Day dawned clear and bright over the Ardennes Forest. Annie awoke with the sun in her eyes. Her first conscious thought was that today she would be back with her unit. Given the past few days, it was the best Christmas present she could have hoped for.

Sitting up, she looked around. She was alone. Karl was nowhere in sight. The litter with the bodies strapped to it was where they'd left it last night. Certainly he hadn't abandoned her after coming this far, had he?

A snap of a branch announced Karl's return. His face was all business.

"We have about an hour's travel left," he said.

He moved to the litter and made a pretense of examining it, checking the ties and the cover. He kept himself positioned in such a way that he wouldn't make eye contact with her.

Annie got up and stretched. The first thing she was going to do when she got back to the hospital was to take a shower and brush her teeth.

Her coat had twisted awkwardly while she'd slept. She straightened it and in doing so her hand felt a bulge in a pocket she rarely used. She felt inside and still couldn't figure out what it was until she pulled the thing out.

A chocolate bar. She remembered sticking it in her pocket when she and the other nurses were hiding the Christmas goodies in hopes they wouldn't end up in German hands.

It looked like a chocolate bar that had been through the war. Its wrapper was torn in places, and a third of it folded over on itself. To call it a bar anymore would be inaccurate. From the feel of it, it was more like chocolate pebbles nestled in a fine dust.

Regardless of how it looked, Annie's mouth watered. Her stomach voiced a gurgle of joy.

Her eyes glazed with tears. She chided herself for getting emotional over a mutilated chocolate bar, but it was a real find. And given the fact that this was Christmas and she hadn't expected to find such a splendid gift, it didn't take much imagination to pretend that Santa Claus had slipped it into her pocket in the middle of the night while she slept.

Karl looked ready to move out. The litter was ready, and he'd adjusted the bandages on his hands and wrestled on his gloves.

Annie approached him just as he was bending down to grip the litter handles.

His voice heavy, his eyes downcast, he said, "It was wrong of me to presume you could ever see me as anything but an enemy. It was just that . . . well, after the last few days, our talks . . . then earlier, seeing how you were with the children, well, I shouldn't have forced you last night. I was being selfish. I'm . . . I'm sorry."

He hefted the litter.

"Karl . . ."

"If it helps," he said, "I think someone ought to pass a law that would prevent people from shooting at each other until they first sit down and get to know one another."

"Karl . . ."

He leaned forward, straining against the heavy load. Annie caught his arm to stop him.

"Merry Christmas, Karl," she said, handing him the chocolate bar.

He stared at her outstretched hand and the dilapidated gift.

"I didn't have time to wrap it," she said.

For every soldier in Europe there were two things more valuable than gold: cigarettes and chocolate.

Karl stared, dumbfounded at the mangled chocolate bar. He blinked back his emotion. "I can't take that from you," he said.

Annie winced with apology. "I forgot I had it," she said.

She tried to hand it to him. His hands remained occupied with the litter.

"Where I come from," she said, "it's impolite to refuse a Christmas gift."

He looked up. It was the first time he'd looked at her since last night when she fled. He lowered the litter.

"Is it impolite to share it?" he asked.

Annie laughed. "No. With chocolate, it's pretty much expected."

With the care of a demolitions expert, he attempted to unwrap the gift. His bandaged hands fumbled badly.

"Let me help you," Annie said.

She folded back the wrapper. The odor of the exposed chocolate crumbs hit her with force, causing her head to swim with anticipated delight.

Taking turns—Karl insisted she go first—they pecked at the crumbs. Licking the tips of their fingers they dabbed the dark brown dust until the wrapper was spotless.

"It's the best Christmas present anyone's ever given me," Karl said with emotion. He neatly folded the wrapper and put it in his pocket.

As the trees began to thin, the snowdrifts got deeper. Annie's heart beat faster with each step and not from exertion only. They were nearing the edge of the forest and the end of their journey.

Gauging from past Christmases, troop movement would be at a minimum as both sides observed an unofficial truce. The timing pleased Annie. Karl should have an easier time getting back to his side of the war undetected.

"Are you going to return to your unit?" Annie asked him.

"I've considered it," Karl said, out of breath. Plumes of frosted breath appeared as he trudged calf-deep through the snow. "It's a risk . . . don't know . . . how much . . . Kleist reported. I may be . . . arrested . . . the moment someone . . . in my unit . . . sees me."

"You can't just wander around the forest indefinitely."

"War can't . . . last forever. Maybe I can just . . . wait it out. Besides . . . I have unfinished business."

"Hans?"

Karl nodded. "I promised him . . . I'd get him home. You taught me that . . . his death doesn't release me from my promise."

"I taught you that?"

Annie felt guilty at the thought of his returning to the forest, knowing that she would soon be safe and warm.

"How much farther?" she asked.

Without slowing, Karl motioned forward with his chin. "See that hillock . . . with the two trees on it, the ones that . . . look like a pair of arthritic hands?"

"I see it."

"The road to Malmedy . . . just beyond it. Once you . . . reach the road . . . you'll have a kilometer . . . two at the most. But a pretty nurse . . . ought to be able to . . . catch herself a ride."

They were closer than she thought.

"Shouldn't you be turning back?"

"Tired . . . of my . . . company?"

Emotion swelled in her throat. She didn't want to say good-bye. Was that crazy? Once they separated she'd never hear from him again. She'd never know if he survived the war, if he made good his promise to Hans, if he was able to continue his music studies or fulfill his dream of playing organ concerts. She wanted to say, You'll write to me, won't you? But who was going to deliver personal correspondence between an American army nurse and a German soldier?

"I'm concerned about you, that's all," she said.

"Really?"

The comment stopped him in his snowy tracks, something he

hated to do, since it meant giving up momentum.

Annie stopped, too. They looked at each other.

"I know I'm probably the . . . last person on earth . . . you want to hear this from," he huffed, "but . . . I'm going to . . . to miss you."

Annie wanted to tell him she'd miss him as well, but the words wouldn't come. It was the uniform that stopped her. The Nazi symbols.

Karl seemed to understand. He said, "I'll go as far as . . . that fir tree. We can place the litter . . . under it for safekeeping. It should be easy enough . . . for you to find it again. It's the one . . . with the broken tip."

Annie looked at the tree. Sure enough, its top had a tip that jutted sideways at a right angle.

With a lunge, Karl put the litter in motion again. By the way he gripped the handles, Annie could tell his hands were hurting. After today, though, they would have plenty of time to heal. Toting the German rifle, Annie walked beside him.

She wondered if, after leaving her, he would watch her from the forest as he did back at Armand and Elthia's farmhouse. Would he wait until an American transport picked her up?

"Halt!"

An American GI appeared from nowhere.

"I said halt!" he shouted.

His voice was high, that of a boy. While he had to be at least eighteen years old, he looked fifteen. Freckles. Round face, nearly as round as his bulging blue eyes.

Karl pulled up, still holding the litter.

"Frankie! Frankie!" the boy yelled over his shoulder but without taking his eyes off Karl. "I got me a Kraut! Frankie, did you hear me? I got me a Kraut!" His feet were dancing in the snow.

"Not funny, Mac. There ain't a Kraut within twenty miles of here."

The voice came from behind the giant fir tree, the one with the broken tip.

Annie had seen her share of new recruits, yet none of them

looked younger or more excitable than Mac. Even his freckles appeared agitated. This being Christmas Day, naturally the greenest recruits were going to pull guard duty.

"I ain't kiddin', Frankie! I just bagged myself a Kraut! Come see! They're gonna give me a medal for this!"

Karl turned his head slightly and said something to Annie. She didn't catch it.

A sandy-headed kid emerged from behind the tree, without a helmet and without a weapon. The top of his head was a wild bush of hair. He was rubbing red eyes with his fist.

"I'm tellin' ya, Mac, there ain't no . . . Why, look at you! You did nab yourself a Kraut!"

Of the two soldiers, the agitated one pointing the rifle at Karl was the calm one. The instant Frankie saw Karl, he slipped in the snow, trying to get back behind the tree. He fell, got up, and slipped again. Giving up on his feet, he crawled crablike back behind the tree. A moment later he reappeared, his helmet on cockeyed and fumbling with his rifle while Mac danced excitedly, yelling at his partner, "I need cover, Frankie! I need cover!"

Karl made a second attempt to say something to Annie, but with the recruit yelling the way he was, she couldn't understand what he was saying.

Running toward them, Frankie slipped again, falling face forward in the snow. He got up sputtering, still fumbling for his rifle. "Tell 'em to put his hands up!" he said with a mouthful of snow.

Mac was growing more excited by the moment, bobbing and weaving now, his feet in constant motion. He thought Frankie's suggestion was a good one.

"Yeah!" he shouted. "Yeah! Put your hands up, you dirty Kraut!"

The barrel of his rifle made crazy loops in the air.

"Put your hands up! Put them up!" Frankie was shouting behind him, still attempting to get his feet beneath him.

"I'll have to put the litter down," Karl said.

Mac's jaw dropped. The flesh behind his freckles turned as white as the snow. "Did you hear that, Frankie? Did you hear? The Kraut spoke to me! He spoke to me in English!"

Frankie was equally dismayed. "It's a trick, Mac! Don't listen to him!"

Slowly Karl lowered the litter. As he did so, he said out of the side of his mouth, "Point the rifle at me."

This time Annie heard him.

With everything happening so quickly she hadn't realized what it must look like, her carrying a weapon, and a German one at that. But if it appeared that she had captured the German . . .

She pointed Karl's rifle at him.

"It's all right, boys," she said. "I'm with the 67th Evac. I captured this . . . this Kraut"—she spit the word—"a short distance from here. He killed my husband and my friend, and now I'm making him haul their bodies back to town."

"What. . . ?" Frankie said.

"I don't know," Mac said. "She wasn't guarding him when I first saw them."

"She wasn't?"

"No! In fact, they was talkin' real casual-like. Like they was friends."

"But that don't make sense, Mac. She's got his gun and everything! And she's a army lieutenant!"

"I know what I saw, Frankie."

"Don't worry, boys. I got things under control," Annie said. "What's he going to do? His hands are occupied. Where's he going to run? I'd shoot him before he took two steps."

"Listen to her. She's telling you the truth," Karl said, his hands raised and his eyes fixed nervously on the weapon pointed at him.

At the sound of Karl's voice, Frankie became agitated. He shouted repeatedly, "Stop talkin' our language! Stop talkin' our language!"

He came up behind Mac, slipping and falling in the snow.

Mac was yelling, too. "Shut up and put your hands up!"

Karl's already raised hands rose higher.

Annie stepped forward. Mustering up her lieutenant's voice, she said, "My name is Annie Mitchell. I'm with the 67th Evac and this is my prisoner."

Mac wasn't listening. His full attention was on Karl, as though he expected the German to spew dragon-fire if he lowered his guard even for a second. Frankie looked equally terrified.

Their terror frightened Annie. She turned to Karl, to order him facedown on the ground, hoping that would defuse the situation.

Karl turned to her. She caught his eye.

Mac kept shouting, "Keep your hands up! Keep your hands up!"

Behind him, Frankie slipped again, this time plowing into his buddy's back. Mac's eyes nearly doubled in size as if a regiment of Germans had just outflanked him. Falling forward, his rifle discharged, once, as he fell, a second time as he struggled to get up.

The first round whistled between Karl and Annie.

The second found its mark in Karl's chest, knocking him backward onto the bodies on the litter.

He slid off, in slow motion. His eyes locked on Annie with an expression that said, Isn't that the dumbest thing you've ever seen in your life? He landed facedown in the snow.

Annie dropped the rifle and ran to him. Falling to her knees, she turned him over. Karl's eyes rolled back into his head. The pristine white Christmas snow was stained crimson.

On the transport back to Malmedy, Annie knelt next to Karl. His eyes were closed, his breathing shallow. She made a pretense of being a nurse on duty. Several times she had to stop herself from gripping his hand.

Riding with them, Mac was telling Frankie how Allentown would probably give him a parade when he got home for his killing a Kraut.

CHAPTER | *33*

*I*n the transport Annie learned that the 67th Evac had returned to Malmedy, same building.

The truck squealed to a stop in front of the hospital.

Annie was home.

"Litter! We need a litter out here!" she shouted, pushing open the front doors.

In her haste she ran headlong into Nina. A platter of Christmas fudge went flying.

Nina's hand flew to her chest, her mouth gaping, and all she could manage to say was, "Oh . . . oh . . . oh . . . oh!"

"Nina, we have an injured soldier in the truck," Annie said. "We need a litter."

Long arms flung around Annie's neck.

"Oh, thank God!" Nina cried. "You're alive! It's a miracle! A genuine Christmas miracle!"

She started crying so hard that her words were nearly indecipherable.

With her touch came a transfer of feeling that almost melted Annie right there and then. How many times had she doubted whether this moment would ever arrive? She was safe now. Home. This was Nina! *Her* Nina!

But as much as she wanted to lose herself in the moment, as much as she wanted to collapse into a chair and sit by the Christmas tree and feast on all the Christmas goodies they'd hid from the Germans, and get caught up with the other nurses, and laugh and cry, and mourn properly for Keith and Mouse—first she had to see to Karl. If she didn't, he'd die.

So she extricated herself from Nina's arms.

"Mouse! Where's Mouse?" Nina cried, looking past Annie excitedly.

Now isn't the time, Annie thought. But she had to say something. She couldn't just let the nurses pull back the canvas from the litter and . . .

"Nina . . . Mouse didn't make it."

Nina stifled a sob with her hands. "Oh no! Mouse!"

"Neither did Keith. Their bodies are on the truck. We brought them home."

"Oh no . . . Annie. Keith, too? Dear, dear Annie . . . you must be devastated!"

She knew she should be devastated, and when there was time, she would be. But right now she had to save the life of the man who had saved her life, and more than once.

"Someone call for a litter?" Two orderlies appeared, one carrying a folded litter.

"On the truck!" Annie directed them. "And hurry!"

She turned to Nina. "We need a surgeon and an anesthesiologist," she said. "Who's on duty?"

"Griffin and Collins."

"Get them. I'll assist."

"But, Annie, you—"

"Hurry, Nina! Please!"

The orderlies climbed into the back of the truck. Annie followed them.

"This is a Jerry!" an orderly said.

One of the orderlies jumped out.

"Wait! What are you doing?" Annie cried.

"I ain't gettin' close to that guy without someone guarding him!"

The other orderly poked his head out the back of the transport and yelled, "Guards! We need a guard here! We have a hostile!"

They stood back and waited.

"Look at him!" Annie shouted. "He's barely conscious! He's no threat to anyone. Now get him into the pre-op!"

"Sorry, ma'am. Not without an armed guard."

Annie looked around helplessly. "Oh, this is ridiculous," she said.

They were wasting time, and Karl didn't have time to waste.

"He's just a Kraut, ma'am," the orderly said.

Finally, two armed soldiers arrived, and Karl was loaded onto a litter. Annie directed the orderlies down the hallway to pre-op just in case they'd forgotten where it was.

Nina caught up with her. She stared down at Karl. "Annie, you didn't tell me it was a Kraut," she said.

"Does it matter?"

Nina looked at her as if she'd lost her mind. "Well, of course it matters! The surgeons aren't going to like having their Christmas interrupted by a Nazi."

He's not a Nazi, Annie thought. She said, "This is a hospital. He needs medical attention."

As Karl was carried into pre-op, a second pair of orderlies followed close behind carrying the other litter.

"The morgue," Annie said to them.

Nina reached down and touched the canvas with her fingertips as it passed. She let out a sob.

"Oh, Mouse . . ." she said.

"Nina, get the surgeons. Tell them to hurry."

Annie turned to enter pre-op when Nina caught her by the arm.

"You've changed," she said.

While Annie scrubbed, she prodded the nurse assigned to prep Karl for surgery.

The woman—Annie didn't know her; Mouse's replacement or

hers?—kept grumbling that it was just like the Germans to ruin their Christmas.

In the OR, Annie stood over Karl as she waited for Dr. Griffin to arrive. Collins, the anesthesiologist, had already sedated Karl. An armed guard wearing a white surgeon's mask stood close by.

Annie had never questioned the presence of a guard in surgery before; today it struck her as absurd. Even if Karl were conscious and alert, even if he were armed, she knew a guard was unnecessary.

Just as she did in the transport, she resisted the urge to take Karl by the hand. Even though he couldn't hear her, she wanted to assure him that everything would be all right.

"Where is he?" Annie said of the surgeon.

"Dr. Griffin was none too happy about having his Christmas cigar interrupted by a Kraut," Collins said.

"I don't care if Dr. Griffin is happy or not," Annie snapped. "This man needs medical attention."

Collins looked at her with raised eyebrows.

The OR doors swung open. A masked surgeon walked through the doors.

It wasn't Griffin.

Annie had spent enough hours next to that masked face to recognize him immediately.

"Dr. Skoglund," she said.

"Annie. Good to see you're not dead."

"I thought Dr. Griffin—"

"You thought wrong."

Annie gloved him. He stepped up to the table.

"What do we have here?" he said.

"A chest wound," Annie said. "He's lost a lot of blood."

"A Nazi," Skoglund said. "Interesting."

Annie held her tongue.

Skoglund extended his hand for the first instrument.

He worked in silence. This was Skoglund's preferred method, unless of course he was badgering a nurse.

"I understand you had a little adventure," he said.

Annie didn't reply.

"You realize, don't you, that I should bring you up on charges. You disobeyed a direct order. Of course, then we heard you were dead, so why bother with all that paper work? But now that it's obvious you're not dead—"

"My husband needed me."

Skoglund interrupted his incision long enough to glance at her. "Your husband. Isn't he the one who's stiff as a Popsicle in the morgue? Doesn't appear you did a very good job of saving him."

"You don't know what happened out there."

He looked at her. "No. No, I don't, do I?" Returning to his work, he said, "Still, there's the matter of the charges."

"Do what you have to do," Annie said. "I did what I felt I had to do."

"And Nurse Hanson . . . would she agree with you that you were doing what you had to do? Seems to me a waste that one person should die because of another person's whim."

Annie bit her lip. Skoglund was a pig to mention Mouse. He knew they were close. He was trying to get to her, to make her cry. He hadn't changed. Annie shook from the effort to restrain herself.

Skoglund held out a hand. He needed forceps. As calmly as Annie could manage, she slapped a pair into his gloved hand.

"It's odd, isn't it," Skoglund said, "to hear an American soldier describe how he happened upon a German soldier pulling two dead Americans on a litter with an American nurse at his side." He directed the comment at Collins. "Not something you hear every day, is it?"

"No, sir," Collins said.

"Makes one wonder what went on in that forest. I mean, Nurse Rawlings here—"

"Mitchell," Annie corrected.

He glanced down at her. "That's right! It is Mitchell, isn't it? Mitchell, as in the name of the dead fellow on the litter, the one that was pulled by our Kraut here."

"Sponge," Annie said. "You need a sponge."

Skoglund looked down at his work. He took the sponge.

"Still, a woman alone in the forest with an enemy soldier . . . sort of makes you wonder what went on. What sort of twisted, wicked things he did to you."

Annie exchanged glances with Collins. His eyes were all that were visible between his surgery cap and mask. Curious eyes. He wanted to know what went on in the forest as much as Skoglund did.

"As an army surgeon, it's only natural for me to ask why you're so insistent about assisting a surgery for this particular patient, without first taking time to refresh yourself."

"I have my reasons."

"Revenge, Rawlings?"

"Mitchell."

"Yes, so you keep insisting. But say, for example, if I were to become distracted for a moment and . . . oh, I don't know, just walk away, turn my back to check on something . . ."

He took a step back from the table and turned away.

"What would prevent you from picking up a scalpel and exacting a little revenge?"

Annie looked up at the guard. He sniffed and then casually turned his back to her.

Collins waited to see what she would do next.

"Doctor . . . your patient," Annie said evenly.

Skoglund returned to the table. The guard resumed his position, appearing disappointed. Skoglund, on the other hand, looked as if he'd solved a puzzle.

"Not in a revenge mood, are we?" he said. "I guess not, this being Christmas and all, a charitable season. Know any Christmas carols, Collins?"

"Just 'Jingle Bells,' sir."

Annie took a deep breath, slow and in such a way that Skoglund wouldn't notice. He was getting to her. Maybe because she was tired. She had to be strong. She couldn't let him get to her.

"Now that I think of it," Skoglund said, "our little Annie is too much of a lady to give in to the pleasures of revenge, wouldn't you say, Collins? Even if she felt inclined, she's not the kind of person who could inflict pain on another person, no matter how much pain he'd caused her."

Just keep pressing, buster, Annie said to herself, *and you'll find out how wrong you are.*

"Whereas I, who have no morals, wouldn't think twice about exacting a pound of flesh. Neither would I think twice about exacting revenge on behalf of a friend who has been grievously wronged."

He reached across Annie . . .

"Doctor?"

What was he doing?

. . . to the instrument tray. Something he'd never done before.

"Dr. Skoglund?"

He picked up a scalpel. It flashed in the light. The surgery didn't require a scalpel. He was ready to close.

"After all," Skoglund said, holding the scalpel over Karl, "we're all patriotic Americans here, who have committed ourselves to the collapse of the Third Reich and the German nation. And haven't we all agreed that in order to win this war, it is necessary for us to kill Germans? So, if a German soldier were to die on the operating table . . ."

He positioned the scalpel at Karl's throat.

". . . because an artery was accidentally nicked . . ."

Collins's eyes grew wide with excitement. The guard grinned.

". . . not only would it serve the cause of the good ol' U.S. of A., but possibly do for a friend what she is unable to do for herself."

The blade touched Karl's throat.

"Doctor!" Annie said.

It pressed against flesh.

"Dr. Skoglund!"

"Merry Christmas, Annie," Skoglund said as a bead of red appeared.

"Doctor!" she screamed, grabbing his arm.

Skoglund looked at her, his eyes merry.

"Why, Nurse Rawlings," he said. "Exactly what did this Kraut do to you in that forest?"

CHAPTER 34

*F*ollowing surgery, Annie took a shower. A long one. It felt wonderful, but that wasn't the reason she stayed in there so long. While she was battling Skoglund in the OR, Mac and Frankie, the two American soldiers, had been narrating their adventure to whoever would listen to them. By the time Annie emerged from surgery, rumors about her and the German had circulated throughout the hospital.

"Is it true they found you kissing the German right next to Keith's and Mouse's bodies?" Nina asked.

"What?" Annie cried.

An assembly of nurses gathered around them. Most of the nurses Annie recognized; a couple of them were new.

"They also said you were carrying the German's rifle and that you handed it to him so he could shoot them."

"Nina, that's ridiculous."

"That's what they told us."

"And you believed them? They're a couple of scared boys trying to make themselves look like heroes! They were planning their own parades once they returned home!"

That was when Annie retreated to the shower. She stayed until the hot water ran out.

In the nurses' quarters Annie sat on a cot and brushed her hair. It wasn't her cot. At the moment she didn't have a cot. It wasn't her hairbrush, either. She had to borrow Nina's.

She was alone. She could hear the other nurses in the ward with the Christmas tree, yet Annie had no plans to join them. All she wanted right now was to find a comfortable, quiet, warm place where she could lie down and sleep for a month.

Despite Skoglund's theatrics in the OR, the surgery went well. Karl was out of danger and recovering, under guard. He was still asleep when she left him.

Captain Maude Elliott appeared in the doorway.

"Mitchell, as soon as you're presentable, in my office."

"Yes, ma'am," Annie said.

This couldn't be good. It was Christmas Day. Any business that could be put off to the day after Christmas was put off.

Annie stroked her hair a couple of times for no other reason than it felt good to have clean hair again. She got up and followed the captain to her office.

Annie interrupted the pacing of an army colonel when she entered Captain Elliott's office. The captain sat behind her desk.

Elliott and the colonel motioned in unison to a straight-back chair. Annie sat.

"This is Colonel Jack Flynn," Elliott said. "He has some questions regarding General Maxwell Conrad's death."

Flynn began firing before Annie had a chance to acknowledge, let alone greet him. His first question was not a question at all.

"You were with the general when he died."

"No, sir. The general was dead when I arrived."

A forward thrust of his lower lip indicated that Flynn didn't like her answer. Annie had heard soldiers occasionally refer to their superior officers as "tough old birds." Flynn certainly fit that description. He had eagle eyes, a thin beaklike nose, and leathery skin. Annie wasn't close enough to see if he had pinfeathers.

"Could you have gotten there sooner?"

Captain Elliott avoided Annie's glance.

Annie wasn't supposed to have gotten there at all, a fact of which the colonel was obviously unaware.

"No, sir. We left immediately after learning of the general's need for medical assistance."

Behind the desk, Elliott breathed easier.

"Why you?" Flynn barked.

Another glance at Elliott. "Upon orders, the staff of the hospital had retreated," Annie said. "A few of us were left behind to care for patients who could not be transported. Two doctors and three nurses."

"Volunteers," Elliott added.

Flynn looked impressed. "Why didn't Dr. Eugene Skoglund go himself?"

Annie was beginning to understand. The army was looking for someone to blame. One of their hotshot generals got himself killed, and they needed someone to hang for his death. Skoglund was an easy target.

Annie stood and faced Flynn directly. "With all due respect, Colonel, it would have been negligent of Dr. Skoglund to abandon his patients here at the hospital. In the field, the important thing is to stabilize the patient, prepare him for transport, and get him to an adequate facility as quickly as possible. That is exactly what Mouse . . . Lieutenant Hanson and I set out to do. If you'll check Lieutenant Hanson's record, you'll see that she was trained to drive an ambulance. But, as I already told you, it wouldn't have mattered who went. The general was already dead when we arrived."

As she spoke she never once broke contact with his steely blue eyes, though not without difficulty. Flynn's gaze was as intimidating as Skoglund's verbal assaults.

"Lieutenant Hanson died during the rescue operation," Flynn said.

"That's correct, Colonel."

"As did Lieutenant Keith Mitchell."

"My husband," Annie said.

"He was alive when you reached the site."

"Yes, sir."

Flynn obviously wanted more.

Annie described the effort to locate the general's jeep as well as the scene when they arrived. She told Flynn how they were attacked by passing German tanks.

"At which time Lieutenant Hanson was killed," she said.

"Not Lieutenant Mitchell?"

"Not at that time, sir. We managed to escape."

"When was Mitchell killed?"

"Later. We happened upon two German soldiers, foraging in the woods. Gunfire was exchanged." She swallowed hard at the memory. "That's when Keith . . . Lieutenant Mitchell was killed, along with one of the Germans."

Hans. Who loves to swim.

"So the Kraut, the one in the ward, he didn't fire on General Maxwell?"

"No, sir. As I said, we encountered him later."

Flynn appeared disappointed. "Your husband was dead, but still you managed to capture the Kraut?"

"Not at first," Annie said.

How much to tell him?

"You were captured."

"Yes, sir."

Flynn's eyes narrowed. "He didn't shoot you outright. Did he abuse you?"

Now Flynn was after Karl. He didn't want to hear how Karl saved her life, that he loved music, that he returned her safely to Malmedy while hauling the bodies of her friend and husband. Annie became acutely aware that anything she said would be used as an excuse to punish Karl.

"No, sir," she said. "He didn't abuse me. He was wounded."

"So you disarmed him."

"Yes, sir."

"How exactly?"

"I kicked him in his wound and took his rifle."

Flynn liked that. His laughing bounced off the walls.

"And then I forced him to carry the bodies of my husband and friend back to Malmedy."

If you can't find someone to blame, Annie thought, *find a hero. It's the army way.*

"According to the two soldiers who found you, your guard was down when you emerged from the forest."

"The man was wounded, sir. His hands were occupied pulling the litter. He wasn't going anywhere I didn't want him to go."

"Outstanding!" Flynn said.

He got exactly what he'd come for—someone to draw the attention away from a bullheaded general who got himself and his men killed.

Flynn stared hard at her, giving Annie one final visual evaluation. Whatever he was looking for, apparently he saw it.

"There's a citation in this for you, Lieutenant," he said.

"I'd rather have my husband back," Annie replied.

CHAPTER 35

*A*fter her interview with Colonel Flynn, Annie returned to the nurses' quarters, where she told essentially the same story. She had intended to tell more, but when Nina said with disdain, "Annie! It sounds like you're fond of the Kraut!" she decided to hold back.

She remembered how she felt when Mouse wheeled the German prisoner into their Christmas party. Let them get to know Karl. Then they'd be more open to the possibility that not all Germans were pit bulls.

She winced when she realized she'd just indicted herself with her own words. Everyone wanted to know what Karl did to her in that forest. He taught her a lesson about humanity—that was what he did.

Annie took her long-anticipated nap and awoke as the sun was setting on Christmas Day. The hospital was quiet, the nurses sitting by the tree and talking about past Christmases in the States. Annie slipped unnoticed into the hallway. Now would be a good time to check on Karl.

Guards stopped her at the entrance to the ward.

"What do you mean I can't see him?" Annie said. "I'm a nurse. He's a patient. Now stand aside."

"Sorry, ma'am. Can't do that."

"You can't deny a prisoner of war medical treatment."

"We're not denying him treatment, ma'am."

"Then let me in."

"We're denying you entrance, ma'am."

"Me?"

"Captain Elliott's orders."

Annie tracked Elliott down, finding her in her quarters. Maude Elliott sat alone on her cot in her robe with an open tin of fruitcake on her lap. Christmas wrapping paper littered the floor at her feet. The civilian robe and casual surroundings made her look older than she was. The last two years of war had aged the woman considerably.

"Have a piece?" she offered when she saw Annie standing in her doorway.

"Why can't I see him?"

The tin hovered between them. When Annie made no attempt to take a piece, Elliott replaced the lid.

"We appreciate the way you handled Colonel Flynn," Elliott said. "He could have made it difficult for us."

Annie was already steaming, and her pressure was rising. "You haven't answered my question."

"Captain Skoglund is grateful to you. They could have hung him out to dry. Though, quite frankly, had I been here, I wouldn't have let you go, either. What you did was foolish and it cost us one of our nurses. Personally, I think you deserve a court martial, not a citation."

Annie folded her arms and waited for an answer to her question. She needn't ask it a third time.

Elliott conceded. "It wouldn't look good," she said.

"I don't accept that. A nurse tending a patient in a hospital wouldn't look good?"

"No. *You* tending *him* wouldn't look good," Elliott shot back. "Look, I don't know what happened in that forest, and I don't want to know. The less I know, the better. What's important is that we have an established story that is acceptable to the army, book closed."

"I just want to talk to him," Annie said.

"Why?"

It was a line-in-the-sand question. Elliott folded her arms, warning Annie that she'd be stepping over the line at her own peril.

Annie hesitated.

"That's what I thought," Elliott said.

"I still want to see him."

"Then answer my question," Elliott pressed. "Why would an army nurse who has just lost her husband want to visit the German soldier who killed him? Why would an army nurse who had just been held captive for a week want to visit her enemy captor? I've been asking myself these questions ever since you returned and the answers I come up with scare me."

Annie didn't trust Elliott enough to be candid with her.

With a groan, Elliott stood. She turned her back on Annie to put her fruitcake tin on a shelf. "You are forbidden access to the German prisoner for the length of his stay, do you understand?"

"Yes, ma'am."

"And you are not to tell anyone what happened in that forest other than the story you told Colonel Flynn, is that clear? If so much as a rumor gets back to headquarters that you have anything other than hostile feelings for that German, it will blow the whole story out of the water, and I won't stand for that." She paused. In a softer voice, she said, "It's Christmas, Annie. Go spend it with the nurses."

Annie started to leave. She turned back.

"Captain Elliott, the . . . the German had a black notebook."

Elliott swung around. "What do you know about it? Colonel Flynn said it was some kind of code, possibly a key to the German offensive."

"I don't think that's what it is," Annie said.

"Well, it's not for us to determine, is it? The book's been delivered to headquarters. Cryptologists are poring over it right now. They'll crack it."

Annie stifled a grin. "I hope they like Bach, ma'am."

"What's that?"

"Nothing. Merry Christmas, Captain Elliott."

Early the next morning, on December twenty-sixth, Annie discreetly inquired about Karl's condition from a nurse who was working in his ward. The nurse told her that Karl was no longer a patient at the 67th.

"They transported him already?" Annie cried. "Where?"

"Wherever they take POWs, I guess," the nurse said. "All I know is that a couple of soldiers came for him and took him away."

CHAPTER 36

Don't get me wrong. Once I was back at the 67th, the full impact of Keith's and Mouse's deaths fell on me like a ton of bricks. Mouse left a void in my heart that has never been filled. Your sister—sorry, but I still can't speak of her without crying; we're going to have to do a repair job on my makeup, aren't we?—but your sister was one special lady. I've never loved another woman like I loved her.

And Keith—he was not only my husband; he was my friend, my confidant. We'd talked about everything with each other since high school. And even though I'd arranged for his body to be shipped back to the States, I kept looking up expecting to see him standing in the doorway like he'd done the night of the Christmas party. I kept thinking we would still make it to Paris. And then, one day, for some reason—I don't know why it finally sunk in—I realized that we never would make it to Paris and that I was a widow. To this day, I can't read the Li'l Abner comic strip without crying. It's the little things that really get to you, isn't it?

But you have to realize what happened in that forest. I felt like it had taken three people from me, not just two. A part of me still hated Karl, but yet I missed him. It surprised me how much I missed him. I wanted to know how his wound was healing, to thank him for bringing Keith and Mouse back and for protecting me from the German spies, and Kleist and Elthia. I wanted to talk music with him. I wanted to hear him play the organ. I know it sounds crazy, but the guy got under my skin.

I told myself to give it time, that it was just the trauma of everything that had happened in the forest that made me feel the way I did, that it would wear off in a week or so.

It didn't. News about Karl's fate was growing into an obsession.

The skies of the Ardennes Forest had cleared, and our planes were in the air again. With air superiority, it didn't take long for our boys to crush Hitler's last-ditch effort to pull victory from defeat. And as we turned the corner into 1945, we were confident that before the year was over, Hitler would be squashed once and for all and we'd all be going home before long.

Two weeks into the new year, Captain Elliott summoned me into her office.

———————

"Mitchell, this has got to stop!" Elliott shouted.

She held up a sheaf of papers. Annie recognized them.

"Simple inquiries," Annie said. "Nothing wrong with that."

"The fact that you can't see what's wrong with it is what's wrong, Mitchell! Colonel Flynn is furious. He's been running all over creation collecting your letters before someone of consequence gets word of them."

Annie had never seen Elliott this angry.

"I just got off the phone to headquarters. That's twice now they've called me wanting to know why one of my nurses wants to be pen pals with a German POW. What am I supposed to say to them?"

"I just want to locate him."

"Why? Why do you want to locate him? Give me a good reason so I can get Flynn off my back!"

Annie looked down. "We've had this discussion before."

"That's right, we have! And you weren't able to give me a satisfactory answer then, either!"

Annie felt badly she'd put Captain Elliott in this position.

"It's personal," Annie said softly. "Look, I can't tell you every-thing that happened in the forest."

"And I told you I don't want to know."

"I know. Captain, believe me when I say nothing sordid or unseemly happened. He didn't make me his slave. He didn't abuse me. He was very civil. All I want to know is whether or not he's all right. Is that too much to ask?"

Captain Maude Elliott's answer was to shove the letters in a file folder, throw them into a drawer, and slam the drawer shut.

"It's apparent to me you have lost all objectivity in this matter, Lieutenant Mitchell," she said. "You've given me little choice. I'm transferring you."

"Transferring me? Where?"

"Back to the States."

Annie's shoulders slumped. Elliott's tone was that of a judge pass-ing sentence. There would be no talking her out of it.

There were only two reasons why an active nurse would be shipped back to the States before the completion of her tour of duty: either she didn't have what it took to be a front-line nurse, or she was a disciplinary problem. This wouldn't look good on Annie's rec-ord.

"It so happens that Dr. Skoglund has received new orders," Elli-ott said, already filling out papers. "He's requested that you accom-pany him. Considering your recent actions, I think it's a good idea."

Annie winced at the bad news. She wasn't only being disciplined; she was being assigned to purgatory.

"You leave in two days."

"Where?"

"Balboa Naval Hospital. You'll be on temporary loan to the navy. Dr. Skoglund has been asked to train their surgeons in some new surgical techniques. You'll assist him."

San Diego. The silver lining. San Diego and Skoglund. Annie thought it would have been fitting had Captain Elliott delivered the news by saying, "I've got good news and bad news. The good news is you're going home to San Diego. The bad news is . . ."

"Yes, ma'am," Annie said.

"Dismissed."

Annie turned to leave.

"Mitchell, one thing more. For the remainder of your time here at the 67th Evac, all mail privileges are rescinded. I don't have the authority to extend that order to San Diego. Once there, you're someone else's problem."

"Yes, ma'am."

Annie felt it was no coincidence when she bumped into Dr. Eugene Skoglund in the hallway outside Elliott's office.

He winked and said, "Once we get to San Diego, everything will work out just fine for us, you'll see."

CHAPTER | *37*

Two months after I arrived in San Diego, the focus of the war shifted to the Pacific. In April, Hitler put a bullet in his head in a Berlin bunker, and the once powerful Third Reich collapsed. So while all my buddies were being shipped home for good, I was still neck-deep in casualties. Same war, different enemy.

The major difference was that I was no longer on the front line, and I wasn't freezing my toes off. Balboa Park Naval Hospital had spilled over into a park area. All the museums were emptied of their artifacts and turned into hospital wards. The Museum of Natural History had 960 beds, the Museum of Man, 759 beds, and the Museum of Fine Arts, 423 beds. The House of Hospitality housed 600 nurses, and the Balboa Park Club was turned into a dispensary. The lily pond became a swimming pool for patients.

I remember thinking that the art museum would be such a strange place to die.

———

Annie Mitchell stepped through the glass doors of the art museum. She checked her watch using the available light spilling out from the interior. It was nearly 2:00 A.M.

Standing on the top step, bone weary, she stretched. The Plaza del Pacifico lay before her, encompassed by old Spanish colonial-style buildings, eucalyptus and palm trees. Overhead, looking like ghostly apparitions, low clouds scudded across the night sky. A moist onshore breeze troubled the palm fronds and deposited a thin layer of the sea on everything it touched. The summer ocean air was a welcome scent after back-to-back shifts of rubbing alcohol and ointment.

Directly in front of her was the Organ Pavilion. She thought of Karl. Every night when she stepped from the ward and saw the Organ Pavilion, she thought of Karl.

Balboa Park had always been a magical place when Annie was growing up, a carnival setting where San Diego had once played host to the world during the California Pacific International Exposition.

Revelers had come to the park from all over the world, including President Franklin Deleno Roosevelt and the first lady, Eleanor. They came to see Alpha the Robot answer questions and respond to commands, stand up, sit down, fire a pistol. They came to see a demonstration of a picture radio called television. Annie's memories included Gold Gulch, a facsimile gold mining camp, riding a donkey, watching money being printed, chewing a stick of Beechnut Gum, and eating a Fischer scone smothered in raspberry jam, which cost her five cents.

It didn't seem right that a place once so magical would become a place of pain and death. Nor did it seem right that a place known for its equitable climate and palm trees would remind her of winter in the Ardennes Forest.

Annie's footsteps echoed against the buildings as she crossed the deserted plaza. She carried with her papers and envelopes. Hospital forms mostly, but also personal letters she'd penned, dictated to her by burn patients.

As she stepped from between the buildings to cross to the main hospital, a din arose from the city streets below. She walked to a grassy bluff, one of the most scenic locations in San Diego. It was a warm August night.

The city below her was ablaze with lights. The El Cortez Hotel dominated the skyline. Being accustomed to blackout conditions all these years, the city looked vulnerable, dangerous. But the danger had now passed. Japan had surrendered. The war was over, and San Diego was celebrating.

She climbed the steps to the hospital administration building. The front desk was deserted. Someone was neglecting their duty, but given the circumstances, she wasn't surprised. Annie placed the reports in the appropriate basket and the letters in the outgoing mail tray. Three of the letters were hers. One to the divisional commander of the First Army, one to the divisional commander of the Third Army, and one to the Red Cross in Belgium. The subject of each of the letters was the same. She requested their help in locating a German prisoner of war.

Stepping back into the night, she wished now she hadn't agreed to meet Stan after her shift. She was tired, but it was more than that. Stan had been showing signs of romantic interest in her, and she didn't want to encourage him. Lately he'd become more insistent.

"You have to meet me," he'd said. *"How many times does a war end?"*

How could she argue with that?

Broadway Avenue was curb-to-curb people. Every light in the city shone or flashed. Confetti twirled like snowflakes, carpeting the streets with color. A bell clanged as the downtown trolley inched its way up the street, revelers hanging out the windows, waving their arms and shouting. Music tumbled out into the street from nearly every open door. Flags fluttered proudly from every establishment.

Women held up their dresses and splashed in Horton Plaza's fountain, while others dangled bare legs and feet from the fire escape on Walker's department store. Everywhere Annie looked there were couples laughing, arm in arm, or embracing and kissing.

Not good, Annie thought. *Too much of that going on. It'll give Stan ideas.*

It was like being at a New Year's Eve party. Following the customary countdown, everybody kissed someone. And now she was standing in the biggest party of the century, and what was she going to do if Stan tried to kiss her?

They'd arranged to meet at Broadway and State streets. When Annie arrived, he wasn't there. She looked around and didn't see him. She checked her watch, thinking she was early. No, she was five minutes late.

After ten more minutes, she decided to leave. Just as well, she told herself. She wasn't in a party mood, and she really did want to get some sleep.

Annie consoled herself that there were any number of reasons that would have kept Stan from meeting her. He could have been called to duty. Surgeons' personal plans are often interrupted. He could have met up with an old buddy and lost track of the time. He could have met another woman, maybe an old girlfriend, or someone who reminded him of an old girlfriend, or who was prettier or more fun to be with.

It takes me off the hook, Annie thought.

She backtracked up Broadway, wading through the bodies and the noise and the gaiety.

Then she saw him. He was fifty feet away. It was as if the crowd was a curtain and he appeared center stage. He walked straight toward her, looking at her, smiling an easy, familiar smile that both attracted and frightened her.

The next thing Annie knew, his arms were around her, and she was bent over backward by the force of his embrace, his lips pressing tenderly against hers.

So much for wondering what she'd do.

For an instant, the world stopped turning. Noises faded. Colors disappeared. Broadway Avenue ceased to exist. The universe stilled, reduced to two souls intertwined.

CLANG! CLANG!

Annie peeked open an eye. The downtown trolley was nearly on top of them. Once again everything was set into motion. Confetti swirled.

Annie felt herself being pulled upright. She was standing in the middle of Broadway Avenue in the arms of Lieutenant Stan Green.

"Couldn't help myself," he said with a lusty grin. "I saw you and . . . something came over me. I just couldn't help myself."

CLANG! CLANG!

Annie looked over Stan's shoulder. The trolley driver was smiling apologetically and waving for them to get off the tracks. Annie blushed.

CHAPTER | *38*

Stan was the driving force that kept me in San Diego after Dr. Skoglund died.

I'd been shipped over ahead of Dr. Skoglund to set up an office and coordinate a teaching schedule with the navy. When Skoglund arrived, the plan was for me to serve as his liaison with the staff at the hospital and assist him during the surgical procedures.

Then his plane went down over the Atlantic. There were no survivors.

You know, as much as I despised the man, news of his death hit me hard. He was a wretch, but he was also the best surgeon I'd ever worked with. I felt guilty because all the time I'd been setting up his office, I was dreading his arrival, thinking that I'd been condemned to spend the rest of my tour of duty fending off his awkward romantic advances.

I couldn't get it off my mind that the last thing he ever said to me was that once we got to San Diego everything would work out fine for us. And then there was that comment about Keith and men dying in war the day after I got married. A hundred twisted scenarios played in my head wondering what Skoglund had in store for me once he arrived.

But I never wished him dead.

Naturally I expected to be reassigned. One week passed, then another, and no orders came. To earn my paycheck, I took a shift *on the ward. They were shorthanded and needed help. At the time, I figured my reassignment had been delayed because of Keith's funeral.*

When his body arrived, I arranged for his interment here. Remember the necklace he gave me at the nurses' Christmas party? I placed it in the casket on the day of the funeral.

I still come here to talk to Keith. It reminds me of the summer evenings in North Park.

Anyway, like I said, I expected new orders. Only, instead of new orders, I got a memo from Lieutenant Stan Green. It said I was to report to him immediately.

Stan was the person who originally arranged for Dr. Skoglund to come to San Diego. He'd read an article Skoglund had written on the discovery of a cryopreservative agent that allowed the freezing of tissue in a viable state. It was a big deal, so he invited Skoglund to teach navy surgeons how to use refrigerated skin as a temporary dressing.

Well, to make a long story short, Stan said that if I was willing, due to a shortage of nurses and an influx of patients, he could arrange for me to complete my tour of duty at Balboa Naval Hospital.

I sensed there were personal reasons behind his offer, but I wanted to stay in San Diego, so I decided to risk it. The paper work was filed, and five months later the war was over.

"Marry me," Stan said.

He held Annie's hand as they gazed out at the sea. The sun was low on the horizon; shadows were long. Waves made one spectacular fireworks display of foam after another against the rocks. Children squatted on the rims of tide pools, poking their hands in the water at the assortment of creatures and squealing with delight. A salty breeze whipped the hem of Annie's summer dress.

This had become *their* spot, the place they would go to get away from the work and laundry and traffic and all the common, mundane details of life. They could stand here for hours and not once think about such things as cleaning kitchen counters, mopping floors, and mowing and watering lawns.

Stan's proposal didn't come as a surprise. It wasn't the first time he'd asked her. The war had been over a year now. Discharged from the military, Annie worked as a civilian nurse at Sharp Hospital. Stan would be discharged in a month. Three local hospitals had made lucrative offers to entice him to join their staff.

And while this wasn't the first time he'd asked Annie to marry him, today's repeat performance wasn't a capricious act. Stan didn't work that way. He was a thoughtful, deliberate, precise man.

Annie, move on with your life!

That was the comment she heard repeated like a broken record wherever she went. Nobody could understand her hesitation.

He's gorgeous!

Truth be told, it was an understatement. Had Annie been able to order a man from the Sears and Roebuck catalog, she couldn't have found a more ideal prospect than Stan Green.

Taking one of those ancient, detailed, marble Greek statues, and giving him a tan, would result in a look-alike of Stan. And while his looks could take a woman's breath away in his dress whites, just a couple of minutes talking to him and she soon forgot the fact that he was so handsome.

One sleepless night Annie pieced together a description of Stan. He had Keith's athletic body, Skoglund's intelligence and surgical skills, and Karl's personality.

She was crazy not to marry him.

And she hadn't ever refused him. Not exactly. It was more like she deferred marrying him. But he was persistent. He knew something had happened to her in Belgium during the war, but he didn't know what. She hadn't told him.

He knew she was sending letters to government officials in several countries and postwar location agencies and various social services, that it was something of a quest for her. But he didn't know whom she was looking for or why. Annie promised she'd tell him someday, and he accepted that.

Fear figured prominently in her decision to keep quiet about Karl. On occasion she'd cautiously lifted the lid on the Ardennes Forest incident to friends and family, only to snap it shut at the first appearance of shock or horror or outrage that she could speak kindly of a German.

If she told Stan, she was afraid she'd lose him. And although she wasn't ready to move on like everyone thought she should, neither did she want to cavalierly toss aside a man for whom she obviously had feelings.

For one thing, he couldn't sing. Stan Green couldn't carry a tune in a hermetically sealed container. People around him cringed when he opened his mouth to sing the national anthem at ball games.

It was such a tiny flaw in the scheme of life, one compounded by a silly fantasy Annie had had years and years ago, a fantasy that had sparked to life for one brief moment in the Ardennes Forest on Christmas Eve, 1944, and died out just as quickly as it appeared. Yet, no matter how hard she tried, Annie could not banish the memory of that night from her mind. Nor could she stop thinking about the man associated with it.

Stan was looking at her. He was waiting for an answer. His sparkling blue eyes—a perfect match for an ocean setting—were hopeful.

"You're such a dear," Annie said, placing a hand against his cheek. "And you know I love you dearly."

"But . . ." he said.

"Can you give me a year?"

Disappointment registered in his eyes.

"I know that's a lot to ask," she said.

"May I ask what you plan to do in that year?" he asked. "A security check on my background? A credit history? Poll my family and former girlfriends?"

Stan tended to fend off disappointment with humor.

"It's not you," Annie insisted. "It's me."

"The unresolved incident in the Ardennes Forest."

That was the extent of Stan's knowledge of Karl.

"I've arranged my vacation next summer so I can go to Europe."

"Do you want company?"

For an instant, an image of a vacation in Europe with Stan flashed in her mind. It was an utterly captivating thought. But that was all it was—an insubstantial thought. And that was all it could be until she finally resolved her feelings for Karl.

"It's so sweet of you to offer," she said, "but this is something I have to do alone." She squeezed his hand, then kissed it. "I'm really not worth this much trouble."

He smiled weakly. "Let me be the judge of that."

Good reply, but then he stiffened.

"It's getting chilly, don't you think? We should head home."

Annie looked at him uncertainly. They always stayed until after the sun set. And if anyone got chilly, it was she who did, not he. The breeze was pleasant.

"Yeah, we should go," she said.

CHAPTER | *39*

In the fall of 1946 I got my first solid lead on Karl. I couldn't believe it. He was here in the States, less than four hundred miles away in Arizona!

I made hasty arrangements for the weekend off and drove to Florence. It's in the desert between Phoenix and Tucson.

———

Annie pulled up in front of the courthouse to get directions. Signs for a junior rodeo tournament were everywhere. That, and a memorial marking the spot where silver screen cowboy Tom Mix crashed his Cord automobile and died, seemed to be the two biggest town attractions.

The courthouse was closed, it being the weekend. Shielding her eyes against the sun, she spied an auto mechanic shop that was open and managed to get directions to the military reservation from a man who was banging the underside of an elevated vehicle, swearing at a muffler that didn't want to come off.

Her heart was skipping like a giddy little girl as she passed through the outer gate and parked in front of the administration building.

"Karl Hausmann," the man behind the counter muttered as he flipped through a thick ledger.

"One *N* or two?"

"Two. Wait. I don't know. I've been using two, but nobody's ever asked me. He's from Riesa, Germany, if that helps."

The counter man glanced up at her with suspicious eyes. He had a pronounced, dimpled chin that worked side to side as he studied her, no doubt wondering what an American woman wanted with a German prisoner of war. Annie had grown accustomed to side-glances. Even when she couldn't see them, she could feel them between the lines of responses to her letters.

"Ah, here he is."

"Really?"

Annie's excitement earned her another questioning glance.

"Right here," the counter man said, pointing to a name in the ledger.

"What do I need to do to see him? Are there forms to fill out?"

The counter man looked up at her with an undertaker's smile. "To see him, you're gonna have to fly to England."

"England?"

The little girl within her stopped skipping, disappointed at the vanishing act made by her chance to see Karl today.

Pointing at the name in the ledger, the man behind the counter slid his finger horizontally across the line. "He went with a bunch of them to England. On March 22, 1946."

"They were released?"

"More like sold."

"Sold?"

"Oh yeah. While they were here, we shipped them around to temporary work sites in Billings, Montana, and Windsor, California. The work dried up, so England bought them."

"Where in England was he shipped?"

Consulting the ledger again, he answered, "Says here, Southampton. But that's just the shipping destination. No telling where he is now."

Annie drove home back across the desert, nursing the pain of knowing that all the time she'd been sending letters to Washington and Brussels and Berlin, Karl had been in Arizona.

So close.

To keep from crying, she planned her trip to England.

CHAPTER 40

*J*ust as Annie was booking a flight to England, she received a reply to one of her letters that changed her plans. The letter informed her that the German prisoners were no longer in England but had been transferred to the military base at Baumholder, Germany.

Annie booked a flight to Germany.

Outwardly, Stan expressed his support. He drove her to the airport and kissed her good-bye. A few minutes before boarding her plane, she saw fear in his eyes. He didn't say it, but she could tell he was afraid this was their last kiss. She couldn't assure him it wasn't.

In Baumholder, between rain showers, Annie was shown the farm where the German prisoners of war had been kept before their being shipped by lorry to Stenay.

Her guide in Baumholder, a gruff sergeant, took pride in showing her the latrine the prisoners had been forced to dig. He laughed when he told her the American guards had convinced the Germans they were digging their own mass grave.

Passing through Belgium, Annie traveled into France, along with memories of Keith and Bastogne and of the Christmas in Paris that never was. She resisted the temptation to visit Malmedy. She had to budget her time.

The prison camp in Stenay lay on a broad meadow along a narrow river. Large, round tents spread across the meadow. They were empty now. Annie felt like she was chasing ghosts.

From Stenay she tracked the ghosts to Cherbourg, a two-day journey through the industrial regions of northern France. While riding in a coach, she learned the prisoners had been loaded in open coal cars, forty to fifty men per car. At the Cherbourg train station they were jeered and pelted with rocks and bottles by the locals.

"Not here, mademoiselle," the stationmaster informed her. He took her out and pointed beyond the seaside cliffs. "Prisoners sent there."

"Are you sure?" Annie asked.

He nodded emphatically, pointing again. The imaginary line of his finger extended across the English Channel to England.

"Do you know what city?"

"*Oui*," said the stationmaster. "Southampton."

For the second day Annie sat in the reception area of the records office in Southampton. She'd spoken to three men who assured her they could help her with locating a German prisoner of war. The three men expressed identical disappointment when she insisted her desire to locate the POW was personal, and then they promptly disappeared and were never seen again.

For the fourth time she was escorted past the counter to a wooden chair beside a desk. The chair was the same. The desk was the same. The person behind the desk was a man she'd never seen before.

Annie's first thought at seeing him was that he was round. His head was a round ball sitting atop a larger round torso ball. His eyes were round, and he wore a pair of round wire eyeglasses. His mouth was small and, well, round. Instead of "umming" when thinking, he "ooooed," appearing to suck air through an invisible straw.

He introduced himself as Thornton Stubbs.

Placing her original letter on the desk for the fourth time, Annie said, "Mr. Stubbs, this is my correspondence with this office from last year, which indicates the man I am attempting to locate arrived in Southampton from Camp Florence, Arizona, in late March. As you can see, it states clearly that he is no longer in Southampton and suggests I look in Baumholder, Germany."

Stubbs studied the letter.

"Oooo, let's see now . . . Egerton. He's no longer with us." He set down the letter. "May I ask the reason behind your request? What is your interest in this German prisoner?"

"My reasons are of a personal nature, Mr. Stubbs."

His eyebrows lowered in disappointment.

"You strike me as a woman with a good story to tell," he groused. "Be that as it may, I believe I can help you locate your . . . your, shall we say, person of interest."

"I'd greatly appreciate your help," Annie said, not getting her hopes up. She'd heard this line before.

"If you'll just wait in the reception area . . ."

Annie made a visible show of nesting. "If you don't mind, Mr. Stubbs, I'll wait right here."

"I assure you, Mrs. Mitchell . . ."

"With all respect, Mr. Stubbs, the men in this office have a tendency to disappear. Do you have a wife and children, Mr. Stubbs?"

Stubbs looked perplexed. "Yes, I—"

"For their sake, then, I will remain here in the hope that I might keep their husband and father from disappearing from off the face of the earth like all the other men in this office seem to have done."

Stubbs gave a *tut-tut* sound. "American humor," he said with distaste before disappearing through a door.

An hour later he returned, plopping a large bound volume on the desk.

"Here it is," he said breezily, as though he'd been gone only a short time. He followed his finger down the page, reading and nodding with an occasional grunt.

A weary Annie watched, her hopes carefully locked away in a deep vault. She'd taken them out too readily too many times.

"Ah! I see Egerton's error," he said. "The chap didn't read down far enough. Quite amusing, wouldn't you say?"

Annie was not amused. "Mr. Stubbs, you're telling me I just spent the last week traveling all over Europe because one of your employees didn't read down the page before responding to my letter?"

"It . . . it appears so. Did you enjoy the countryside as you traveled? It is lovely this time of year, isn't it? Not exactly a waste of time, then, wouldn't you say?"

Annie fumed. "Does that book say where I might find Karl Hausmann?"

Stubbs adjusted his round glasses and looked. "According to this record, he is in Hampshire in the town of Romsey."

"Is this record current?"

Stubbs took offense. "Why yes, Mrs. Mitchell, all of our records are current."

"Does it say what he is doing in Romsey?"

"Not specifically, but I can tell you that most of the prisoners in Hampshire are hired out to farmers."

Annie's time was running out. She had less than a week to locate Karl and get back to San Diego. She bought a train ticket and set out immediately for Romsey.

Upon arrival she found an old-fashioned town with row after row of small houses with cramped gardens. The people were friendly enough but strangely reserved. They moved at an unhurried pace.

Annie found a man who thought he recognized Karl's description, saying that he worked out at Preston Marshall's farm, only a two-mile walk away.

Bag in hand, Annie set out for the Marshall farm.

Preston Marshall remembered Karl. A nice chap. But he'd been transferred to an outcamp in a beautiful old country house called Hazelhurst, near the village of Corhampton.

"Hausmann? Fine musician. Hard worker, too," said Thurmond Fitzwarren of Hazelhurst. "Told him if he ever wanted to come back to England, there was a job waiting for him here."

"Do you know where Mr. Hausmann went from here?" Annie asked.

"Most certainly, young lady. He was sent back to Southampton to be released. Go to the records department on—"

"Thank you. I know where the records department is," Annie said.

"Ah yes, here it is," Laine Hayward of records said. "Karl Hausmann. He was released two weeks ago."

Hayward was a genial sort.

"Don't know what Stubbs was thinking. It's right here." He looked up and smiled. "A bit of bad luck for you, wouldn't you say?"

Annie was too tired to slap him.

"Does it say where he went?"

"Well, no, it wouldn't say that now, would it? We don't keep tabs on the men after they've been set free, don't you see."

Annie walked out of the records office with two days remaining before her flight back to the States. With little time left for travel, she bought an airline ticket for Germany.

CHAPTER 41

*A*nnie recognized Riesa from Karl's description, counting herself lucky that she'd made it, given her time constraints. And, fortunately for her, Riesa was in the American sector.

When she arrived she found a city struggling to recover from the demands of Hitler's power-hungry war machine. Riesa's river port, rail junction, and industrial center were silent and abandoned. Everyone she met spoke softly and with downcast eyes, laboring under a collective guilt from the suffering they'd caused Europe and the world.

Walking the roads of Riesa, she came upon the Elbe River, where she saw a band of boys beating summer's heat by swimming along the bank. She stood here for a time and watched them dive and splash and laugh.

Few people in the town spoke English. Those who did told stories of sons and brothers who had been killed in Russia, in France, at Normandy, in the Ardennes Forest. The town's male population had been decimated. All that remained to rebuild were old men and boys.

At Trinitatis Kirche, Annie found an elderly priest who spoke broken English. When she asked him if he knew Karl Hausmann, he pulled her by the arm out to the church cemetery, got down on his knees and patted a fresh grave.

"Hausmann," he said.

"Karl Hausmann?" Annie repeated, refusing to believe she'd come all this way, followed Karl's trail all over Europe, only to have it end here.

"*Ja*. Karl Hausmann," he said again, patting the grave.

Panic rose like floodwaters. She refused to believe it. It just couldn't be, not after all he'd been through. For Karl to survive the Russian winters, the atrocities of war, years as a prisoner, to come home and die? No. It just wasn't possible.

"When?" she asked.

The priest held up two fingers.

"Two what? Two days ago? Two weeks ago?"

He nodded. "*Ja*," he said.

Which was it? The grave was too fresh to be two months old.

"How? How did he die?"

The priest's fingers became a walking man. His other hand, held firm and straight, some kind of force that plowed over the fingers.

"An accident? He was hit by something? A car? A train?"

"*Ja*," the priest said as he patted the grave. "Hausmann."

With less than a day remaining, Annie found no one who could confirm or deny what the priest had told her. She tried the police, neighbors, shop owners, the boys at the river, anybody who would talk to her.

While everyone was friendly, the people who might know something were either gone for the day, or couldn't speak English, or instead wanted to tell her stories of the war. At any other time, Annie would have loved to listen to them, and she didn't want to be rude, but right now she just didn't have time.

She tried to locate Karl's parents, but there must have been a dozen or more Hausmanns in Riesa. So she decided she'd just have to come back, possibly next summer. She cringed at the thought of what it would do to Stan if she asked him to wait another year.

But she'd have to cross that bridge when she got back to San Diego. Right now she had one more stop to make.

Annie stood on a bluff overlooking the city of Riesa. Below her the town appeared to be sleeping. The Elbe River tiptoed by so as not to wake it.

The sun felt warm on her face. A pleasant breeze rose up the hillside from the river. Annie imagined what the city would look like at night under a blanket of snow.

Alone, she sang:

> *"Silent night, holy night,*
> *All is calm, all is bright,*
> *Round yon virgin mother and Child.*
> *Holy Infant, so tender and mild,*
> *Sleep in heavenly peace,*
> *Sleep in heavenly peace."*

When she had finished singing, she descended the hill to return home to San Diego. And Stan.

CHAPTER 42

*W*ell, there you have it," Annie said. "That's my sordid tale. I'm crazy, aren't I? Tell me that I'm crazy not to marry Stan."

"You're crazy not to marry Stan," Celia said.

"Thank you. Just what I needed to hear." Annie gathered up her wedding dress and stood with difficulty, unaccustomed to managing so much material.

Celia had an easier time of it. She was younger. Besides, a bridesmaid's dress wasn't as cumbersome.

"I mean, Karl's dead. End of story," Celia said.

Annie stared at her. "But I don't know that," she said. "Not for sure."

"But you said the priest told you that Karl was dead!"

"He was old, and I don't know how much English he understood. He just kept grinning and patting the ground. For all I know, he might have thought I was shopping for a grave for Karl."

Celia cocked her head. "Annie, be realistic. You don't know when to give up, do you?"

Annie's hands dropped to her sides. "I just can't get him out of my mind, Celia."

"You told me you didn't love him."

"That's just it, I don't! At least, I keep telling myself I don't. But how can I know?"

Celia sighed. "It sounds to me like you're in love with the possibility of being in love with Karl. You know what I think? I think that if you ever did find him, after one day you'd be scratching your head and wondering what you've been thinking all this time."

Annie stared out at the Pacific horizon. "I think I'd like to live that day," she said. "At least then I'd know."

Celia looked at her watch. "Annie, we've got to go. The wind has played havoc with your hair, and your face is a disaster area—major makeup repair needed."

She turned to lead the way back up the hill to the car and ran into a man who looked like a grounds keeper. His trousers were brown and baggy, and he wore a brown long-sleeved shirt that hung on him loosely, and a fedora hat.

"I'm sorry!" Celia cried. "I didn't know you were there."

The man didn't seem to hear her. He was looking past her.

"Hello, Annie," he said.

He extended his hand. In it was an old, wrinkled chocolate bar wrapper.

Celia looked at it, then up at him. "Oh!" she said. "Is that what I think it is?"

"Hello, Karl," Annie said.

CHAPTER 43

hile Celia waited in the car, Annie and Karl strolled along the edge of the cemetery grounds. A crisp October wind blew in off the ocean. Below them, waves crashed against the rocks.

"It's beautiful here," Karl said. "I can see why you love it so much."

He was thin. Too thin. He almost didn't look like the same man. His voice, however, was Karl's voice. If that wasn't enough, the scar on his cheek served as identification.

Annie's mind was jumbled, unable to sort out this time conundrum life had just handed her. She'd just been talking about Karl and now here he was! She didn't know what to think. She didn't know what to say. She didn't know how to feel. All she knew for sure was that her heart was beating in her throat.

She held in her hand the wrapper from the chocolate bar they'd shared Christmas Day in the Ardennes Forest, the last time she'd seen him.

"I didn't know if you'd remember me," Karl said, referring to the wrapper. "And if you did remember me, I didn't know if you'd want to see me."

"How . . . how have you been?" Annie said.

"I'm doing well. Look, if this is a bad time . . ."

"I have a few minutes," Annie said.

Karl took a good look at her and smiled. "You know, over the years I've imagined what you would look like, if I ever saw you again. But I never imagined this. A bridal gown in a cemetery. Is that an American tradition or something?"

Annie smiled. "Not so much. I was just stopping by to see Keith."

"Me too," Karl said. He pulled a folded sheet of paper from his shirt pocket. Annie saw that it was a map of the cemetery grounds, given to visitors when they inquired about the location of a partic- ular grave.

"You came to pay your respects to Keith?" Annie asked.

"Ja. Well, actually, I came looking for you, and my plane just got in, so I thought I'd come here this afternoon and then see you tomorrow. Call first. That way, if you didn't want to see me, you know, it would be easier for you to tell me. But then I saw a woman in a wedding dress, and we don't see too many women in wedding dresses at cemeteries in Germany, and . . . well, you just sort of stood out. And then I saw it was you."

"You came looking for me?"

"Ja."

They walked in silence for a time. A stiff breeze whipped Annie's wedding dress.

"They wouldn't let me see you at the hospital," Annie said. "In Malmedy."

"I know."

They walked a little farther.

"It really is beautiful here," Karl said.

"Yeah, it is, isn't it?"

Celia came bounding down the hill.

"Annie, we really need to be going!" she called.

Annie Mitchell took a deep, ragged breath. She looked at Karl, then back at Celia.

"Can you do something for me, dear?" she said.

"Annie . . ." Celia cautioned.

"Can you call Stan for me and give him a message? Tell him I'm going to need one more day."

ACKNOWLEDGMENTS

Special thanks to—

Elizabeth Ernst, my talented daughter, for reading through an early version of the story and providing invaluable feedback. I look forward to seeing your name on the spine of your first novel.

Bethany House Publishers, especially my editor, Luke Hinrichs, for his patient perseverance.

ABOUT THE AUTHOR

JACK CAVANAUGH has been studying the craft of novel writing for nearly a quarter of a century. The author of twenty published novels, his books have received both Christian and secular awards, including two Christy Awards for excellence in Christian fiction. Jack and his wife, Marni, live in Southern California.

A GRAND SERIES
OF FAITH AND HISTORY!

Epic in scope, Gilbert Morris's HOUSE OF WINSLOW series is nothing less than the compelling story of the forces and people that shaped American history. Each book has a plot that takes you away to another time with characters whose lives are examples of heroism, courage, faith, and love.

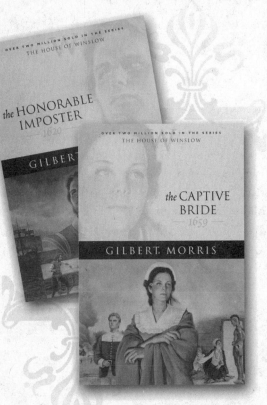

The Honorable Imposter
The Captive Bride
The Indentured Heart
The Gentle Rebel
The Saintly Buccaneer
The Holy Warrior
The Reluctant Bridegroom
The Last Confederate
The Dixie Widow
The Wounded Yankee
The Union Belle
The Final Adversary
The Crossed Sabres
The Valiant Gunman
The Gallant Outlaw
The Jeweled Spur
The Yukon Queen
The Rough Rider
The Iron Lady
The Silver Star
The Shadow Portrait
The White Hunter
The Flying Cavalier
The Glorious Prodigal
The Amazon Quest
The Golden Angel
The Heavenly Fugitive
The Fiery Ring
The Pilgrim Song
The Beloved Enemy
The Virtuous Woman
The Gypsy Moon
The Unlikely Allies (Fall 2005)

"It's hard to sustain momentum in a series, but...
Gilbert Morris delivers everything his fans have come to expect:
romance, mystery, exotic locations, and spiritual epiphanies,
all infused with strong moral messages."
—AMAZON.COM

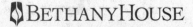
BETHANYHOUSE